SCHOOL'S OUT

I grasped the rifle tight and closed my eyes. I steadied my breathing and opened them again. The madness scampered around the periphery of my vision, but I found that I had, for a moment at least, clarity.

Maybe it was the recklessness of drugged-up mania, or perhaps I was simply so far gone that I had ceased to worry about the consequences of my actions; whichever it was, I didn't hesitate for an instant. In a heartbeat I did the one thing I had been trying so hard to avoid these long months since The Cull had made each man, woman and child the sole guardian of their own morality; the one thing I had feared the most because of what it would say about where my choices had brought me and what I was truly capable of.

I squeezed the trigger and ende~~d~~ ~~a~~ ~~~~ ife.

Finally, I was a killer

An Abaddon Books™ Publication
www.abaddonbooks.com
abaddon@rebellion.co.uk

First published in 2007 by Abaddon Books™, Rebellion Intellectual
Property Limited, The Studio, Brewer Street, Oxford, OX1 1QN, UK.

Distributed in the US and Canada by SCB Distributors.15608 South
Century New Drive, Gardena, CA 90248, USA.

10 9 8 7 6 5 4 3 2 1

Editor: Jonathan Oliver
Cover: Mark Harrison
Design: Simon Parr & Luke Preece
Marketing and PR: Keith Richardson
Creative Director and CEO: Jason Kingsley
Chief Technical Officer: Chris Kingsley
The Afterblight Chronicles™created by Simon Spurrier and Andy Boot

ISBN 13: 978-1-905437-40-5
ISBN 10: 1-905437-40-4
A CIP record for this book is available from the British Library

Printed in the UK by Bookmarque, Surrey

THE AFTERBLIGHT CHRONICLES

SCHOOL'S OUT

Scott Andrews

Abaddon Books

WWW.ABADDONBOOKS.COM

For Katherine Pearson, Winnie Thomas and
Bryan Banks, with thanks. Also for all the kids
I taught; I learnt far more from them than they
ever did from me.

With thanks to my wonderful wife, without
whom I couldn't possibly have written this, and
my trusty readthrough crew:
Justin, Simon, Griff, David, Chris and Danny.

In the first decade of the new millennium a devastating plague swept the planet, killing all but those with the blood group 'O negative.' Communities crumbled, society fragmented and in its place rose the rule of tyrants and crazed cults lead by dangerous religious revolutionaries.

This is the world of *The Afterblight Chronicles* and this is the story of an unusual group of survivors...

LESSON ONE:
How To Be A Killer

CHAPTER ONE

I celebrated my fifteenth birthday by burying my headmaster and emptying my bladder on the freshly turned earth. Best present a boy could have.

I found his corpse on the sofa in the living room of his private quarters. I'd only been in that room once before, when I was among a group of boarders who pretended to play chess on his dining table while he stood behind us beaming benevolently as part of a photo shoot for the school prospectus.

He didn't look so smug now, curled up under a blanket clutching a whisky bottle and a handful of pills. I reckoned he'd been dead for about two weeks; I had become very familiar with the processes of bodily decay in the preceding months.

I opened a window to let out the stink, sat in the armchair opposite and considered the fate of a man I had hated more than I can easily express. At moments like this the novels I had read always portrayed the hero realising that their hatred had vanished and been replaced by pity and sadness at the futility of it all. Bollocks. I still hated him as much as ever, the only thing missing was the fear.

The corridor that ran alongside the head's living room was walled by a thin wooden partition and the dormitory I used to share with three other boys lay on the other side. At night the four of us would lie awake and listen to our headmaster drunkenly arguing with his wife, our matron. We liked her. She was kind.

He had been no nicer to the boys in his care. His mood swings were sudden and unpredictable, his punishments cruel and extreme. I don't mean to make St Mark's sound like something out of Dickens. But our headmaster was a bully, pure and simple. Far worse than any of the prefects he'd appointed, with the possible exception of MacKillick; but he was long gone, thank God.

I was glad the head was dead, even gladder that his death had come at his own hands. I enjoyed imagining his despair. It felt good.

Perhaps I should have worried about my mental state.

I considered pissing on the corpse there and then, but decided it would be crass. Pissing on his grave seemed classier. I was just about to get on with the grisly task of hauling him downstairs when I heard a low growl from the doorway to my right.

Shit. I'd forgotten the dog.

Nasty great brute called Jonah. An Irish wolfhound the size of a pony that liked to shag our legs when Master wasn't around to kick some obedience into it. Always had a hungry look in its eyes, even back then. I didn't want to turn my head and see how it looked after two weeks locked in a flat with a decaying owner.

Two things occurred to me: first, that the dog's fear of its master must have been intense to prevent it from snacking on the corpse, and second, that by the time I was able to rise from my seat it'd be upon me and that would be that.

The headmaster's wife left him in the end. One Saturday morning while he was out taking rugby practice she rounded up all the boys who weren't on the team and together we helped move her stuff out of the flat into the transit van she had waiting downstairs. She'd kissed us all on the cheek and driven off crying. When he returned and found her gone he seemed bewildered, asked us if we'd seen her go. We all said "no sir".

Perhaps I could roll off the seat to my left, use it as a shield and beat the dog back out of the room. Who was

I kidding? It was an armchair; by the time I'd managed to get a useable grip on it I'd be dog food. Despite my probably hopeless position there was an absence of fear. No butterflies in my stomach, I wasn't breathing faster. Could I really be so unconcerned about my own life?

Our new matron had a lot of work to do to win over those of us who'd been so fond of her predecessor. For one thing, she didn't look like a matron. The head's wife had been middle-aged, round, rosy cheeked and, well, matronly. This imposter was in her twenties, slim, with deep green eyes and dyed red hair. She was gorgeous, and that was a problem – she acted more like a cool older sister than the surrogate mum we all wanted. No teenage boy really wants to hang out with his older sister. I liked her immediately, but everyone else kept their distance. They called her Miss Crowther, refusing to call her Matron, but she won them over eventually.

Two months into spring term we all went down with flu. There were only eight of us in residence that weekend but since the sanatorium had only four beds the headmaster decreed that we should all remain in our dormitories, in our own beds, in total silence until Monday. Miss Crowther wasn't having any of that, and confined us all to sickbay, enlisting our help to carry in chairs and camp beds. Then she set us up with a telly and rented us a load of DVDs.

The headmaster was livid when he found out, and we sat in the San and listened to him bawling at her. *How dare she subvert his authority, who did she think she was? He had half a mind to show her the back of his hand.* It all sounded very familiar. But she stood up to him, told him that the San was her jurisdiction, that if he interfered with her care of sick boys she'd go to the governors so why didn't he just shut up and back off? Astonishingly, he did, and Miss Crowther became Matron, heroine to us all.

The dog's growl changed tenor, shifting into a full snarl. I heard its claws on the floorboards as it inched its way inside the room, manoeuvring itself to attack. I'd foolishly left my rucksack in the hallway; anything I could have used to protect myself was in there. I was defenceless and I couldn't see any way out. There was nothing else for it, I'd just have to take the beast on bare fisted.

When the plague first hit the headlines Matron reassured us that antibiotics and effective quarantine would keep us all safe. The World Health Organisation would ensure that it didn't become a pandemic. Boy, did she ever get that wrong. But to be fair, so did everyone else.

There was a big meeting with the governors, parents and staff, and even the students were allowed a say, or at least the sixth-formers got to choose a representative to speak for them; fifth-formers and juniors didn't get a look in. A vocal minority wanted the school to close its gates and quarantine itself, but in the end the parents insisted that boys should be taken home to their families. One teacher would remain on site and look after those boys whose parents were trapped abroad, or worse, already dead. Matron said she had nowhere else to go, and she remained to tend any boys who got sick. The teacher who stayed alongside her, Mr James, was a popular master, taught Physics, and there had been rumours of a romance between him and Matron in the weeks leading up to the dissolution of the school. One of the boys who stayed behind told me he was secretly looking forward to it. They'd have the school to themselves, and Matron and Mr James were sure to be good fun. It would be just like a big holiday.

I had passed that boy's grave on the way up the school driveway an hour earlier. Mr James's too. In fact almost all the boys I could remember having stayed behind seemed to be buried in the makeshift graveyard that had once been the front lawn. Neat wooden crosses bore their names and dates. Most had died in the space of a single week, two months ago. Presumably the headmaster had returned from wherever he'd been lurking shortly thereafter, had hung around for a while and then topped himself.

My father was overseas when The Cull began, serving with the army in Iraq. Mother took me home and we quarantined ourselves as best we could. Before communications gave out entirely I managed to talk to Dad on the phone and he'd told me that the rumour there was that people with the blood group O-neg were immune. He and I were both O-negs, Mother was not. Ever the practical man, Dad demanded we discuss what would happen if she died, and I reluctantly agreed that I would return to the school and wait for him to come get me. He promised he'd find a way, and I didn't doubt him.

So when Mother finally did die – and, contrary to the reports the last vestiges of the media were peddling, it was not quick, or easy, or peaceful – I buried her in the back garden, packed up a bag of kit and started out for school. After all, where else was there for me? And now, after cycling halfway across the county and surviving three gang attacks *en route*, I was probably about to get savaged and eaten by a dog I'd last seen staring dolefully up at me with its tongue lolling out as it made furry love to my right leg. Terrific.

Jonah had now worked his way into the room and stood directly in front of me. His back was hunched, his rear legs crouched down ready to pounce. Fangs bared, eyes wild, feral and furious. This was a very big, very vicious looking beast. I decided I'd go for the eyes and the throat in the first instance, and try to kick it in the nuts at the same time. I didn't think I could kill it, but with any luck I could disable it enough to force it to retreat and then I could grab my bag, leg it out of the flat and shut the door behind me, trapping it again. The headmaster could bury his own damn self for all I cared. I'd have enough to do tending my bite wounds.

And then the dog was upon me and I was fighting for my life.

I wasn't wearing my biker jacket, but the lighter leather coat I did have on provided some protection to my right forearm as I jammed it into the dog's gaping mouth. Forced back in my chair by the strength of the attack, I tried to raise my feet to kick the beast away, but its hind legs scrabbled on the hard wood floor, claws clattering for purchase, and I couldn't get a clear shot.

I felt the dog's hot, moist breath on my face as it worried my arm, shaking it violently left and right, trying to get past it to the soft flesh of my throat. I brought my left arm up and grabbed it by the throat, squeezing its windpipe as hard as I could; didn't even give the beast pause for thought.

My right forearm was beginning to hurt like hell. The teeth may not have been able to break the skin but the dog's jaws were horribly powerful and I was worried it might succeed in cracking the bone.

We were eye to eye, and the madness in those great black orbs finally gave me the first thrill of fear.

I grappled with the dog, managing to push it back an inch or two, giving me room to bring up both my feet and kick it savagely in the hind legs. Losing its balance, it slipped backwards but refused to relinquish my arm, so I was dragged forward like we were in some ludicrous tug of war.

I kicked again, and this time something cracked and the dog let go of my arm to howl in anguish. But still it didn't retreat. I could see I'd damaged its right leg by the way it now favoured its left. Undaunted, the dog lunged for my throat again.

This time I was ready for it, and instead of using my arm as a shield I punched hard with my right fist, straight on its nose. It yelped and backed off again. Thick gobbets of saliva dropped slowly from its slavering jaws as it panted and snarled, eyeing me hungrily. It couldn't have eaten in two weeks, how could it possibly still be so strong?

Before I had time to move again Jonah tried a different tack, lunging for my left leg and worrying it savagely. This time I screamed. Cycling shorts don't give the best protection, and his teeth sank deep into my calf, giving the animal its first taste of my blood. I leaned forward and rained punches down on his head. I realised that I'd made a fatal mistake about a tenth of a second after Jonah did, but that was enough. He released my leg and sprang upwards towards my exposed throat, ready to deliver the killing bite. I didn't even have time to push myself backwards before a loud report deafened me.

When my hearing faded back in all I could hear was the soft whimpering of Jonah the dog, as he lay dying at my feet. I looked towards the door and there, silhouetted in the light, was the figure of a woman holding a smoking rifle.

"Never did like that bloody animal," she said, as she stepped forward into the room. Grimacing, she lowered the rifle, closed her eyes, and pulled the trigger again, putting the beast out of its misery. She paused there for a moment, eyes closed, shoulders hunched. She looked like the loneliest woman in the whole world. Then she looked up at me and smiled a beautiful, weary smile.

"Hello Lee," said Matron.

I winced as Matron dabbed the bite wound with antiseptic. The sanatorium was just the same as it had been before I left – the shelves a bit emptier and the medicine cabinet more sparsely stocked, but otherwise little had changed. It still smelt of TCP, which I found oddly comforting. Matron had changed though. The white uniform was gone, replaced by combat trousers, t-shirt and jacket. Her hair was unkempt and make-up was a distant memory. There were dark rings under her eyes and she looked bone tired.

"The head turned up here about a month ago and tried to take control," explained Matron. "He started laying down the law, giving orders, bossing around dying children, if you can believe that."

I could.

"He tried to institute quarantine, though it was far too late for that, and burial details made up of boys who were already sick. He seemed quite normal until one day, out of nowhere, he just snapped. No build up, no warning signs. He told Peter... Mr James, to help bury one of the boys, but he was already too ill to leave his bed, and refused. I thought the head was going to hit him. Then he just started crying and couldn't seem to stop. He went and locked himself in his rooms and wouldn't come out. I tried, a few times, to coax him out, but all I ever heard was sobbing. Then, after a few days, not even that. I didn't have the time to see to him, there were boys dying every day and the head was O-neg so I just figured I'd deal with him when it was all over. But when I tried the door all I heard was the dog growling and I, well, I just couldn't be bothered. Plus, really, I didn't want to have to bury a half-eaten corpse. Still can't believe the dog left him alone. Weird.

"Stupid pointless bastard," she added. "What a waste."

I didn't think it was much of a loss, but I didn't say

so.

"Did you dig all those graves yourself, then?" I asked.

"No. Mr James helped. At first."

"But you can't have been the only one who survived. Some of the boys must have made it."

I didn't want to ask about Jon. He'd been my best friend since we both started here seven years earlier, and he'd stayed behind when his parents couldn't be located. Mother had offered to take him with us, but the head had forbidden it – what if his parents came looking for him?

"Of the twenty who stayed behind there are three left: Green, Rowles and Norton."

Jon's surname had been Swift. Dead then.

"Oh, and Mr Bates, of course."

"Eh? I thought he'd left?"

"He did." Matron placed a gauze dressing over the wound and reached for the bandage. "But he came back about a week ago. I haven't asked but I assume his wife and children are dead. He's a bit... fragile at the moment."

Bates was our history master. A big, brawny, blokey bloke, all rugby shirts and curry stains; fragile was the last word you'd use to describe him. He was well liked by sporty kids but he had little time for bookish types, and his version of history was all battles and beheadings. He was also the head of the army section of the school's Combined Cadet Force, and he loved bellowing on the parade ground, covering himself in boot polish for night exercises and being pally with the Territorial Army guys they trained with every other month.

My dad didn't think schools had any business dressing fourteen-year-old boys up in army gear, teaching them how to use guns, making war seem like the best possible fun you could have. He had made sure I knew the reality of soldiering – blood, death, squalor. "Don't be like me, son," he'd told me. "Don't be a killer. Don't let your life be all about death. Study hard, pass your exams, get yourself a proper job."

So much for that.

I remember one Friday afternoon Dad stood at the side of the concrete playground we used for parade and watched Bates bluster his way through drill practice. At one point Bates yelled "RIGHT FACE!" especially loud, holding the 'I' for ages and modulating his voice so he sounded like a caricature sergeant from a *Carry On* film. Dad laughed out loud and everyone heard. Bates went red in the face and glared at him until I thought his head was going to explode. Dad just stared him down, a big grin on his face, until Bates dismissed us and stomped off to the staff room.

Anyway, Dad didn't approve of the CCF, but Community Service for three hours every Friday afternoon sounded really dull – helping old ladies with their shopping might be character building but, well, old people smell – so I joined the RAF section. There was a lot less drill and shouting in the RAF section.

My special area of responsibility was weapons training – I taught the fourth-formers how to strip, clean and reassemble the Lee-Enfield .303 rifles that were kept in the weapons store next to the tuck shop; Matron's rifle stood in the corner as she taped up the bandage on my leg, so Bates had obviously opened up the armoury. Made sense. I'd had a few close calls with gangs and vigilante groups on my journey back to school.

"There, all done," said Matron. "You'll be limping for a while, and I want you back here once a day so I can check for infection and change the dressing. Now, you should report for duty! Bates will want to see you. We've all moved into the staff accommodation block, easier to defend, so he reckons." She noticed my curious expression and added, "He's gone a bit... military. Overcompensating a bit. You should go see for yourself while I clean up here. Just remember to call him sir and salute and stuff. Don't worry though, he's harmless enough, I think. He's been very good with young Rowles."

"Okay." I got up, winced again, and sat back down.

"Sorry," said Matron. "No painkillers left. They're on the shopping list for the next expedition, but 'til then I'm afraid you'll just have to grit your teeth. I may be able to rustle up some vodka later, if you're good." She winked and grinned, then handed me a crutch. I hobbled away. *Jesus, my leg hurt.*

As I was turning the corner at the end of the corridor she popped her head out of the sickbay and called after me.

"Oh, and Lee?"

"Yes?"

"It really is very good to see you. We could use some level heads around here."

Trying not to let my level head swell to the size of a football, I blushed and mumbled some thanks.

The staff accommodation was situated in the west wing of the main school building, an old stately home from the 1800s that was turned into a school about a hundred years ago. It was imaginatively referred to as Castle – not The Castle, or Castle House, just Castle. The two towers on either side of the main entrance made it kind of look like a castle, with mock battlements on the roof, but inside it was wood panelling, creaky floorboards and draughty casement windows.

The central heating in our dormitories was provided by huge, old metal radiators that wheezed, groaned and dripped all winter. The paint on them, layers thick, would crack and peel every summer, exposing the scalding hot metal underneath. Some prefects' favourite method of torturing junior boys was to hold their ears to an exposed bit of radiator metal. It'd hurt like hell for days afterwards. MacKillick liked this technique, although he had allegedly once used a softer and more sensitive part of one boy's anatomy, and I don't even want to think about how badly that must've hurt. The radiators were cold now, and the air was chilly and damp.

The school was eerily quiet. I paused in the main assembly hall, breathing in the smell of floor polish and dust. At one end stood the stage, curtains closed. The sixth-formers had performed *A Midsummer Night's Dream* there last term, God knew when it'd see use again. Halfway up the wall, around three sides of the hall, a gallery walkway joined one set of classrooms to the library and staff areas. I limped up the stairs and used it to make my way through into the wing normally reserved for teachers.

I found Bates in the staff room, giving what appeared to be a briefing to the three remaining boys, all in their school uniforms, as if attending a lesson. Bates was stood by a whiteboard, drawing a simple map with arrows showing directions of approach. The central building on the map was labelled 'Tesco'.

The door was open, so I knocked and entered, making Bates jump and reach for his rifle before he recognised me, clocked the crutch, and came over to help me to a seat.

"Kevin isn't it?"

I sighed. "No sir. It's Keegan, sir. Lee Keegan."

"Keegan, right. Well, welcome back Keegan. Been in the wars?"

I've buried my mother, cycled halfway across the

county, been attacked three times on the way, eaten ripe roadkill badger for breakfast and then been savaged by the hound of the bloody Baskervilles. I'm covered in mud, blood, bruises and bandages, and I am on crutches. Of course I've been in the damn wars. You prick.

"Little bit, sir."

He had the good grace to look sympathetic for about two seconds.

"Good to have another senior boy back. RAF, weren't you?" He said RAF with a hint of distaste, as if referring to an embarrassing medical complaint.

"Yes sir. Junior Corporal."

"Oh well. You can still fire one of these though, eh?" He brandished his .303.

"Yes sir."

"Good, good. We'll get you sorted out with at the billet later. I was just outlining the plan of attack for tomorrow. Take a seat."

Bates looked weird. His hair was slicked back with gel (or grease?) and he was dressed in full army gear. His boots shone but he hadn't shaved in days, his eyes were deep set and bloodshot. His manner was different, too. The blokey jokiness was gone and instead he was acting the brisk military man. Grief, did he really think he was a soldier now? I bet he'd even started using the 24-hour clock. He resumed his briefing.

"We assemble by the minibus at oh-six-hundred." *Knew it.* "The primary objective is the tinned goods aisle at Tesco, but matches, cleaning fluids, firelighters and so forth would come in handy. Yes Green?"

The sixth-former had raised his hand.

"Sir, we've already visited... sorry, raided... Sainsbury's, Asda and Waitrose. They were all empty. Morrisons wasn't even there any more. Why should Tesco be any different?"

For the briefest of instants a look of despair flickered across Bates' face. It was gone in a moment, replaced by a patronising smile. God, he really was in a bad way. It'd been hard enough for me to bury my mother but it was, after all, the natural way of things – children mourn their parents. I couldn't begin to imagine what burying his wife and children had done to him; he seemed broken.

"Got to be thorough, Green. A good commander leaves nothing to chance. Nothing!"

"Right sir!" The boy shot me a glance and rolled his eyes. I grimaced back. I knew Green reasonably well. He was in the year above me, but was in my house and had helped organise our annual drama show last term. He was a high achiever in exams, and always put himself front and centre in any play or performance, but get him near a sports field and he looked like he wanted to run and hide under a bush; smart, but a wimp. Exactly the kind of boy Bates wanted nothing to do with. He was tall and lean, with dark hair and brown eyes, and the lucky bastard had avoided acne completely. No such luck for me.

I had been in the Lower Fifth before The Cull. Rowles was a second-former and Norton, sat next to Green, was Upper Fifth.

I barely knew Rowles. He was so much younger than me I'd never had anything to do with him. Even for his age he was small, and his wide eyes and freckled cheeks made him look like one of those cutesy kids from a Disney film, the kind who contrive to get their divorced parents back together just by being awfully, grotesquely, vomit-inducingly sweet. He was looking up at Bates, eyes full of hero worship. Poor kid. Bad enough losing your parents, but to latch onto Bates as your role model, now that was really unfortunate. I realised he was young enough that the world pre-Cull would soon come to seem like a dream to him, some fantasy childhood too idealised to have really occurred.

Norton, on the other hand, was all swagger, but not in a bad way. He was confident and self assured, a posh kid who affected that sort of loping Liam Gallagher strut. Well into martial arts, he had the confidence of someone who knew he could look after himself, and spent most break times smoking in the backroom of the café over the road, chatting up any girls from the high school who bought his bad boy act. Although he fitted the profile, he wasn't a bully or a bastard, and I was pleased to see him; things could be fun with Norton around.

What a gang to see out the apocalypse with – an aspiring luvvie, a wideboy hardarse and an annoying mascot child, overseen by a world weary nurse and a damaged history master who thought he was Sgt Rock. Still, it could be worse – the head could be alive and MacKillick could be here.

Just as that thought flickered through my brain I heard someone behind me clear their throat. I cursed myself for tempting fate and turned around knowing exactly which particular son of a bitch would be standing behind me.

"Hi sir," said Sean MacKillick. "Need a hand?"

"Oh fuck," said Rowles.

CHAPTER TWO

Sean MacKillick was Bates' golden boy, and the highest ranking boy in the army section of the CCF. He was Deputy Head Boy and captain of the rugby team – three successive county trophies. He was also a Grade A, platinum-plated bastard.

Because of his sporting achievements the school authorities thought the sun shone out of Mac's jock-strapped arse, but when the teachers weren't around he was the worst kind of bully – sadistic, vicious and totally random. Jon always said it was because he was so short. Even now, at nineteen, he was shorter than everyone in the room, even Rowles, but he was built like a brick shitter and his head was so square it had corners. His thighs were meaty and his legs so stumpy that he kind of waddled – some of the juniors had christened him Donald Duck – but there was no mistaking the raw, squat power of the man.

His eyes were piercing blue under close-cropped blonde hair, and his face was heavily freckled, but there was cruelty in the curl of his mouth, and his eyes were all cold calculation.

Mac was a posh kid. His father was in the House of Lords until they did away with hereditary peers, but he had adopted the persona of an East end gangster. Born into the aristocracy but he acted like Ray Winstone. Pathetic, really.

Most of his classmates worshipped him, but beyond that he'd been almost universally hated, especially in the CCF. He saw the uniform as a licence to do whatever he pleased, and although he was a bully on school grounds, that was nothing to how he behaved when the army section was away on camp or manoeuvres. Army summer camp last year had reportedly turned into an endless round of forced marches, press ups and endurance tests, all overseen by Mac and ignored by Bates, who seemed to think it was just good, clean fun.

At the last camp, an outward bound week in Wales doing orienteering and stuff, he actually threw a boy into a river and then held his head under the water until he lost consciousness. When they fished him out and revived him Mac made him finish the exercise with them, sodden and disorientated. This was winter, halfway up a mountain, so by the time they made it back to the rendezvous he was literally blue; ended up in hospital with hypothermia. Too scared to tell, he pretended he'd slipped and fallen in. The other boys in the squad kept quiet too – Mac had a little gang of hangers-on and if you didn't want to end up black and blue, you didn't mess.

He and his lackeys would strut (well, they'd strut, he'd waddle) around the school laying down the law, but whenever a teacher appeared Mac would smile and fawn. The head loved him. He was only relegated to Deputy Head Boy because the Head Boy's dad had just donated a new chemistry lab. Matron loathed him. She was always cleaning up the wounds he inflicted, but the head waved away her complaints muttering platitudes about youthful high spirits. Wanker.

There were dark rumours of a death too, a long time ago, back when Mac was a junior. But as far as I knew that's all they were – rumours.

Mac had left school the term before The Cull started, won some big prize on speech day for being king of the brown-nosers, and Jon had keyed his car during the ceremony. Jon who was now dead. We were so relieved to see the back of Mac, so sure he was gone forever.

Basically, Sean MacKillick was the last person on the earth you wanted looking after a group of vulnerable kids in a post-apocalyptic wasteland.

Bates gave an exclamation of joy and – God help us – hugged the bastard.

"Welcome back, Mac," he said. "Now we can really get started."

Over the next few weeks we had a steady influx of people taking up residence. There had been over a thousand boys in the school and at 7% survival rate that left about seventy alive. Of these about forty turned up in the weeks following my return. Some brought brothers or sisters, mothers, grandparents, uncles, aunts and friends. Only one boy arrived with his father, but the man died the next day of pneumonia. Bates was especially good with the boy – Thackeray, his name was – and I saw a whole other side to him. He was caring, kind and thoughtful; surprising. All in all we were forty-six by the end of the month and it felt like life was returning to the old buildings.

Everybody who returned brought their stories with them. Wolf-Barry, a skinny sixth-former who was a bit of a computer geek told of bodies littering the streets of London, rats emerging from the sewers to feast in broad daylight. Rowles had seen mass graves and power stations converted into huge furnaces to burn the dead. 'Horsey' Haycox, imaginatively nicknamed because he was obsessed with horses, had encountered a group of born again fundamentalist Christians who had declared holy war on anyone not of their faith, by which they basically meant anyone non-white. Speight, another sixth former, told a very similar story, but his local

God-bothering nutters were Muslims. There were many other tales of shell-shocked survivors turning to extreme perversions of religion to try and make sense of what had happened, and charismatic leaders building power bases while beheading, hanging or even burning anyone they deemed impure or unclean.

A generator was set up and fuel was collected from a nearby petrol station. We emptied a Blockbuster and most evenings we ran the power for a couple of hours and watched a movie. Television and radio were pretty much dead by this point, although we kept scanning the airwaves for signals. Some satellite stations were still broadcasting as far-off generators slowly ran down, but mostly they all just broadcast muzak and test cards apologising for the interruption in service. An Italian channel played an old dubbed episode of *Fawlty Towers* on a continuous loop for three weeks. One by one all the stations faded away to dead air. The last live station broadcasting came out of Japan, where one guy ran a daily news show. He showed footage of distant explosions and gun battles, empty streets and haunted, echoing city canyons. We watched him every day for a month until one day he just wasn't there any more.

Bates and Mac took charge and organised everyone into work groups, and we started to feather our nest. A spotty little Brummie called Petts prepared a section of land to be a market garden come spring; after all, our supplies of tinned and dehydrated food were running low and soon we'd need to start growing our own.

The main kitchen was a useless modern gas range, but in one of the outbuildings we found a turn of the century kitchen with a long-forgotten wood burning stove. We cleaned it up and had hot food once a day, prepared by one of the boy's aunts, who we started to call the 'Dinner Lady', although her name was Mrs Atkins. Lots of the dorms had old, bricked-up fireplaces, so we took a sledgehammer to those, opened up the chimneys again, harvested some grates from an abandoned hardware store in Sevenoaks, and slept snug every night. The woods in the school grounds provided all the fuel we needed.

We even set up a paddock and rounded up a cow for milking, two pigs and three sheep. Being a posh private school, St Mark's had no shortage of wannabe gentleman farmers and two had survived and returned – Heathcote and Williams took to their tasks like pigs to swill.

The school came to seem like a haven. We organised football and rugby tournaments, started having assembly after breakfast; hell, we even had campfires and sing-alongs. The big stone wall that enclosed the grounds on three sides, and the River Medway which marked the school's southern border, kept the outside world distant and held it at bay. We felt safe and insulated, and Bates and Mac were fine as long as that lasted. Sure the scavenging parties were a little too soldiery to take seriously, but without his cronies Mac seemed almost normal, and Bates gradually settled down. He relied heavily on Mac to organise things, but sorting out the rota for planting spuds and milking the cow doesn't really provide much opportunity for megalomania.

It was surreal. The world had died and here was this tiny, insular community of grieving children carrying on as if everything was fine. And for a while, just for a while, I allowed myself to be lulled by it, allowed myself to think maybe things would be all right, maybe the world hadn't descended into anarchy and chaos and cults and blood and horror, maybe the rest of the world was like we were – hopeful and coping. Maybe this little society we were setting up would work.

What an idiot I was. A community is only as healthy as the people who lead it. And we had Bates and Mac.

I should have realised we were fucked before we even began.

We could only keep the madness at bay for so long. We were living in denial, and Mr Hammond's arrival changed everything.

Norton and I were in the south quad working on a madcap contraption designed by some fifth-form chemistry 'A' student called Dudley, designed to harvest methane gas from animal shit, when we heard the first gunshots. They echoed off the walls and we couldn't tell where they were coming from. There were sharp repetitive sounds too, which we quickly realised were hooves on tarmac, and distant shouts. *The front drive!*

We ran through the buildings to the front door and looked out at the long driveway that led from the front gate up to the school. An old man was running as fast as he could up the drive towards us, holding hands with two boys. All three were shouting for help. Behind them, just inside the gate but gaining fast, were a man and a woman on horseback. Both carried shotguns. The woman took aim at the fleeing trio. She fired and one of the boys stumbled and fell forwards onto the gravel. The old man hesitated, unsure what to do.

"Run, you idiot, run," whispered Norton.

The old man ushered the other boy towards the school and as the child continued running the man turned back to get the wounded boy. He crouched there protectively shielding him from the approaching riders as they reigned in their steeds and loomed over them. The woman took careful aim at the running boy.

While all this was happening boys had come running up to the door one by one, drawn by the noise. Bates arrived last, carrying his rifle. He pushed to the front and went to open the door just as the woman fired and the running boy threw up his arms and tumbled head over heels onto the cold drive. He lay there for a moment and then started crawling towards us. We all gasped, horrified. The woman started her mount trotting towards him.

I glanced up at Bates but the look on his face said it all; he was frozen, unable to make a decision. We weren't going to get anything useful from him.

"Where's Mac?" he asked.

"Scavenging party, sir," I replied.

"Oh. Right. Ummm..."

Shit. I had to do something.

"Sir, give me the gun sir," I said.

"What?"

"Give me the gun, sir." I didn't shout, that wouldn't have worked. I was just quietly insistent, assuming authority I didn't really feel. He handed me the rifle just as Matron came running. She too was armed.

"Matron," I said. "Get out there and talk to them. Just give me two minutes."

Startled, she looked to Bates for confirmation, but he was just staring out the window, biting his lip. She looked back to me and nodded, then stepped out onto the front steps, rifle ready but not presented for firing.

The horsewoman had dismounted and was standing over the injured child, who continued to crawl away from her, whimpering and crying, leaving a thick red snail trail behind him. Her colleague was still mounted, covering the other two, about twenty metres behind her.

I turned away from the door, pushed through the crowd of boys, and ran up the main stairs. I needed to get to a good vantage point.

I heard a shot behind me and my stomach lurched. Jesus, she'd executed the boy.

I reached the first floor landing and ran into the classroom that looked down over the driveway. Dammit, the bloody windows were closed. I laid the rifle on the window seat and tried to pull up the sash. No use, it was painted shut and wouldn't budge. I looked down, saw Matron, and realised with relief that it was she who had fired, a warning shot. The wounded boy was still crawling. The horsewoman's shotgun was now aimed square at Matron.

I could have shattered one of the small panes of glass, but I didn't want to draw attention to myself, and I needed to be able to hear what was being said. I cursed, grabbed the gun, and ran back to the staircase. I was losing seconds I couldn't afford. I sprinted up the stairs to the second floor. The front room here was a dormitory with beds lying underneath the windows, one of which was already open. I muttered silent thanks and lay down on the bed, brought the rifle up and rested the barrel on the window frame. I nestled the stock deep into the soft tissue of my right shoulder. The .303 kicks like a bastard, and if you don't seat it properly you can give yourself a livid purple bruise to the collarbone that'll leave you hurting for weeks. Believe me, I know.

I lifted the bolt, drew it back and a round popped up from the magazine to fill the void. I then pushed the bolt forward again, smoothly slotting the round into the breach, snapped the bolt back down and slipped off the safety catch. I took careful aim and calmed my breathing, steadied my hands, focused on the woman with the shotgun.

"...looters, plain and simple," she was saying. She stood about five metres in front of Matron. The boy was still crawling, still whimpering, halfway between the two women.

"Looters?" replied Matron, incredulous.

"They were seen taking food from a newsagent's in Hildenborough. An old man with two boys. No doubt. We've been tracking them for the past hour."

"And who the hell says they shouldn't take food where they find it? You may not have noticed, dear, but our debit cards don't work any more."

The boy kept crawling.

"We control Hildenborough now," the woman said. "Our territory, our rules."

"And who's we?"

"The local magistrate, George Baker, took charge. He's the law there, and if he says you're a looter, you're a looter."

"And you shoot looters?"

"The ones who run, yeah."

"And the ones you catch?"

"We hang them."

Matron leant down to the boy, who had now reached her and was clawing at her shoes.

"I know this boy. He's thirteen!" she shouted.

The horsewoman shrugged.

"Looter is a looter. And people who shelter looters are no better."

Matron stood up again, raised her rifle and walked right up to the horsewoman. I thought the rider would fire but she kept her cool, confident that her colleague would deter Matron from firing the first shot.

The two women stood face to face, one raised gun barrel length between them.

"Well this," said Matron, "is my territory. And here I am the law. You leave. Now."

The horsewoman held Matron's gaze for a long minute. I had to shift my aim; Matron's head was blocking my shot. I sighted on the horseman instead.

The horsewoman called Matron's bluff.

"Oh yeah," she sneered. "And who's going to make me? You and whose army?"

She pushed the barrel of Matron's rifle aside, raised her shotgun and, before I could react, clubbed Matron hard on the head with the stock. Matron slumped to the ground, stunned.

This was it, the moment of truth. I'd fired this rifle countless times on the range, blasting away at paper people, but I'd never fired at a real, breathing, living human being. If I could list my unspoken ambitions in life one of them, which I think most people probably share, was to never actually kill someone. I didn't want anybody's blood on my conscience, didn't want to stay awake at night playing and replaying my actions, seeing someone die again and again at my hands.

I'd heard my dad wake up screaming.

I knew what becoming a killer meant.

But there and then hesitation meant that other people, people I cared about, would die. I didn't have time to consider, philosophise or second guess. As the horsewoman lowered her gun to point at Matron's head, I took careful aim at her chest and gently squeezed the trigger.

But before I could shoot, before I could take my first life, someone else opened fire at the man who sat covering the other two 'looters'. The man spun in the air, tumbled off the horse and lay still. The woman turned to see what was happening. Matron, injured but mobile, gathered the wounded boy into her arms and began staggering towards the school. The man's horse took fright and ran left onto the grass, whinnying and rearing, revealing Mac, stood at the school gate with a smoking rifle held firm at his shoulder.

The horsewoman gave a cry of anguish and ran towards Mac. She fired her shotgun once, causing the old man to duck, but the shot went wide, and then she too was felled by a single shot from Mac. Her momentum carried her on a few steps and then she fell in a heap alongside the two looters she'd been pursuing.

Her horse now took fright and bolted, racing, head down, towards Matron, threatening to trample her and the boy she was carrying.

Without a second's thought I re-sighted and fired.

The rifle kicked hard into my shoulder and the explosion deafened me. But the horse went down, clean shot, straight to the head. It was the first time I had ever shot a moving target. The first time I'd ever shot anything alive.

I lay there for a moment, shocked by what I'd done. I could see Mac looking up at my window in surprise.

My hands were shaking.

I wasn't really a killer.

Not yet.

I walked back down the stairs, unsteady on my feet, wobbly with adrenaline comedown. The entrance hall was in commotion. Matron had already gone; run straight through the crowd on the way to the San, and Norton had taken control of the situation.

"Heathcote, take some boys and get these fucking horses out of sight," he was saying. "Williams you take care of the bodies. The last thing we need is their friends finding their corpses on our front door."

The two farmboys gathered groups of older boys and hurried outside to begin cleaning up.

I stood there, letting the noise and confusion wash over me. It took me a moment before I realised that Norton was talking to me.

"Lee. Lee!"

I shook my head to clear away the fog. "Yeah?"

He put his hand on my arm, concerned. "You okay?"

"Yeah." I nodded. "Yeah, I think so, yeah."

"Good. Come on, let's get the other wounded boy inside."

"Yeah, sure."

Outside the sky was clear blue, the air crisp and fresh. The gravel crunched underneath my feet as we ran to the fallen boy and the old man who was tending him. All my senses seemed heightened. I could hear my heart pounding, see far off details with crystal clarity. I could smell the blood.

We ran past the dead horse, next to which stood three boys debating the best way to move the great beast. I slowed and stopped. I stepped around the animal and knelt down beside it, reaching out to touch its still warm neck. Its eyes stared, mad and sightless, and its mouth lay open, tongue lolling out, teeth bared in fright. There was a neat hole above its left eye, from which black and grey matter oozed onto the drive.

I felt its fading body heat and tears welled up in my eyes. My stomach felt hollow, my head felt tight, and all I wanted to do was curl up in a dark hole and cry. It was the first real emotion I had felt since my mother died.

I forced the feelings down. Time for that later; things to do now. I muttered "sorry," and then rose and ran after Norton, wiping my eyes as I did so.

As I approached the looters I was shocked to recognise the man. It was Mr Hammond, our art master. I knew the boy too, by sight. He was a third-former, I think, but his name escaped me. Hammond was an old man, seventy-five and long overdue for retirement, but he looked about ninety now. His face was pale and unshaven, his cheeks hollow and shadowed. His clothes, so familiar from countless art classes, were ragged and torn. He had a deep gash across his forehead that streamed blood down one side of his face.

He didn't look like he'd endured the easiest apocalypse.

Williams lifted the dead woman and pushed past me as I approached. Norton was helping Hammond to his feet, Mac was lifting the wounded boy. Bates was standing there too, staring at the pool of blood on the ground, eyes glazed, expression blank. When I reached him he didn't look up.

"Sir," I said. No response. "Sir."

Bates snapped out of his reverie and looked up at me. "Hmmm?"

"Your rifle, sir," I said, and handed it to him. He looked down at it in horror, as if I'd just offered him a severed human head. Then he reached out and took it.

"Thank you," he murmured.

Norton and Hammond moved off back towards the school, and Mac handed the boy, bleeding but breathing, to a couple of fifth-formers who carried him away.

So there we were; me, Bates and Mac, stood around two pools of blood, all unsure exactly what to say to each other. It was only now that I noticed that Mac had dried blood smeared across his combat jacket. I studied him closely. I had just killed a horse and I was a wreck; he'd just gunned down two people and he didn't seem in the least bit concerned. I may not have been a killer, but he was. And something about his reaction, or lack of it, told me this was not the first time he'd taken a life.

"What happened to you?" I asked. "Where are the others?"

Bates looked at Mac and seemed to regain his senses. Mac was watching him carefully, and his cool appraising stare made me feel deeply uneasy.

"Yes, Mac," said Bates. "You left with McCulloch and Fleming. Where are they?"

He would have answered but he was suddenly surrounded by a crowd of sixth form boys, eager to congratulate him. Wolf-Barry slapped his back and punched the air, Patel kept saying that it was "so cool", Zayn just looked awed.

Great, he'd got a new fan club.

We gathered that evening in the main common room after a subdued dinner of curried horse. I didn't eat.

Bates was first to speak.

"You're all aware of the incident that occurred this afternoon. Matron is even now working to save the lives of the two boys who were shot. These boys are Grant of 2B and Preston of 4C."

One boy in the second row gave an audible gasp at this news. A classmate, probably.

Bates seemed more sure of himself in this safe, controlled environment. All trace of his earlier loss of composure was gone. He stood erect, in full uniform, with his arms behind his back, like a regimental Sergeant-Major.

"I'm going to hand over to Mr Hammond at this stage, who will tell you what happened. Dennis..."

He gestured to his colleague to take over, and resumed his seat. Hammond stood and surveyed the room, scanning our faces, mentally noting which of us he knew, seeing who had survived and who, by omission, had not.

"Boys, it's good to be back. It's good to see so many of you again. It gives me hope that..." He trailed off, momentarily overcome.

"Preston and Grant lived near me in Sevenoaks, and they both arrived at my house together a few days ago.

It was my suggestion that we return here. If we'd stayed where we were, maybe... Anyway, we ran out of petrol just as we entered Hildenborough. But it's only an hour's walk to the school so we weren't worried. Grant was hungry so we stopped at a newsagent's and rummaged around for something to eat. The place had been pretty thoroughly cleaned out, but we found chocolate bars underneath an overturned cupboard. We considered ourselves lucky, and set off again. But within minutes there was a hue and cry. The shout 'looter' went up and we saw a man running towards us, so we just ran for our lives.

"Preston knows the area very well and thanks to him we were able to elude our pursuers, although we never seemed able to completely shake them off. They finally caught up with us at the gate and you know the rest.

"If it hadn't been for Matron and MacKillick here..." Again he trailed off into silence.

You would have expected Hammond to have been grateful to the man who had saved his life, but the look he flashed Mac was one of distaste and suspicion.

Bates stood again, thanked Hammond, and handed the floor to Mac with an alarming degree of deference. Norton and I exchange worried glances. Mac had cleaned up and changed his uniform, but he still sported combats and camouflage.

"Thank you, sir" he said, with perhaps the tiniest hint of sarcasm. "I'll be brief. Fleming, McCulloch and me left this morning to scavenge in Hildenborough. As you know the shops have all been cleaned out, so we had to go house to house. Not the prettiest work. Those houses that haven't already been got at have normally still got occupants. You need a strong stomach."

What a smug, self-satisfied, aren't-I-hard sod he was.

"We found one house full of stuff we could use and we started carrying it out to the minibus. I was inside when I heard shouting. I went to the window and saw three men, all carrying guns, coming at McCulloch and Fleming. Our boys weren't armed, they'd been surprised, they didn't stand a chance. I watched as they were led away and then I followed, dodging house to house and keeping out of sight. They took the lads to a big house down a side road, an old manor house I think. I didn't even have time to sneak up and look through a window before they were brought out again. The three men and a new guy, some posh lord of the manor type in tweeds and stuff. They led our boys round the side of the house and I followed, hiding behind the hedges. And there, like it was the most normal thing in the world to have in your garden, was a gallows.

"McCulloch started screaming, so they did him first. It was all over in an instant. Then they did Fleming. He'd wet himself before they even put the noose around his neck."

Bloody hell, Mac. No need for the fucking details. I clenched my fists angrily. He was enjoying this.

"I didn't stick around after that. But as I was leaving town I saw some guys putting up a new fence across the road and a sign saying 'Hildenborough Protectorate. Governor: George Baker. Traders welcomed. Looters hanged.'

"I had to try another way out of town and found guards posted at all the exit points around the perimeter. So I dealt with one of them and came back here. Just in time too, I reckon."

'Dealt with one of them'. That explained the blood on his jacket. So he'd killed three people today and he looked for all the world like he was having the time of his life. I felt sick.

He sat back down and Bates took the floor again.

"Boys, I know this is hard, but we have to accept the

reality that we may be, um, at war."

There were murmurs of disbelief.

"I know it sounds ridiculous, but consider the facts. A hostile force has established a base of operations practically on our doorstep. They've killed two of us and wounded two more; we've killed three of them. We know they're armed, entrenched, and determined. We must assume they will attack, and we must be ready."

I raised my hand to ask why he thought they'd attack.

"Put your hand down, Keegan," he barked. "I didn't throw the floor open to questions. And that goes for everyone. If we're to survive this we need to be focused, united, organised. There needs to be a clear chain of command and all orders will need to be followed promptly and without question. Is that clear?"

"Well, really," said the Dinner Lady. "I don't expect to be talked to like that."

"Ma'am," snapped Bates. "You are welcome to remain at St Mark's but I am in charge here and if you accept my protection I'm afraid you accept my rules."

And just like that Bates declared martial law.

I looked over at Mac. His face was solemn but his eyes told a different story. They shone with glee.

Hammond spoke up.

"I say Bates, are you quite sure you need to..."

Bates leaned forward and hissed something peremptory at Hammond, who fell silent.

He went on: "We need to secure our perimeter, post guards, organise patrols and so forth. To this end we are re-establishing the CCF and every boy will be expected to do their bit."

Broadbent raised his hand and began bleating before Bates could stop him.

"But sir, I was excused CCF because of my asthma. My dad wrote a note and everything."

"I said no questions, boy!" Bates yelled. "And no excuses either. If you're old enough to dress yourself you're old enough to carry a gun."

You could feel the shock in the room as everybody's eyes widened and their shoulders stiffened. Bates breathed deeply and visibly calmed himself.

"I know it's not how we want things to be, but it's the way things are," he reasoned. "It's my job, and Mac's, to keep you safe. I failed in that today. Not again.

"As of now you will all refer to me as Colonel and Mac as Major. Is that clear?"

I wanted to laugh in his face. I wanted to stand up and shout "Are you fucking joking? You're a history teacher, you deluded tinpot tosser". But I didn't. It was all too tragic for that. Tragic and – I glanced at Mac – sinister.

"I said is that clear?"

Some boys muttered "yes, Colonel" unenthusiastically. I thought Bates was going to push it, but he must have realised the time wasn't yet right.

"Good," he said. "Now, I want Speight, Pugh, Wylie, Wolf-Barry, Patel, Green, Zayn and Keegan to stay behind. The rest of you are dismissed for the evening."

Norton whispered "Good luck" as he got up to leave. Everybody else shuffled out leaving myself, Bates, Mac and the six other boys whose names had been called. They were all the remaining sixth-formers; I was the only non sixth-former there.

When everyone else had left, Bates gestured for us all to come and sit together at the front, and sat to address us.

"You're the senior boys here, and a lot of the responsibility of this is going to rest with you. We'll be assigning ranks in the coming days but for now you'll all be acting corporals. Major Mac will be managing you directly and I want you to follow his orders promptly and without question at all times. Is that clear?"

"Yes Colonel."

"Good lads," said Bates. He smiled what he probably thought was a reassuring smile, but he actually looked more like a scared man presenting his teeth to a sadistic dentist. He patted Mac on the shoulder.

"All yours, Major," he said, and left the room.

Mac glared at us and grinned a sly, feral grin. He didn't look impressed by us, but he did look pleased with himself. He pulled his chair around so that he was facing us.

"Right, I've killed three fuckers today and if none of you want to be number four you'll keep your ears open and your mouths shut. Clear?"

Oh yeah. Here he was. This was the Mac I remembered. All these weeks of playing nice and sucking up to Bates, he was just biding his time, waiting for the right moment. Now Bates had shown weakness, there was blood in the water, and Mac was the shark.

Things were going to get ugly.

CHAPTER THREE

I saw Mac with his father once, on speech day. Jon and I walked behind them for a while, fascinated by the way they talked. His father, being a Lord, was all fruity vowels and wot-wot, and the brilliant thing is that Mac was too. He was all 'Gosh Daddy' and 'Super' and 'Cripes'. Once he actually said "Oh, my stars and garters!" Jon and I had to walk away at that point because we were finding it impossible to stifle our giggles.

I looked at the wannabe gangster who sat in front of me now and all I could think was: *what would your father think?* And also: *I know you, fraud. Everybody else may think you're a hard nut but underneath it all you're just a spoiled upper class daddy's boy overcompensating for the silver spoon you've got shoved up your arse.*

"Right," he said, in his broad cockney accent. "From now on, as far as you're concerned I am your fucking God. I am the law. Proper Judge Dredd, that's me. What I say goes and you don't question a fucking word, got it? You are mine."

He paused for effect and graced us with a menacing leer.

"But I'm not unreasonable," he lied. "I'm not unfriendly. Stick with me and you'll be all right. I'll take care of you. I like loyalty. If you're loyal we'll rub along just peachy, clear?"

Again, we nodded.

"Right. So. The Colonel has made me second-in-command and you lot are my officers. You're my go-to guys. You'll be able to give orders to all the other scrotes and you'll carry weapons at all times. I'll be doing some extra training with you over the next few days –

leadership, strategy, warcraft, that sort of shit. And you'll be leading scavenging groups, raiding parties and any other kind of operation too fucking menial for me to dirty my lilywhites with.

"Stick with me and you'll be in clover. Fuck with me and you'll be pushing it up.

"Now, most of you were in the CCF under me, so you know how I like things done. Those of you who were fucking flyboys will learn."

I'm sure we will, I thought.

"Keegan!" he bellowed suddenly, making me jump.

"Yeah?" I stammered. He glared at me dangerously. "I mean, yes sir?"

He nodded, letting it go this once.

"You showed a lot of initiative this afternoon."

"Thank you, sir."

"For a flyboy," he added. "And a fifth-form scrote. Bloody good shooting too. Almost as good as mine, eh?" He laughed at his little joke. Pugh sniggered sycophantically until silenced by a contemptuous look from Mac.

"We're going to need you, Keegan, if things get sticky," he went on.

He turned his attention to the others and I sighed heavily, suddenly aware that I'd been holding my breath.

"The rest of you could learn from this one. Proactive is what he is."

He leaned in close to me, his hot sour breath in my face, and hissed: "But not too proactive, yeah? Don't want to be too smart for your own good, do you, Keegan?"

"No sir," I said, crisply. He leaned back and smiled.

"Right, let's get you lot into patrols."

As the briefing got underway I realised that I was being given an opportunity. If I was to be part of the officer corps then I could get close to Mac, and if I could get close to him perhaps I could influence him, divert him, maybe even, if the need arose, deal with him.

I prepared myself to be Mac's bestest of best mates: reliable, steadfast and sneaky as a bastard.

Speight and Zayn got first watch, the rest of us were dismissed. I'd be reporting for guard duty with Wolf-Barry first thing in the morning so I wanted to get my head down.

The difference between night and day used to be blurred by electricity; streetlights turned the night sky orange and blotted out the stars; electric lights in the home allowed people to keep doing whatever they wanted all night long; car headlights made travel in the darkness a cinch. Things were different now. Battery torches were only used when absolutely necessary, so any light after dark had to come from flame. People were returning to the old rhythms of day and night, rising and retiring with the sun.

Nonetheless, the old term-time routine of lights-out was still being being preserved by Bates; juniors in bed at 8, fourth and fifth-formers by 9:30, seniors by 11. So normally I'd need to be tucked up by 9:30, but I'd been told that as an honorary senior – with all the duties that implied – I could observe senior bedtime, so I had some time in hand and there was someone I wanted to see.

The door of the sanatorium was closed, but the candle light flickering through the frosted glass windows revealed Matron moving around inside. I knocked and I saw her freeze. She didn't respond. Perhaps she wanted to be left alone. I knocked again.

"Matron," I said, "It's me, Lee. I just wanted to see how you are."

Her silhouette relaxed.

"Come in Lee," she said.

I pushed open the door and entered to find Matron standing at the side of the padded table she used for examinations. There was a livid purple bruise on her forehead where the horsewoman had clubbed her, and for an instant I was so furious I wished I had shot the bitch after all. Matron was dressed in medical whites and an apron stained with fresh blood. Her sleeves were rolled up and she was wearing thin rubber gloves which she was removing as I entered. Her face was as white as her clothes.

Four bodies lay on the floor, covered with sheets. Both boys had died then.

I stood there in the doorway, unsure what to say. She broke the silence.

"Too many pellets," she said simply. "Not enough anaesthetic."

Next to the table stood a complicated system of tubes suspended from a metal stand. She must have been giving transfusions.

She followed my gaze and nodded.

"Atkins gave blood first, then Broadbent, Dudley and Haycox. They were so brave, but it just wasn't enough." Her voice caught in her throat and she leaned against the table as if light-headed. Then she looked up, remembering.

"Oh Lee, I forgot to thank you. You saved my life, didn't you?"

I nodded, still unsure what to say.

"Bless you. You saved me, but I couldn't save them." She slumped to the floor. "What a fucking waste. To survive the end of the world just to be murdered for a Mars bar." She hid her face in her hands and wept.

I walked over to her, knelt down, and gingerly reached

out to touch her shoulder. As I did so she leaned forward and embraced me, burying her face in my neck, soaking it with tears.

We sat there like that for quite some time.

With the bodies buried, one horse butchered and salted, and the other released ten miles down the road, we removed all evidence of the confrontation on the school drive.

The minibus that had been abandoned in Hildenborough was thankfully not one of those with the school name and crest painted on the side, so no-one could trace it back to us without checking the registration plate with the DVLA, and they weren't taking calls. We just had to hope that McCulloch or Fleming hadn't revealed our location to our neighbours before they were hanged. However, Bates wasn't prepared to take any chances, and the next afternoon he called all the officers to the common room. He got straight to the point.

"We need ordnance," he said simply. "Our armoury holds ten rifles and a few boxes of rounds, but if it came to a shooting war we'd be lucky to last a day. Of course with law and order entirely broken down there are weapons and ammunition there for the taking, if you know where to look. And I do. So we're going on a field trip."

He took out his whiteboard pen and started drawing a map.

Pugh and Wylie stayed behind to guard the school. Mr Hammond was planning to teach a class, so most boys would be safe inside. Meanwhile the rest of us hit the road, with Mac and Bates each driving a minibus. In full combats, all armed, and with mud and boot polish rubbed into our face, we were off to get ourselves an arsenal and we were ready to meet resistance.

Giving Hildenborough a wide berth we headed out into darkest Kent. The only cars we passed had been abandoned, and the roads were well on their way to becoming impassable. With no council workers to operate the hedge trimmers or clear fallen trees, the narrow country lanes were rapidly disappearing under the greenery. On some roads the hedgerows scraped along both sides of the bus. A couple of summers and they'd be buried forever.

We passed through picturesque villages with large greens, their cricket squares so neat for so long, now shaggy and unkempt. We saw ancient churches with their stained glass windows smashed and their huge, centuries-old oak doors hanging off thick, bent hinges. We drove past fields of cows, most dead or dying, suffering agonies because they'd been bred to produce milk that nobody was around to extract.

There were some signs of life: a man driving a horse and cart carrying a crop of leeks; the occasional cottage with a column of thin smoke snaking up into the dull grey sky; a village hall ablaze. In one hamlet a gang of feral children heaved bricks at us as we drove past. Mac fired some warning shots over their heads and laughed as they ran for cover.

When we were half a mile from our destination we pulled into a farmyard. Mac and I swept the buildings to ensure they were empty, and then we stashed the buses in a barn. From here we were on foot. We split into two groups. Me, Mac and Green went one way, Bates, Zayn and Wolf-Barry went the other. Speight and Patel stayed to guard the transport. The intention was to approach the target from different directions.

We headed off into thick forest. One startled, honking partridge could reveal our presence, so we trod lightly. We did startle a small family of deer, but they ran away from our objective, so we reckoned we were okay. Off to our right a brace of pigeons noisily took flight and flapped away; Bates' group were clearly less covert than they thought they were.

As we approached the edge of the trees we fell to our stomachs and crawled through the wet, mulchy leaves, rifles held out in front of us. Eventually Mac held up his hand and we stopped. He took out his binoculars and studied the terrain beyond the tree-line for a minute or two before handing them across to me.

"What do you see, Keegan?"

I took the glasses and looked down onto the Kent and Sussex Territorial Army Firing Range and Armoury.

A chain link fence stood between us and the complex. A burnt-out saloon car was wedged into one section directly in front of us, presumably the result of someone's ill-advised attempt to ram their way in. It was riddled with bullet holes. There were plenty of possible entry points; the fence wasn't much of a barrier, it was falling down in various places, but the state of the car implied that the complex had been defended at some point. Was it still?

Off to our right were the firing ranges. A brick trench looked out onto a long stretch of grass with a huge sandbank at the far end. Propped up in front of the sand stood the fading, tattered shreds of paper soldiers, stapled to wooden boards. Many had fallen to the floor, or hung sideways at crazy angles as if drunk. Both the trench and the sandbank could provide excellent cover for attackers or defenders.

Directly in front of us stood the main building. It was two storeys high, brick built, with an impressive sign hanging across the large double doorway proclaiming its military importance. Many of the windows were smashed, and the far right rooms on the top floor had been on fire in the not too distant past; streaks of black scorching stretched from the cracked windows to the roof.

The car park in front of the building was empty except for one shiny BMW which, bizarrely, appeared untouched, still waiting patiently for its proud owner to return. Beyond the car park, to our left, was the driveway, lined with single storey outbuildings which appeared to continue behind the main building; there was more of the complex out of sight, presumably a parade ground and maybe an assault course.

There were two sandbag emplacements at the entrance to the main building, but there were no men or guns there. They were the remains of a previous attempt at defence, long since abandoned.

If I were defending this place where would I station myself?

I scanned the roof and windows of the main building but could see no signs of life or other, more recent fortifications – no sandbags, barriers or not-so-casually placed obstacles behind which to hide. The firing range appeared empty, as did the outbuildings lining the drive. Perhaps any defenders would be stationed behind the main building, but that would leave them unable to cover the most obvious routes of approach, so that seemed unlikely. So either I was missing something, or the place was deserted.

I was just about to hand the binoculars back to Mac when I caught a glimpse of a brick corner poking out behind the portico entrance to the firing range trench. I shuffled left a bit to get a better view and found myself gazing at a solid, brick and concrete Second World War pillbox. Anyone in there would have a 360° view of pretty much the entire complex, a mostly unimpeded line of fire, and bugger all chance of being killed by some yokel looter with a shotgun.

I pointed to the pillbox and handed the glasses back to Mac, who nodded; he'd seen it already or, more likely, been tipped off by Bates earlier.

"Bit obvious, though, innit," he whispered, handing the glasses to Green, who took his turn scanning the area. "I'd have someone somewhere else too, covering the approach to the pillbox. Now, where would that fucker be, d'you think?"

"Sir," whispered Green. "The car in the fence. Rear right wheel." He passed back the binoculars and Mac took a look. He grinned.

"Not too shabby, Green. Not too shabby at all." He passed the binoculars to me. Sure enough, just visible poking out from behind the rear wheel was a boot. As I watched it moved ever so slightly. There was a man under the car. Between him and the pillbox all the open spaces in the complex were exposed to crossfire.

We didn't have walkie-talkies, so the next thing was for Green and Wolf-Barry to skirt the complex, staying in the woods. They'd meet halfway between our positions and compare notes. Green scurried away while Mac and I shuffled back from the edge of the wood into deep cover and sat up against a couple of trees. Mac took out a battered packet of Marlboros and offered one to me.

"They might see the smoke, sir," I pointed out. Mac glared at me, and for a moment I thought he was going to pitch a fit, but eventually he nodded and put away the packet.

"Fair point," he said. He regarded me coolly. "Yesterday, why didn't you just shoot that bitch?"

Because I'm not a murdering psycho whose first instinct is to open fire.

Breathe. Calm. Play the part. Earn his trust.

"Wasn't sure that I'd be able to get her mate before he shot Hammond and the others. Didn't want to shoot first, I suppose. But I was just about to pop her before you did. So thanks. Saved me the trouble." I grinned, trying to make out I thought it was funny. "Good shooting, by the way."

"Had lots of practice, ain't I."

Oh very good, hard case. Make out that you shoot people all the time. I know where you got your practice – shooting pheasants on Daddy's estate in your plus fours and Barbour jacket.

Then again, not too fast. I didn't know what happened to him during The Cull. I didn't know what he'd been doing for the last year. He could have been on a killing spree. After all, who'd know? He may have been a pampered Grant Mitchell clone, but I knew it would be dangerous to underestimate him.

"Killed many people since The Cull started, have you?" Casual, unconcerned, sound interested not appalled.

"A few." Cagey, giving nothing away. "No-one who didn't have it coming, anyway. First time's the worst. Easier after that."

"So who was first, then?"

Long silence.

Green emerged, limping, from the trees and the moment passed.

"What the bloody 'ell happened to you?" said Mac.

"Slipped, sir. Think I've twisted me ankle."

"Fuck me, Green, I'd have been better off sending my little sister. Right, sit down. What do they reckon?"

"The parade ground round back is deserted and they can't see anyone, so it's probably just the man under the car and the one in the pillbox. The Colonel and his men are going to take up firing positions in the main building, on the top floor left. Our job is to take out the guy under the car without drawing the attention of the pillbox. He said that's your job, sir."

But Mac was already moving. He'd pulled a vicious looking knife from his backpack, placed it between his teeth, and was crawling away on his belly.

"Cover me, Keegan," he whispered as he slithered out of the woods and began inching his way towards the car, which sat about fifty metres away and down a slope. The long grass provided good cover.

I took up position at the tree-line, nestled the rifle into my shoulder and scanned the area for nasty surprises. The place was as quiet as the grave.

And then, just as he made his final approach to the car, Mac burst out of the grass and ran as fast as he could back towards the trees, blowing our cover completely. I thought he'd lost the plot until the car exploded in a sudden blossom of flame and smoke, flinging Mac forward onto his face. He staggered upright again and continued running. No-one opened fire, and he made it back into cover safely. He sat next to me panting hard.

"Fucking tripwire," he gasped. "There wasn't a man under the car at all. Just a fucking leg, attached to a piece of wire that some bastard was tugging. Lured me in and I didn't see the booby trap 'til I crawled right into it. Fucking amateur!" He threw his knife in fury. It thudded into a tree, thrumming with force.

"Where's the puppeteer then?" I asked.

"The wire leads off to the left, so anywhere between the car and the main gate I reckon. But we're blown now. There could be any number of hostiles in there and they know we're here. We need a rethink."

At that moment there was a crackle of static and an ancient tannoy system hissed into life. A man's voice echoed tinnily around the buildings.

"This facility is the property of His Majesty's Armed

Forces and is defended. In accordance with emergency measures, and standing orders relating to Operation Motherland, any attempt to infiltrate this facility is an act of treason. Any further incursions will be met with deadly force. This is your first and last warning."

The speakers fell silent, as did we.

"What the sweet holy Christ," said Mac eventually, "is Operation Motherland?"

He bit his lip and surveyed the complex nervously.

"Right. That place is full of ordnance and I'm bloody well having it, standing orders or not."

"We could wait 'til after dark, sir," offered Green.

"And if they've got night goggles we hand them a major advantage, numbnuts. Nah, we need to do this quickly." He pulled out the binoculars again.

"Two wires we need to trace. The tannoy ones and the puppet one. Let's see where they go."

As he tried to trace the tannoy wires back to the mic I caught a glimpse of a flash from the top floor of the main windows. I looked closer and there it was again. I tapped Mac on the shoulder and pointed it out. He took a look.

"It's Bates," he said. Not 'the Colonel' I noticed. Interesting. "Signalling us with a mirror. Bloody idiot, keep your head down." But it was too late. A burst of machine gun fire raked across the face of the building, splintering the window frame and spraying the remaining shards of glass inward at Bates and the others. The pillbox was manned.

"I think someone's hit, can't see who," said Mac. "Fuck, this is a shambles. Right, enough of this." He handed the binoculars to me. "Green."

"Sir?"

"The tannoy wires go to the pillbox and the puppet wire leads down to the main gate. I think there's a man in cover there, probably a sniper in camouflage. You could probably walk right up to him and not see him, if he knows his job. But I want you to keep in the trees and move down to cover the area. He won't risk a shot until he sees a target the pillbox can't deal with, so I need you, Keegan, to draw his fire."

"Sir?" I asked, trying not to sound incredulous.

Mac grinned. "I know you're the better shot, Keegan, but Green's not going to be doing the 100 metre sprint anytime soon, are you Green?"

"No sir," he said, abjectly.

"And you can shoot that damn thing, right?"

"Yes sir."

"Well then. You're the bait, Keegan, and Green shoots the shooter. Sorted."

"And what will you be doing while I'm being shot at, sir?" I asked.

He opened his backpack, pulled out a stick of dynamite and waved it in my face. "Passed a quarry on my way back to Castle, didn't I? I'm going to blow that fucking pillbox wide open."

"And the Colonel?"

"Fuck him, if he's not been shot already he deserves to be. We're dealing with this. With me?"

"Yes sir!" yelped gung-ho Green.

Oh yeah, this was going to end well.

We synchronised our watches and then, always staying in the trees, Green and I went left, while Mac went right, towards the pillbox. Green took up position covering the long grass near the main gate and I kept going. I travelled some way past the complex, out of any possible sniper's line of sight, and scurried across the road leading to the gate. I made it safely into the trees on the other side and started to move back towards the fence. It didn't take long to find a breach and I snaked under the chain link and crawled through the grass until I was behind the first outbuilding on the opposite side of the road to Green.

Even higher on my list of Things-I-Never-Want-To-Do than 'shoot somebody' was 'be shot by somebody else'. So I wasn't entirely comfortable with Mac's plan that I should run up and down in plain view of a sniper, presenting a nice juicy target for a thumb-sized piece of supersonic, superheated lead that could push my brains out through my face.

I lay there for a minute, breathing deeply, calming myself, considering. Should I leg it? Just cut my losses and run? Go it alone? Did I need to remain at the school, taking orders from nutters and idiots, getting involved in unnecessary gunfights and risking my life... for what? For the school? For Matron?

But where else could I go? And if I left, how would Dad find me?

No, there was no choice. I'd made my decision to return to the school and I was stuck with it. I just had to stay alive long enough for Dad to come get me, and then I could split and leave Mac and Bates to their stupid army games. Until then I had to play along. After all, there was supposed to be safety in numbers, wasn't there?

I checked my watch. Time to go. I walked forward slowly. The gap between this outbuilding and the next was about ten metres. I had to cover that distance slowly enough to allow the sniper to notice me, sight, and fire, but sufficiently quickly that he didn't quite have time to take aim accurately enough to kill me. I'm sure an experienced SAS man would be able to do some calculation based on distance, running speed and firing time and tell you, to the second, how long he should be visible for. I was just going to have to guess using my vast experience of watching DVDs of *24*.

Fuck it.

I ran.

Three steps, that's all it took. Three bloody steps and I was flat on my face unsure what had hit me, and where. My mouth was full of grass before I even heard the shot.

And then, as I tried to work out if I was bleeding to death, a burst of machine gun fire and a huge explosion from up ahead. Shards of pillbox brick impacted all around me.

And then, before the dust had settled, a series of sharp reports off to my right, as the sniper and Green exchanged fire.

And then a scream.

And then silence.

CHAPTER FOUR

The problem with being in a battle is that if you get killed you never know whether your side wins or not. Sacrificing your life in a blaze of heroic glory is fine, but only if you're willing to accept that it might not have achieved anything.

Movie battles have a good solid story structure – beginning, middle, end – and the audience gets to see how it all works out, how the actions of certain characters shape events, how their deaths either do or don't have any meaning. But as I lay there in the cool grass, shot, bleeding, going into shock, I realised that the characters in those films, the ones who save the day by charging the machine guns or providing diversions so their mates can escape, the ones who say 'leave me, I'll only slow you down' or 'I can delay them, give you time to escape,' die alone, clinging to the hope that maybe they've made a difference but not really sure if they've just thrown their lives away for no good reason.

I had no idea if Green had shot the sniper or vice-versa. Even if Green had shot him, our 'side' might still not get the weapons. And if we did get the weapons we still might not survive the coming year. In which case what possible point did my slow, silent, blood-soaked death on a patch of scrubland between two prefabs actually have? How had I helped? Would I be remembered as a hero who sacrificed himself for the greater good, or would I just end up a leg attached to a piece of string underneath a car somewhere, luring other poor bastards into an ambush?

Luckily, the thing about shock is that pretty quickly you stop giving a toss about much of anything, so I soon stopped philosophising. I then briefly, dispassionately, considered giving up or going on, and then began crawling towards cover.

The sniper must have been aiming for my upper body. I wasn't sure whether I was lucky that he'd only hit my left thigh, or unlucky that he'd hit me at all. A thigh wound might sound painful but non-threatening – all that muscle to absorb the slug, no major organs to hit – but you've got arteries running through your legs, and if the bullet had hit one of those I wasn't going to be around for much longer, no matter how much cover I found.

I made it into the shade of the next outbuilding without being shot again. I propped myself up against the wall and examined my leg. It was bleeding freely but not spurting. Lucky. I pulled my belt out of my trousers, looped it around my leg just above the wound, and pulled it tight. Up to now there'd been hardly any pain, but as the belt dug in I had to work hard to stifle a scream.

I fastened the belt and tried to stand, using my rifle as a crutch. As soon as I was upright I had a massive headrush and tumbled back onto the ground.

I may have blacked out, I don't know.

Deep breaths. Focus. Get back up.

I hobbled away towards the main building. Dear God my leg hurt. Jonah had taken a chunk out of it and it hadn't hurt half as badly as this. Matron would be pleased, assuming I ever made it back to the sanatorium.

As I approached the gap between the next prefab and the one beyond I heard the unmistakeable snap of a twig. There was someone coming. If I tried to shoulder my rifle I'd topple over, so I propped myself up against the wall and raised the weapon, waiting for my stalker to break cover.

My vision was starting to blur.

Green hobbled from between the two buildings. He had

one hand above his head but the other arm hung limp at his side, dripping fresh blood. Score two to the sniper. But the sniper obviously thought I was dead, because he strolled out in front of me, bold as brass, keeping his rifle aimed square at Green's back.

Two things occurred to me. Firstly, they must have marched right across the road in full view of the pillbox, so the sniper didn't think there was any threat to him from that direction, which might mean Mac was dead; secondly, I was once again being offered an opportunity to become a killer.

"Hold it."

The sniper froze, staring straight ahead. Green, on the other hand, jumped out of his skin.

"I could shoot you right here and now," I said. "You'd be dead before you hit the ground." I was lightheaded, all right, please forgive the clichés. "I really don't want to do that, but please believe me when I say that I won't hesitate for an instant if you do anything at all to make me nervous. I've lost a lot of blood and I'm not sure I'm thinking clearly, so you'd better not make me jump."

The sniper was well camouflaged. His face and hands were daubed in black and green paint, and he had webbing hanging off him like a cloak, with pieces of greenery, twigs, leaves and ferns sticking out of it. He was carrying an L96 sniper rifle and had various other pieces of kit in pouches and holsters. He was about 40 and middle aged spread had taken hold. Hardly Hereford material, probably some weekend warrior TA guy who worked in accounts during the week.

"All right," he said, still not moving an inch. "Now calm down, son. I had no idea I was shooting at kids. I'd never have opened fire if I'd realised. There's no need for any more shooting, okay?"

"Not if you drop your gun, there isn't."

"Can't do that, laddie. Orders is orders, y'know."

I raised the rifle, pointed it straight at his head, and shuffled forward until the muzzle gently kissed his temple.

"Last chance. Drop it, or I drop you."

The cocky bastard actually thought about it for a minute, but then he lowered his gun and let it fall to the ground.

Thank you. Still not a killer.

Green staggered sideways and slumped against the wall of the opposite prefab. He was hyperventilating and glassy-eyed.

"On the floor, face down, hands behind your head."

"Now listen, can we not..."

"On the floor!"

The sniper complied.

"Green. Green!"

"Um, yeah? Yeah? Lee? Lee, I'm shot, Lee. He shot me, Lee."

"I know, but you're fine, doesn't look too serious. You're going to be fine."

"But he shot me, Lee. In my arm. He shot my arm. I've been shot. In the arm."

"He's going into shock. Let me help," said the sniper.

"Shut the fuck up," I barked. "Green, I need you to focus on me. Green. Green. Focus on me." His eyes swam around in his head but eventually they locked onto mine. "I want you to go into the main building, head to the top floor and find the Colonel. He's got a med kit. Tell him what's happened. But Green, keep behind these prefabs and enter the main building from the rear, don't expose yourself to the pillbox, understand? Understand?"

He nodded listlessly.

"Okay, off you go. Quickly now."

He lurched away like a zombie in a bad horror film.

Once I was sure he'd gone the right way, I turned my attention back to my captive.

"TA, right?"

"Is this an interrogation?" He sounded amused. I kicked him. Bad idea. My wounded leg buckled underneath me. He was moving before I even realised I was falling. But he was fat and slow, and I was lucky. I fell in such a way that the rifle remained pointing at him, and as my back hit the wall I was left slumped but upright, with my gun pointing square at his chest. He was on his knees, one hand reaching for a holster on his hip, but he knew he'd never make it. He widened his arms, smiled, and shuffled backwards until he was leaning against the opposite wall. I rested my rifle on my good knee, finger still firm on the trigger.

"Mind if I smoke?"

"Be my guest."

He reached slowly into a webbed pocket, took out a kit and began the rollup ritual. As he did so he considered me.

"How old are you, son?"

"Old enough."

"Fourteen, fifteen? What you doing running around playing soldiers, eh?"

I was not in the mood to be interrogated.

"I want you to very slowly take out the handguns and toss them over to me. Slowly."

He put the ciggie in his mouth, lit it, and then casually tossed me two shiny new Browning L9A1 sidearms.

"Here, have the ammo as well. Call it a gift. Plenty more where that came from." He threw me four clips of 13 rounds. I stashed the guns and ammunition in the big pockets on my trousers. No need for anyone else to know I had them. Insurance.

"What's that you've got, old .303? Where d'you get

that then?"

I didn't answer.

"Let me guess. CCF, right? You're from one of those posh schools where the kids play dress up. Listen son, I dunno who's giving you orders but they're fucked in the head if they think that storming a military facility is a job for teenagers. You should be holed up somewhere learning to rub sticks together to make fire, not creeping around the countryside shooting at adults."

"Maybe. But adults keep shooting at us and I feel a lot safer knowing I can shoot back."

He thought about this for a moment and then nodded. "Fair enough, I s'pose."

"And anyway, I'm the one holding the gun and it sounded to me like your pillbox got blown to pieces, so I wouldn't underestimate us, mate. We're not playing games here."

He grinned. "Again, fair point."

"So what's Operation Motherland when it's at home?" I asked.

"Exactly what I want to fucking know," said Mac.

The armoury was a room in the main building's basement, one end of which housed a huge vault door. The sniper and two other men were tied to chairs in front of the door. One of the captives from the pillbox had a nasty head wound and was only partially conscious. The other was covered in brick dust but looked fine.

Mac himself was also covered in dust and had a large purple bruise on his forehead. He'd been knocked out by a piece of brick sent sky high by the explosion, but he'd come round first and pulled these two from the wreckage.

"Pillboxes are fucking solid, right," he'd explained. "So I had to use a lot of geli. I managed to lay the charge without them spotting me, but they clocked me as I was crawling away and I had to hit the detonator before I was fully clear otherwise they'd have killed me."

The rest of us were gathered around the door too, sitting on chairs or lounging on the cellar steps. Wolf-Barry was dressing Green's wound, Zayn was seeing to mine. Bates, Zayn and Wolf-Barry's faces were all covered in tiny cuts where the glass from the window had shrapnelled into them, but none had serious injuries. Apparently they'd still been sitting up there trying to formulate a plan when Mac blew the pillbox and all the shooting happened. Nice one Batesy, leading from the front.

"Dave, I'm sorry about this," said Bates, addressing the conscious man from the pillbox. "But we've got a situation and I need those weapons. Didn't think there'd be anyone defending the place. Not my intention to have any shooting, but you shot first and my boys have a right to defend themselves. All you need to do is tell us how to open the vault and no-one else needs to get hurt."

The man didn't even try to hide his contempt.

"What the fuck do you think you're doing, Bates? I mean, you always were a jumped up little tosser who thought he was a soldier, but seriously, what the fuck is this? Colonel? You're a Colonel? Don't make me laugh. All those times we let you come down the boozer with us after manoeuvres so you could tell us all about the SAS stories you used to read. We were laughing *at* you, you moron, not *with* you. Do you really, seriously think that..."

He trailed off as a loud, sickening gurgle came from the semi-conscious man tied up next to him. All heads turned in time to see Mac pull his knife out of the man's neck. Blood gushed out over his hands, and down the man's jacket. We all sat there in stunned silence as the man shook and jerked in his bonds as he frothed, spluttered and wheezed. It took him a horribly long time to die, and none of us said a word.

Again, the hollowness in my stomach and the deep, sick sense that everything was spiralling out of control. But I was weak from blood loss, light-headed and mildly in shock. My reactions were muted. I could do nothing but watch.

"You're next," said Mac, simply. He then wiped the knife blade on his sleeve and sat back down, staring straight into Dave's terrified eyes with something that looked awfully like lust.

Zayn ran up the stairs. The sounds of him retching echoed back down to us.

Bates was white as a sheet. He hadn't ordered Mac to do that. Even through layers of shock I realised that if he let it go unremarked then Bates' authority would be gone forever and it would only be a matter of time before Mac made his move. I willed Bates to shout at him, to demand his weapon, to dress him down and seize control. But he didn't have it in him. Bates so desperately wanted to be a strong military leader but he was weak, indecisive and vulnerable. And with his next words he doomed all of us.

"Well, Dave?" he whispered, unable to conceal his shock but trying to play along and follow Mac's lead. "What's it to be?"

Dave held Mac's gaze, his eyes full of disbelief and horror. And, I noticed with surprise, tears. He told us the combination.

Mac smiled. "Thanks, mate," he said. He looked up at Bates. "Want to do the honours, sir?"

Bates seemed to be looking right through Mac at something terrible in the distance, but he nodded and mumbled "Yes, thank you Major." Now he was thanking his subordinate for giving him permission to open a door.

He stepped forward and entered the combination, swung the huge lever handle and pulled the heavy door open to reveal racks upon racks of armaments and stacked boxes of ammunition. Mac gave a low whistle of appreciation.

"Lovely jubbly," he said.

We brought the minibuses up to the front door and started loading the weapons into the back. Green and I sat in the front seats watching the others do all the heavy lifting. There were about fifty SA 80 Light Machine Guns, ten boxes of grenades, three more Browning sidearms and four 7.62mm General Purpose Machine Guns, the kind you would mount on a jeep or in a pillbox. There was also more ammunition than we could carry, so there would have to be a second trip. With this amount of firepower, properly used, we'd be a pretty formidable opposition.

"We could even go on the offensive," said Wolf-Barry. "Take the fight to those Hildenborough fuckers. Mac'll see us right, he'll make sure we do what's necessary to protect ourselves."

In his mind Mac had replaced Bates already. I wondered how many of the others felt the same way. And I wondered how long it would be before Mac's assumption of power became official. What would that would mean for poor usurped Mr Bates?

When the buses were loaded Patel opened the driver's door, excited. "You're going to want to see this," he said. "Mac's doing an interrogation."

In fact this was pretty much the last thing I wanted to

see, but somehow I felt I should. I was responsible for capturing the sniper, whatever happened to him would be, to some degree, on my conscience. I hopped out of the bus and continued hopping 'til I was back at the vault door.

Mac had the two surviving TA men sitting facing each other, with himself circling around them.

"... got what we came for," he was saying. "But we want to be sure we haven't missed anything, and the only thing more useful than guns is intel, right?"

Neither man moved a muscle, but they were rigid with fear and determination.

"So what I need to know, sorry, what *we* need to know," he gestured at Bates, who was sitting on the steps, reduced to the role of bystander, "is what Operation Motherland is and what it could mean for my merry little band. So who wants to tell me? Dave? Derek?"

So the sniper was called Derek. I almost wished I hadn't known that.

Neither said a word.

Mac started twirling his hunting knife around in his right hand.

"If no-one tells me then I'm going to have get a little cut happy. Now, I must admit, I'm looking forward to that, so I'd encourage you to hold out for a while. Been some time since I gave any fucker a really good cutting."

"Fuck you," whispered Dave.

"Oh goody, here I come a-cutting," said Mac, with the most malevolent grin I'd ever seen. He advanced towards the captive, knife raised.

"All right, all right," said Derek. "Just, leave him alone, okay. There's no need for any of this."

Mac stopped and turned to face Derek.

"Says you," he replied. He stood for a moment, considering, and then decided to give Derek a chance.

"Okay then, spill."

But Derek had got the measure of the man, and he cocked his head to one side as he regarded his would-be torturer. I saw all hope go out of his eyes and resignation and defeat set in. He'd realised what I'd long ago worked out – Mac was never going to let him get out of here alive, no matter what he said. He stared into the face of the man who he knew would soon be his murderer and found a depth of resolve that no amount of threats could break.

"Operation Motherland," he said, "is your death, little man. It's your big, hairy, motherfucking slaughter. It's coming for you and you won't even know it's arrived until you're dangling from a rope, kicking in the air and shitting yourself as your eyes pop out and your tongue turns black and you realise in your final moments that all you ever were was a sad, frightened child who wants his mummy. Operation Motherland is our justice and our justification and our vengeance. And that's all you're getting from either of us, cunt, so cut away."

Mac stood there staring at Derek, looking sort of impressed.

"Oh well," he said. "It was worth a try."

And he pulled out a handgun and shot both men in the head.

"Right then, back to Castle with the booty," he said, and walked up the stairs past us, whistling, leaving behind the corpses of three more soldiers who'd never know how the story ended.

CHAPTER FIVE

Nobody spoke much on the drive home, all of us trying to process what had happened. I would soon come to learn that the lesson the others took from the day was as simple as it was stupid: Mac is the boss, he is hard and cool and if you stick by him you'll be fine. That day Green, Zayn, Wolf-Barry, Patel and Speight all became, to a greater or lesser degree, Mac's devoted disciples, his power base, and everybody else's biggest problem.

What lesson Bates took away with him I'll never know, but it was a different man travelling back to school with us from the one who'd set out that morning. He'd appeared broken before, now he seemed to be a shadow.

When we got back to the school I was ferried up to the sanatorium with Green, and Matron swabbed and stitched and bandaged us. Green was allowed to go, he only had a flesh wound, but my injury was sufficiently severe that I was confined to a bed in the San. Matron warned me that as it healed it would hurt much more, and that if I wanted to recover fully then I must at all costs avoid splitting the stitches. I was prescribed bed rest for a week and a wheelchair for a fortnight thereafter.

It was my second day in the San when Mac came to visit.

"I tried to buy you some grapes, but they'd sold out." He laughed at his own joke, and I cracked a grin. He pulled a chair up next to my bed.

"Listen, Lee, what you did back there – risking your life, getting shot, saving Green, capturing that bastard sniper – that was hardcore shit. I reckon you're probably the hardest person here. Next to me, obviously. And you can really shoot."

Flattery now?

"The rest of my lads are loyal and all that, but, y'know, they ain't exactly Einsteins. If I'm to run this place...", and just like that he admitted he was planning to do away with Bates, "... then I need a lieutenant, a second-in-command, someone I can trust to watch my back when things get nasty. Someone with initiative. And I reckon that's you, mate."

Bloody hellfire. Okay, careful, think this through. Mac's not stupid. He knows to keep his enemies closest so maybe he realises I'm a threat and just wants to keep an eye on me. At the same time, I want to keep him close too, precisely because I am a threat. Then again, if I'm his trustworthy right hand man then it should make it easier for me to keep secrets from him, subvert him and bring him down. Easier and far more dangerous.

My head hurt just trying to work out all the wheels within wheels this conversation was setting in motion. But really, I had no choice whatsoever.

"Wow, Mac, I dunno what to say. I mean, I'm only a fifth year and the others are sixth-formers. I don't think they'd like me lording it over them."

"Let me worry about them. They'll do as I say."

"Okay, well, wow. Um, yeah, I'm flattered you think I'm the man for the job and I'll try not to let you down."

"So you'll do it?"

"Yeah, bring it on." Just the right mix of reticence and gung-ho. I should be on the stage.

Mac held out his hand and I shook it. I waited for the warning, the lean-in and hiss, the 'but if you...' It didn't come. Maybe he was sincere. He smiled.

"That's that then. Now all we need is for you to get better and we can really start sorting this fucking place out."

"What you got in mind?"

"Oh you'll see, you'll see."
Yeah, I thought. *I'm sure I will.*

After being in the thick of things for a few days it was odd to be cocooned in the San while the school went about turning itself into an armed camp, and Mac and his newly acquired groupies started to swagger and strut around Castle like they owned the place. Which, given that they were the only ones allowed to carry guns at all times, they did. They soon started dishing out punishments for supposed transgressions – lines, canings, laps before breakfast. It wouldn't be long before more inventive, sadistic punishments. The bullying was beginning.

Norton visited me regularly and kept me up to date with what was going on, and I was able to pass him my handguns and ammo to be stashed somewhere safe. Through him I learned that a new armoury had been set up in the cellar of Castle, with an armed guard on duty at all times. Bates and Mac carried handguns, but the rest of the senior officers carried rifles.

"Hammond's started giving lessons, if you can believe that," Norton told me. "Survivalist stuff, like water purification, how to trap and skin a rabbit, firemaking, that sort of thing. It's like being in the bloody Boy Scouts again. Oh and he's got these DVDs of this awful old telly show about survivors after a plague and he makes us watch it and 'discuss the issues'." He mock yawned.

"But that's not the best thing," he went on. "He's making a memorial. He won't let any of us see it, but knowing him it'll be some daft modern art sculpture. A ball with a hole it or something. Anyway, he's planning a big ceremony to unveil it the day after tomorrow, so we'll get you down in the wheelchair for that."

"I can hardly contain my excitement," I said.

I had told Norton all about events at the TA centre and he agreed with me that Mac was becoming a serious problem. If it had only been Mac then we might have used our guns to drive him out, or worse. But now he had a new gang of acolytes it was going to be much harder to unseat him. We would have to be cunning, bide our time, wait for the right moment, recruit other boys who would help us when the time came.

"Wylie is the biggest problem right now," said Norton. "He's taken a fancy to Unwin's little sister and he's not taking no for an answer. There've been a few slanging matches, but so far he's not threatened Unwin with his gun, but I reckon it's only a matter of time." He paused and looked at me worriedly. "She's 13, Lee."

"And what's Mac's reaction to this?"

"Seems to think it's funny."

"Look, do you think you'd be comfortable carrying a gun yourself?"

Norton looked surprised. "Me? Yeah, I suppose."

"Good, then find a way of carrying one of the Brownings with you, out of sight, and keep an eye on Unwin and his sister. You may have to intervene if things get nasty. But listen – only if there's no-one else around. If you can get away with doing something then do it, but if you run the risk of getting caught then do nothing."

I was appalled at what I was saying, but if Norton was shocked by the suggestion he didn't show it. Maybe the desperation of our situation hadn't quite sunk in yet, or maybe he was just a cooler customer than I had realised.

"God knows what Mac'd do to you if he found you threatening one of his officers," I went on, "and we have to keep an eye on the big picture here. Mac's our prime target, we can't do anything that jeopardises our plans to take him down."

"We have plans?"

"Um, no, not yet. But we will have. Wait and see. Big, clever plans. Schemes, maybe even plots."

"I like a good plot."

"There you go then."

As Norton and I cemented our friendship with conspiracy, Matron and I also grew closer. I would sit in the San with her as she did her morning surgeries, and she began teaching me the rudiments of first aid and medicine.

We hadn't only found weapons at the TA HQ. On the trip to collect the remaining ammunition Bates had ordered a full sweep of the facility and had found a well stocked medical centre, the contents of which had been brought back and given to Matron. She was ecstatic that now she had some proper painkillers, antibiotics, dressings and stuff. It wouldn't last long, but it provided temporary relief at least.

So in the afternoons I helped her catalogue the haul and she talked me through each drug and what it did. I carefully noted any drugs that could be used as sedatives or stimulants, just in case.

And as we did this she talked to me about books, films and music. She never mentioned her family or her life outside the school, but then I'd never known her to leave the grounds, even on her days off. Maybe she didn't have a life outside the school.

Somehow we managed to do a lot of laughing.

Mr Hammond had been a popular teacher. He expected the class to rise to their feet when he entered the room, wore a long black gown to teach lessons, and you got the sense that there were times he longed to pull a boy up to the front of the class by their sideburns and give them six of the best like he was allowed to do when he was a younger man. But we respected and liked him because you always knew where you stood with him. The rules of his classroom were clear and simple, he never lost his temper, and never gave out punishments just because he was having a bad day – if you did cop it from him he always made sure you knew why.

His lessons were interesting if not exactly thrilling, and his obsessive passion for all things Modern in art meant that anyone seeking enlightenment about mundane stuff like life drawing or sculpture could feel his frustration at having to teach what he considered backward and irrelevant skills. Cubism and Henry Moore's abstracts were all he lived for. I thought it was all meaningless, pretentious crap, if I'm honest, but it's hard not to warm to someone who's so genuinely enthusiastic.

He studied here as a boy and had returned to teach here immediately he qualified, so apart from his first five years, and three years at art college, he'd been ensconced in Castle for his entire life. He was an old man who should have retired years ago but he was such a fixture of the place that no-one could imagine him leaving. At the age of seventy-five he was still teaching art and had looked likely to do so until he dropped.

Although he was the senior master there had never been any question of his challenging Bates' authority, he just wasn't the type. Teaching lessons in post-apocalyptic survivalism sounded like just the kind of thing he'd come up with, and I wished I could have sat in on just one. Norton told me that there were a large group of younger boys who adored him utterly. He was playing granddad to them and they were lapping it up. After all, Mac wasn't exactly the approachable type, and Bates, despite his initial rapport with the younger boys, was increasingly isolated and distant.

In some ways you could say that, in a very short time, Hammond had cemented himself into the position he had held for so many decades before The Cull – the heart of the school, its conscience and kindness.

And of course, there was no room for such things in our brave new world.

The first snow of the winter fell the night before the great unveiling ceremony, making the school and its grounds shine and glitter. Norton turned up to collect me in his CCF uniform, which was unusual, but I didn't say anything. He and Matron lifted me out of my bed and into a wheelchair. My leg was in constant pain, a low dull throb that flared into sharp agony with the slightest movement, but in the absence of the proper hospital kit some of the boys had used cushions and planks to rig up a horizontal shelf for my leg to rest on, so once I was safely aboard I could be wheeled about without screaming all the time. Which was a plus.

With Norton as my driver we crunched through the snow to the front lawn where the school had assembled. I couldn't believe my eyes. Instead of the rag-tag gaggle of boys in what remained of their uniforms, I was confronted by fifty or so boys of all ages in full army kit. On the younger boys it looked comically large, but their trousers had been turned up and the huge jumpers tied with belts. Obviously the berets were a problem, so the younger boys either went bareheaded or wore baseball caps that had been painted green.

Not only were they dressed like soldiers, they were standing at ease in a nice square little cadre. And – my already cold blood ran ice – all of them held SA80s.

"What the fuck is this?" I whispered to Norton.

"I was going to warn you, but I figured you needed to see it for yourself. I can see it and I still don't believe it."

"So he actually did it, all the kids are in the army now?"

"Uh huh. As of this afternoon there's going to be compulsory drill and weapons training for all boys, as well as lessons on tactics, camouflage, all that shit. They've even tapped me to teach martial arts."

In front of the assembled troops was an object, about head height, draped in a sheet. Bates and Hammond stood either side of it, with Matron and the five remaining grown-ups – an old aunt and three grandparents – sitting on a row of chairs to the left; Green, his arm still in a sling, sat with them. To the right stood the remaining officers in two rows, like an honour guard, all holding .303 rifles.

Norton wheeled me up the row of chairs and positioned me on the end, next to Green. He then marched to the ranks and took up his position in the troops. As he stood at ease he winked at me and gave the smallest of shrugs as if to say 'I know, what a farce'.

Once Norton was in place, Bates stood. He looked even worse than he had when I'd last seen him. Although he was clean shaven his face was a mess of red spots and slashes where he'd cut himself. It wasn't hard to see why – his hands, which gripped a swagger stick behind his back so hard that his knuckles had turned white, were shaking. His eyes lacked focus; as he spoke he never seemed to be looking directly at anything or anyone, but to a point slightly to their left or right, or somewhere through and behind them.

Mac stood to attention in front of the troops, facing Bates. He stared straight into Bates' eyes, unwavering.

Bates never met his gaze.

The boys stood to shambolic attention at Mac's instruction, and Bates began to speak.

"At ease, men. Stand easy." The boys, many unsure what this meant, shuffled nervously in the cold. "When I was a boy my grandfather used to tell me tales of the Second World War. Stories of heroes and derring-do, secret missions, cunning generals, evil Nazis. It all seemed so simple. Good against bad, good wins, bad loses, everyone's happy..."

He lapsed into silence and stared off into space. As the seconds ticked past it became clear that this was more than just a dramatic pause. It soon became a very awkward silence, and then people started looking at each other out of the corners of their eyes and grimacing. Embarrassment set in, and then genuine discomfort. It must have been about a minute before he started again and everyone's shoulders relaxed.

"But the world isn't like that, is it men?" His voice was harder now, more assured. He started to increase his volume until he was on the verge of shouting. "Now it's just survival. Kill or be killed. It's hard and cruel and violent and wrong, but it's the world we have to live in and we have to be as hard as it is if we're to survive.

"We've all lost people, I know that. But they won't be forgotten. As we build our perfect home here in the grounds of our beloved school we carry with us the memories of those who have fallen before us, to the plague or the madness that followed it."

He paused again but this time, thank God, it was a dramatic flourish.

"My colleague Mr Hammond, who has given his life to this school, has constructed a monument to our fallen dead. Mr Hammond..." He gestured for Hammond to take his place, and sat down.

Hammond rose and walked to the same spot Bates had spoken from.

"Um, thanks Bates." He paused a second to collect his thoughts and then, to my surprise, he looked up at the crowd with a strong, clear gaze. There was a sense of purpose in his eyes and his jaw was set with determination. The feeble pensioner we'd rescued on the driveway had been replaced by the firm disciplinarian of old. "But I'm afraid I can't agree with your sentiments.

"You see, I remember the war. I was only a boy at school but even I could see that it wasn't glorious. When my parents were burned alive in their house they weren't heroes, they were victims of indiscriminate slaughter. Hundreds of thousands of people died in England during the Blitz, died in their beds, died at their breakfast tables, died on their way to work or in the pub or in the arms of their lovers. And that was hard and cruel and violent and wrong. But do you know how we fought it, hmm? By rising above it! We chose decency and kindness and community, we cared for each other. We refused to become the thing we were fighting and *that's* why we triumphed."

This was rousing stuff. Blitz Spirit! Triumph through adversity! Battle of Britain! Never in the field, etc. I was sitting there thinking of all the bombs we dropped on German cities – what can I say, I'm a cynical sod sometimes – but I was more interested in the reaction of Bates and Mac to this diatribe. Mac's face gave nothing away, but Bates' eyes were finally focused, and he looked furious.

"But you, Bates, what are you offering these children in the face of all this horror? More death! You can't meet violence with violence; you can't fight plague, fear, panic and desperation with a gun! If you want to build an army you need to arm them with knowledge that can help them rebuild, that can help them to help others to rebuild. Then maybe you can hold back the tide. But what you're offering us here, with your uniforms, guns and marching is nothing but an opportunity to die for no reason when we should be looking for a way to live!

"And that's why I made this."

He turned and pulled the sheet off the sculpture to reveal a figure made of white plaster that shone in the reflected snowlight. It was a boy of about twelve, dressed in school uniform. Under one arm he carried a pile of books, and in the other hand he held a satchel with a vivid red cross on it. Beneath the figure was a plinth bearing the inscription 'Through wisdom and compassion, out of the darkness', and underneath that a list of the dead.

We all stared at this gleaming statue, amazed. It was beautiful and awful. I didn't think Hammond had it in him to produce something so good. And judging by the expressions on everyone's faces, nobody else did either.

"This school has been a home to me all my life," said Hammond. "It represents everything I believe in and cherish – kindness, duty, learning and respect. Turning it into an armed camp cheapens everything it stands for, and I will not allow that to stand."

Someone started to clap. It was Matron. She rose to her feet and applauded. Then the four other grown-ups followed suit, and then the Dinner Lady.

Bates was crimson with fury, staring at these insubordinate ingrates, but he was frozen by the moment, shocked into inaction by the open defiance of what he was trying to achieve.

And then one, then two, then ten, then most, then all of the boys began clapping as well. This could be it, I realised. This could be the moment when we pulled back from the brink, abandoned the army game and reclaimed a little bit of sanity and humanity; the moment we pulled the rug out from under the feet of Bates and Mac and took charge. Everything depended upon how our glorious leaders responded to this insurrection.

Bates rose to his feet and strutted towards Hammond, who stood his ground.

"Oh shit," I whispered. "Here we go."

"I should shoot you here and now for insubordination," he hissed. The applause died away as people noticed that Bates' hand was wrapped tightly around the handle of his still-holstered sidearm.

"Insubordination?" mocked Hammond. "I'm not subordinate to you. I don't take orders from anyone, let alone a deluded history teacher who thinks he's Field Marshal Montgomery."

I could have hugged him for that. It was all I could do not to cheer. Still Mac was unmoving, at attention, staring straight ahead. The officers, who had not clapped, also stood still, but I could see they were nervous, uncertain what to do. They looked to Mac for a lead, but he was giving them nothing, letting the scene before him play out uninterrupted. The situation, and the school's future, was balanced on a knife edge.

"These boys need a strong hand, they need to be protected." Bates was trying not to shout, but even so his words carried clearly in the sudden silence.

"Yes they do. From you, and that psychopath there!" He pointed at Mac, who didn't move a muscle. "Look at what you've achieved since you've been in charge, eh? Two boys hanged in Hildenborough, two more shot and wounded in a stupid act of military adventurism. Your second-in-command has murdered four people that I know of in the last two weeks. And this school, which is supposed to be a haven of safety and learning, which could be offering sanctuary and succour to all the lost children wandering around out there in the chaos, has been turned into a bloody fortress. We should be sending out expeditions to retrieve children not armaments. Can't you see that?"

Bates had drawn his gun. It was hard to tell whether he'd done it consciously or not, but he stood there face to face with Hammond, his pistol held tight, shaking with barely contained fury and madness.

I saw Green take a step forward, as if to intervene, but Mac caught his eye and flashed him a look of warning. Green, cowed, stepped back into line.

"Mr Hammond, I am afraid that you are no longer welcome at this institution. You are ordered to leave."

Hammond laughed in Bates' face.

"You can't order me to leave. This is my home far more than it's ever been yours. I was here when your father was in nappies, young man. This is my school, not yours, and you'll have to kill me to get rid of me."

"No, I won't," said Bates.

Bates turned to Mac.

"Major, you and your men escort Mr Hammond from the premises immediately," he said.

"Yes sir!" barked Mac, and nodded to his officers, who raised their rifles and walked forward.

At this point Matron stepped forward to intervene, but Mac blocked her way and hissed into her face "Sit down, bitch, or else". She sat down, ashen-faced.

Seeing Mac advancing towards him, Hammond straightened his back and stuck out his chest. He wasn't going to be intimidated.

"You can't hand me over to this man, Bates," he cried. "We both know I'll be dead within the hour. And these boys won't let it happen, will you boys?"

Oh, what a misjudgement that was. Because the boys didn't make a sound. They were too afraid of the raised guns of the officers, too cowed by the horrors that had overtaken their lives in the last year, too conditioned to fear Mac. They'd enjoyed a mad moment of rebellion but once they'd stopped applauding their own terror had crept in to fill the silence.

Norton looked over at me desperately, seeking guidance. If I gave the nod he'd speak up.

Should I have given the signal? I still wonder about that. If I had, if Norton had stepped forward and rallied the boys, maybe things would have been different. Maybe all the blood and death could have been prevented. But I was unsure. It seemed too risky. I shook my head, and Norton clenched his jaw and remained silent. In that moment of uncertainty and cowardice he and I condemned us to all that followed.

Faced by Mac's slow, menacing approach, and the silent acquiescence of the boys, Hammond began to appreciate the gravity of his situation.

"You can't do this, Bates. For God's sake man, look at yourself, look at what you're doing!" There was a desperate, pleading note in his voice now.

"Mac's orders are to expel you," said Bates, "and that is what he'll do, isn't it Major?"

"Yes sir!"

Mac, approaching from behind Bates, bared his teeth at Hammond, and winked. Bates stepped forward, his pistol raised to cover Hammond and deter him from running. Hammond contemptuously batted the pistol aside. Bates brought it to bear again. Hammond batted it aside again. Bates raised the pistol to hit Hammond with it, but the old man grabbed Bates' arm to counter the blow.

You've seen the movies. You know what comes next. The two men grapple for possession of the weapon, they huddle in tight, almost embracing, as they strain and clutch and struggle for leverage. Then a shot – shocking, sudden, echoing off the buildings and trees, repeating again and again and fading away as the two men stand stock still, frozen, the horrified spectators waiting to see which one of them will topple.

Hammond backed away from Bates, his face full of confusion and fear. Then he fell sideways into the snow, and twitched and shook and died.

Bates stood there, the smoking gun in his hand. He stared at Hammond's body and seemed frozen, rooted to the spot.

Rowles broke ranks and ran towards the school, crying. Without a moment's hesitation Mac drew his sidearm and fired into the air.

"One more inch, Rowles, and I'll have you up on a charge of desertion!" he yelled.

Rowles turned back, his face streaked with tears and snot, utterly terrified. His lower lip trembled.

"Back in line, boy, now!"

Rowles shuffled back, wide-eyed, and rejoined the serried ranks of boys, all of whom mirrored his fear and uncertainty.

"You are on parade. You do not leave until you are dismissed. Understand?"

The boys stood in silence.

"I said," bellowed Mac, "do you understand?"

A half-hearted "yes sir".

"I bloody well hope so."

Mac turned to his officers. Patel and Wolf-Barry were restraining Matron, who had attempted to run to Hammond when he had been shot.

"Zayn, Pugh, take Hammond's body to the San." They did so.

Bates was still standing there.

Mac addressed the troops.

"The Colonel is right. There's no room here for charity, no food for freeloaders, no beds for fucking whingers. We stay tight, we stay hard, we stay alive. Hammond thought otherwise and look where it fucking got him."

"That's Mr Hammond to you, McKillick," shouted Matron, straining against the boys who were holding her back. Mac turned and walked slowly towards her. He had still not holstered his gun. He leaned forward so there was only an inch at most between their faces.

"Now you listen to me and you listen well, bitch," he whispered. "I run this place now. My gaff, my rules. And if you don't like that you can piss off. But while you stay here you do exactly as I say or so help me God I will fucking gut you. I *own* you, bitch, and don't you fucking forget it."

He leered at her and then raised his free hand and ever so softly caressed her cheek.

And for the first time ever I genuinely wanted to kill someone.

Matron spat in his face. There was an audible intake of breath from the boys.

Mac smiled.

"Take her away boys," he said. "Find somewhere safe and lock the cow up. I'm sure we can find a use for her."

"Sir?" Pugh, having a moment of conscience.

"Yes Corporal?" The danger in Mac's voice was unmistakeable.

"Nothing sir."

"Good, then carry on."

The two boys marched Matron away towards the school.

Bates still hadn't moved.

Mac walked over to Hammond's statue and kicked it hard. It slowly toppled over and fell into the bloodstained snow. Another failed attempt at decency and compassion, white on red.

CHAPTER SIX

The court martial of Mr Bates began the next morning.

Most of the officers were present, including myself, in my wheelchair, sitting at Mac's right hand. Only Green and Wylie were absent, running exercises with the boys. Mac, sporting a huge bruise on his left cheek which he made no reference to, took the chair. We were to be Bates' judges and jury.

Bates sat before us, hands bound. He was deep in shock and hadn't said a word since the shooting the previous day.

I don't think I've ever felt as powerless as I did in that room. Officially I was now one of the three most powerful people in the school, but this was a pantomime of Mac's devising and we all knew what was expected of us. Step out of line, challenge Mac in this context, and I had no doubt I'd share whatever fate he had in store for Bates. This was to be the culmination of Mac's ascent to power and we had to rubber stamp it, no matter what. Our lives depended upon it.

"Colonel Michael Bates, you are arraigned here today to answer the charge of murder."

Mac was even putting on a plummy voice, pretending to be a High Court judge. Actually, not 'putting on' at all; 'reverting to', more like.

Bates mumbled something inaudible in response.

"Speak up, Colonel," said Mac.

Bates looked up at Mac. The depth of despair in those eyes was like a physical blow.

"I said sorry," he muttered.

Mac snorted. "I'm afraid sorry just isn't going to do.

You are accused of a criminal offence of the most heinous type and you must answer for it before the court."

"So sorry," he whispered again, and his head slumped forward as his shoulders began to heave. He began to sob.

Mac was unmoved.

"Do I take it to understand that you are throwing yourself upon the mercy of this court, Colonel?"

But the only sound that came from Bates was a deep, hoarse moan.

"In which case we shall retire to consider our verdict."

As Mac rose Bates looked up and began to speak.

"All I wanted," he sobbed, "was to help."

"Well I think that..."

"All I wanted," Bates interrupted, "was to look after them. To make them safe, to protect and care for them, that's all I ever wanted, even before. But it was always so hard. They never understood what I was doing, never understood that it was all for their own good. Never understood. Nobody ever understood."

He started to speak more loudly now, passionately pleading with us to understand his choices and failures.

"Do you know what it's like to try and help someone who doesn't want to be helped? Do you? To try and persuade them that you know best? It's impossible. But it was my job, my duty, I couldn't just give up, could I? I had to make them see. I had to keep them safe. 'Arm ourselves', I said. 'The school will be safe', I said. 'Sanctuary', I said. But they wouldn't believe me. Wouldn't do things my way. Had to challenge me, always had to challenge me. Undermine, countermand, mock and ignore. All I wanted, all I ever wanted, was to be a hero, their hero."

Mac started to giggle. A man was falling to pieces in front of him and the sick bastard actually thought it was funny.

"And now I never will be, will I?" Bates looked up at Mac again, suddenly clear-eyed and focused. "Because you're going to kill me, aren't you, Mac?"

Mac met his gaze, but said nothing.

"Yeah, of course you are," said Bates. "You've been building up to this from the moment you arrived. Just biding your time, waiting for me to make a mistake. Well, good for you. Good for you. Made it easy for you really, didn't I? Got it wrong every step of the way and you just let me get deeper and deeper into the shit until it was time to make your move. And now you've got your lackeys and your weapons and your army. But what are you going to do with it all? What's the point of all the power? Do you even have a point, or is it just for its own sake, just because you can? You don't care for these boys, you don't care for their wellbeing or safety. You just want to be in control of them. And now you are. My fault, again. My fault."

He took a deep breath and calmed the final sobs that had interspersed his little speech. He raised his bound hands and wiped his eyes and nose on his sleeve, sat upright and stared straight ahead, trying to find some final shreds of dignity.

"Before you pass sentence I want to make a final request." He turned his gaze to me. "I don't know why you're allying yourself with this bastard, Keegan, but I've been watching you and I think you're better than this." *Oh shit, thanks. Blow my cover, why don't you?* "I want you to do something for me, if you can."

"What's that then?" I tried to sound casual and unconcerned. Mustn't let Mac know how much I was hating this.

"I want you to find my sons and tell them what's happened."

"What?" I couldn't keep the surprise out of my voice.

"They're alive?"

"Oh yes, they're alive. What, you thought I'd buried them? No, they were both O-neg. But they weren't mine. Carol and I adopted. Pure chance they had the same blood type. All I ever wanted... sorry. Anyway, find them. Apologise for me. They're with their mother at a farm just north of Leeds. Ranmore Farm, it's on the maps."

"So why did you come back here? What happened?" asked Mac, intrigued, in spite of himself.

"They left me." He gave a bitter laugh. "I was the luckiest man in the world, you see. Only child, so no brothers or sisters to lose. Both my parents already dead. My wife and kids all immune. My whole family, everyone I loved, survived The Cull. Luckiest man in the world. But then... they just left me. No reason left to pretend, she said. Not our real dad anyway, they said. And gone. All I ever wanted was to make them safe, be a hero to them, to my boys. But they hated me. All that love and now... just... nothing."

Suddenly Bates was transformed, suddenly he made sense. I felt desperately, achingly sorry for him.

"Wow," laughed Mac. "You're an even bigger loser than I thought!"

"Yes," said Bates, thoroughly broken. "I suppose I am."

"Well, the sentence is death, obviously. But I need a bit of time to consider how, so we'll just bung you back in a locked room for a bit while I work it out, yeah?"

While Bates languished under lock and key and Mac worked out which form of painful death most took his fancy, the day proceeded as normal. Norton wheeled me back to the San where I was still sleeping, despite Matron's incarceration.

"She's in one of the rooms upstairs," Norton said. He'd been snooping around for me, trying to find out where she was being kept. "Mac's old room, actually. The door's not locked as far as I can tell, but he's got Wolf-Barry on guard outside."

"Has she... has anything..." I couldn't quite bring myself to put my fears into words.

"I only found out where she was this morning, and as far as I know no-one's been in to see her since. But I don't know about last night, Lee."

I didn't want to think about what Mac might have done to her. I recalled the mysterious bruise on Mac's cheek.

Norton handed me the two Brownings that he'd hidden for me and I pocketed them both.

"Right, we need to get Wolf-Barry away from that door. I need to get in there."

"I might have an idea how we can do that," said Norton. "You might even call it a plot. But how are you going to manage? You can barely walk."

I lifted my good leg off the wheelchair rest and placed it on the floor, levering myself upright. I gingerly put my bad leg down and allowed it to take the tiniest fraction of my weight. Not so bad. A bit more. Bearable. I tried a step and it was like someone had shoved a hot metal bar straight through my calf. I grunted in pain and clenched my jaw. But I could do it. I had to.

Norton looked at me doubtfully.

"Piece of cake," I lied.

With the arrival of winter the school had become bitterly cold, and fires were kept burning in most grates throughout the day. Norton snuck into the dorm along the corridor from where Matron was being kept and nudged one of the logs out of the grate and onto the floor where it began to smoulder on the old waxed floorboard. The dorm door was open so we were counting on Wolf-Barry smelling the fire and raising the alarm before it really took hold. Last thing we wanted was to burn the school down.

Norton wafted the fumes towards the door then nipped out the dorm's back door and down the fire escape. It didn't take long for Wolf-Barry to cotton on, and he ran off shouting. I had managed to hop my way up the back stairs and as soon as he was out of sight I pushed open the stairwell door and hopped to Matron's room. I tried to ignore the blood that was beginning to trickle down my wounded leg, and the spots that were appearing at the edge of my vision.

I pushed the door – not locked, thank Christ – and lurched into the room. It was only my unsteady footing that saved me from receiving a floorboard to the face.

"Hey, hey, it's me, Lee," I whispered urgently.

Matron was stood just inside the door holding her improvised weapon. Her face was one big bruise. One eye was swollen shut, her lips were blue and bulbous. There was blood underneath her nose, which bulged where I think it had been broken. Her clothes were torn, too. She was breathing hard and her teeth were bared and bloody.

"What kept you, Lee? Come to take your turn?"

No time to dwell on what that implies. Focus. Concentrate. Things to do.

"Matron, we need to get you out of here now."

"And why should I trust you? They told me, you're his loyal second-in-command now!" She was fighting back tears, her words coming out in a furious mix of anger and pain.

There was no time to explain myself. The corridor would

be swarming in seconds. I pulled one of the handguns from my pocket and held it out to her.

"Take it."

She looked down at it, confused.

"Take it!"

She dropped the floorboard, grabbed the gun and then looked up at me. I couldn't read the expression on her wrecked face.

"Now come on!" I grabbed her hand and turned, gently pushing the door open as I did so. But we'd lingered too long. There was already a crowd of boys arguing over which colour of fire extinguisher they should use. Norton was nearest the door, bathed in a dim orange light, trying to take control but also keeping an eye out for our escape. Not only was he providing a distraction for us, he wanted to be closest to the danger, didn't want anyone else getting burnt because of his actions. My admiration for him grew hugely.

I pulled Matron behind me and dashed for the stairwell. We feel through the door and it closed behind us. We'd made it unseen.

It was only when I stopped inside the door that I realised I had run along the landing. Adrenalin is a great painkiller, but I knew I'd pay for that later. I could hear footsteps coming up the stairs below us; someone taking the back route to the fire. Matron and I flew down the flight of stairs and flung ourselves through the door of the next floor down, just in time to avoid being seen.

My leg buckled underneath me, and Matron helped me along the corridor to the San, which was almost directly beneath the burning dormitory. Smoke was beginning to seep through the ceiling from above.

"We don't have much time," I said. "Someone will be coming to get me to safety soon. They can't find you here and they mustn't suspect that I can walk yet. Help me into bed." Matron did so, and her hands came away from my leg covered in blood. She gasped.

"Lee, you must let me see to this, you could be crippled."

"No time. Now take the gun and go. Run. Find somewhere and hole up. This school isn't safe for you any more and I can't deal with Mac if he has you hostage. So go, please."

She hefted the Browning. Then she popped out the clip, checked it was loaded, slammed it home, cocked the gun, chambered a round and slipped off the safety catch. She knew exactly what she was doing. How the hell was a boarding school matron so familiar with a firearm?

"I'm not going anywhere." She was breathing hard and even through the bruises there was no mistaking the look of fury and determination on her face.

"And what are you going to do?" I demanded. "Shoot them all? You don't stand a chance. There are six of them, not to mention Mac, and after what they've done do you think they'll hesitate to shoot you? This school needs you – I need you – to be safe, so that when we finally get rid of that fucker you're there to help us pick up the pieces."

Her eyes burned with hatred, but I could see she was beginning to hesitate. I pressed my advantage.

"If you go after him now you'll be dead within the hour. Or worse – locked up again. Please, just run."

She hesitated, her hand upon my arm. If I'd been in her shoes I don't know if I'd have been able to beat down the desire for vengeance, but somehow I got through to her. I looked up at her ruined face and saw tears of frustration welling out of her swollen eyes.

I had so much I wanted to say to her but this was not the time.

"Please, Jane, just run. Be safe."

She leaned down and kissed me gently on the lips.

"You too," she said, and ran out the door.

I thought she'd make straight for freedom, but once again I'd underestimated her determination. In fact she took refuge in a deserted classroom until the early hours of the morning and then crept out to implement her plan.

The boys were sleeping in five dorms of about ten each, and each dorm had one officer sleeping there as well, as a deterrent against night-time escape attempts. But the four girls who had taken shelter at the school slept in their own dorm, along with the old aunt and one grandmother. They were unguarded and in a different part of Castle to the boys.

Under cover of darkness Matron snuck in, woke them, got their bags packed and provided armed escort as they slipped silently out of the school and into the night. Although prepared to forgo her revenge, she nonetheless ensured that no other girl or woman would have to endure what she had.

When I found out about Matron's night raid I couldn't help but smile. She was certainly audacious. I didn't want to think about where she and the girls were going or how they'd fare. All I knew was that they were safer elsewhere, and were one less factor I had to consider when it came to planning Mac's downfall.

However, I needed Matron's medical skills more than ever; my leg was wrecked. The stitches had split, the wound was oozing blood and the pain was unspeakable. I started to worry about things like gangrene and amputation. I did the best I could to sort myself out with antiseptic, fresh stitches and dressings.

Have you ever stitched your own wound? I don't recommend it. Once I was finished I lay back and hoped for the best. With any luck I'd be able to stay off it for a while now, and would be able to let it heal.

The big question now was what would happen to Bates. We got our answer the next morning, and it was worse than anything I could have imagined.

Behind the main school building were two sports pitches and a cricket square, all ringed by woods. The school had favoured rugby over football, and there were huge H-shaped rugby posts at either end of each pitch. Mac had a detail of boys cut down one of the rugby goals, dismantle it and reassemble it in the shape of a cross, which lay flat, ready to be re-erected using one of the vacated postholes.

He was going to crucify Bates.

"We can't let this happen," said Norton, urgently, when the truth became apparent. We were sitting in the San staring out of the window at the ghastly construction and all it represented. "If we let him do this then... I don't know what. But it ain't good."

"And how do you suggest we stop him?" I replied. "He has a cadre of permanently armed boys who are fiercely loyal. At first through stupidity and now, after what they did to Matron, they're as guilty as he is and they know it. He owns them and I don't think they'll hesitate to shoot any one of us dead if Mac orders it. Not now."

Norton nodded. "I've asked around, as discreetly as I can, but no-one saw anything that night. I can't find out which boys went into that room."

Alone in the San, my mind focused by the pain, I'd had plenty of time to dwell on what had happened to Matron. "Come to take your turn?" she'd asked. At first the implication of that question made me sick with horror, but then, as the long night wore on that disgust turned into a deep burning pit of anger, a fury I didn't know I had it in me to feel. It changed me. It made things simple.

"Then we assume they all did," I said. "Every one of those bastards is responsible for what happened to Matron, and every single one of them will pay for it. They crossed a line when they went into that room. He initiated them."

I was actually grateful for being bedridden, and that gratitude made me guilty. Had I been expected to participate I would have either gotten myself killed trying to prevent it, or been forced to take part at the point of a gun. I knew this, but still I felt that I should have been there to protect her, that I could have done something, anything.

"They're like him now," I went on. "He's made them that way, and we mustn't underestimate any one of them. They're loyal and stupid and, we now know, capable of pretty much anything. We have to be so careful. Play the long game."

"Bates won't be around that long."

"No," I admitted, matter of fact. "He probably won't be."

Norton looked at me askance.

"So we do nothing? We just let them do this?"

I looked at the cross and considered my options.

"No. No, we don't. But I can only see one course of action that doesn't get us crucified too. I don't like it, and neither will you."

All the blood drained from Norton's face as I told him what I wanted him to do.

"Coming to join the party?" asked Mac, as he pushed the wheelchair to my bedside. "I promise you, son, it's gonna be massive!"

"Wouldn't miss it for the world, sir." I smiled my most feral smile and for the first time it didn't feel forced or fake. I felt like a hunter, felt that ruthlessness, that focus, that calm.

"Attaboy, Lee." He playfully punched me on the arm and then helped me into the chair. I didn't bother disguising my discomfort and pain; if my plan didn't work and I had to resort to plan B, I would need Mac to know just how bad my leg really was.

"Still bad, eh?"

"Yeah. Little bit. Wish Matron was here, I don't want it going gangrenous."

"That bitch is long gone, but we'll find her. Just for you Lee, we'll find her."

He pushed me out the door and down the corridor to the stairs, where Patel was waiting to help carry me down.

"Actually, Lee, you missed some fun the other night, y'know."

Staying calm in the face of moments like this was becoming easier; the anger gave me more control.

"Really? What was that then?"

We reached the top of the stairs and Patel took the front wheels.

"What do you say, Patel? The other night. Quality times, yeah?"

Patel looked momentarily uncomfortable, but it might just have been the weight of the chair.

"Yes sir. Top quality," he replied.

"We taught that bitch a lesson all right. Let her know who's in charge around here. You should've been there, Lee. I reckon you always fancied her, am I right? Shame you missed your chance to take a pop, yeah?"

I fantasised about taking a knife, driving it deep into his beating heart and smiling into his dying eyes.

"Now that," I said enthusiastically, "would have been

worth getting gangrene for!"

Mac and Patel laughed. All three of us, partners in crime.

We reached the bottom of the stairs and I was wheeled out through the courtyard to the back field.

"The girls legged it during the night, by the way. Don't worry, we'll find 'em. And we've got night patrols now, and sentry boxes. No-one else is getting out of here. Isn't that right, fat lady?" This last to the Dinner Lady, who stood to one side, arms folded, trying defiance on for size, but unable to disguise her uncertainty and fear. She slept alone, above the kitchen, directly opposite the windows of the boys' dorms. Matron must have considered it too risky to wake her.

"She tried to leg it this morning," said Mac, "but she's too big to be proper stealthy. Anyway, what'd we eat if she vanished? You're precious to me, Mrs Dinner Lady, you are. Got to keep you close to home."

He leaned down and whispered to me. "Plus, you know, with Matron gone, we gotta have options for entertainment, yeah."

Norton was stood on the edge of the ranks closest to me. He glanced at me as I was wheeled past and nodded almost imperceptibly. I sighed with relief. Mission accomplished.

Mac parked me and took his place in front of the troops, the cross looming above him.

"It gives me no pleasure, what I'm about to do," he said.

Oh fuck off, I thought.

"But a strong leader must be ruthless in the pursuit of justice and safety. Anyone who harms one of mine will suffer the consequences, and they must know that I will be unswerving in their pursuit. There is no room here for mercy or forgiveness. The only sacred thing here is justice. If you kill one of the people under my protection you kill a part of me. And so help me God, you will do penance for your sins."

This was a new line, this holy righteousness bollocks. I hoped he wasn't going to get a messiah complex. On cue, Mac took out a Bible and began to read aloud as Zayn and Green emerged from the building escorting Bates.

"The path of the righteous man is beset on all sides by the iniquities of the selfish and the tyranny of evil men," read Mac, channelling Samuel L. Jackson. "Blessed is he, who in the name of charity and goodwill, shepherds the weak through the valley of darkness, for he is truly his brother's keeper and the finder of lost children. And I will strike down upon thee with great vengeance and furious anger those who would attempt to poison and destroy my brothers. And you will know my name is the Lord when I lay my vengeance upon thee."

Mac was really hamming it up. This was taking a turn for the weird. Whatever, I had to compliment him on his choice of reading; it was at least appropriate.

The boys led Bates up to the cross and he didn't struggle at all. Even when he saw the construction upon which he was to be mounted, he didn't show the least surprise or concern. I didn't think there was much left of Bates to kill.

Mac walked over to him and forced him down onto his knees, and then his back. He tied his wrists and feet to the improvised crucifix in silence. Then he got the hammer and nails. He looked disappointed when Bates didn't cry out in pain as they pierced his flesh.

He stood back and seized one of the ropes that were attached to the cross. Zayn and Pugh took the others, and together they heaved the construction upright. It was difficult. The heavy structure swayed and warped as they manhandled the post into the hole. They stood back and looked up at their handiwork.

It's a potent image, a man on a cross, possibly the most iconic there is. It's full of associations and meanings, mythic resonances of sacrifice and martyrdom. I looked up at Bates, whose head lolled drunkenly onto his shoulders, glassy eyed. Here was no sacrifice. He was no martyr. He was just a weak man who'd tried to be strong and had failed. No great tragedy, just another failed hero.

Mac seemed unsatisfied by the spectacle. I think he'd expected some wailing and moaning, begging and pleading. He'd been looking forward to this moment and now it had arrived his subject wasn't delivering the goods. Where was the catharsis? Where was the triumph? How could he gloat over a man so rag-doll limp that he was barely even present at his own execution?

I felt a tiny glow of satisfaction. The sedative that I'd taken from the San was doing its work. Norton had ensured that he was chosen to take the condemned man his final meal. He'd relayed my promise to find Bates' family and inform them of his death, before offering him a syringe. Bates had obviously accepted the escape route we'd offered him, and had injected himself. If I'd judged the dosage right he would lapse into a coma and die within a couple of hours and no-one would be any the wiser. Mac would think the crucifixion had been quicker than expected, probably assuming heart failure and shock, while Bates surfed out of this life on a warm wave of drug-induced bliss.

It was the only mercy we could offer him.

The boys were dismissed and they marched away in silence.

Mac took one last look at Bates and then walked over to me and began to wheel me towards Castle, leaving his one-time mentor to what he believed would be a slow and agonising death.

I took some satisfaction in knowing that I'd cheated Mac of that, at least. It was not much of a victory, but it was something, some small scintilla of compassion.

Now that I was his second-in-command I needed to find a way of talking to Mac, of being his mate. It was difficult to know which tack to take but I decided to brazen it out and be chummy and sarcastic and hope he went with it and didn't take offence. I gulped and took the plunge.

"You," I said witheringly, "have seen *Pulp Fiction* way too many times."

He chuckled and replied "I got pre-mediaeval on his ass."

And then Bates began to scream.

"At last," said Mac, with satisfaction. But he kept wheeling me onwards and he never looked back.

The scream of a dying man is a terrible thing to hear. It cuts right through you, strips you of all your illusions of immortality, removes any comfort you take in your own existence and reminds you, in the starkest way possible, that we all survive the day at the merest whim of fate and happenstance. It's humbling and horrifying and once you've heard it you never forget it. But at least it's normally over quite quickly.

I lay in the San listening to Bates scream for about an hour before I decided that I could stand it no longer. Either I'd got the dosage wrong and he had come around, or he was suffering the worst trip imaginable. Whatever. I'd either not helped or, perhaps, had made things worse. I wasn't prepared to live with that. Time for Plan B.

I levered myself off the bed and hopped across to the medicine cabinet. My leg was so bad now that even hopping was almost unbearable. But what did my pain compare with that of the man outside screaming into the face of inevitable death? I opened the cabinet and sorted through the little bottles until I found the right one. I grabbed a syringe, filled it, and jammed it straight into my wound. For a moment there were two men screaming, but then the sweet morphine did its work and my leg felt warm and clumsy and twice its normal size. But at least it bore my weight. I had no idea how long it would take for the drug to affect my senses, but I knew I had to be fast. I limped to the door and checked the corridor. Empty. Thank heaven for small blessings. My rifle stood against the wall in one of the corners, untouched since I'd put it there when I was brought into the San wounded, what seemed like a lifetime ago.

I picked it up and limped to the back stairwell. Again, no-one around. I hit the stairs and climbed. I was starting to get dizzy. I held tight to the railing as I made my way up to the locked door that gave out onto the roof. Two hard blows from my rifle butt took care of the lock, and I was out, underneath the low grey clouds.

I made my way to the edge of the roof, which felt springy underneath me, like I was walking on a duvet. The sky above me began to spin and I felt a hot flush rise up my body and face, like a cartoon character who's just eaten a hot chilli. I walked right to the edge and looked down, swayed unsteadily and leapt back. Carefully.

I lay down, assumed firing position and sighted my rifle on the chest of the man so far below me, who screamed and screamed and screamed.

I tried to focus on my task but the roof felt as if it was swallowing me up, engulfing me like quicksand. My head felt tight, my vision swam, my hands shook.

I grasped the rifle tight and closed my eyes. I steadied my breathing and opened them again. The madness scampered around the periphery of my vision, but I found that I had, for a moment at least, clarity.

Maybe it was the recklessness of drugged-up mania, or perhaps I was simply so far gone that I had ceased to worry about the consequences of my actions; whichever it was, I didn't hesitate for an instant. In a heartbeat I did the one thing I had been trying so hard to avoid these long months since The Cull had made each man, woman and child the sole guardian of their own morality; the one thing I had feared the most because of what it would say about where my choices had brought me and what I was truly capable of.

I squeezed the trigger and ended a man's life.

Finally, I was a killer.

LESSON TWO:
How To Be A Traitor

CHAPTER SEVEN

Before The Cull, back when St Mark's was just another boy's school and I was just a fourth-former trying to pass my exams, I got on the wrong side of Mac once.

It was Friday lunchtime and I had cycled into town to buy myself a bag of chips and pick up a magazine. Popping out at lunchtime wasn't forbidden but it was tight, time-wise, and if you dawdled you ran the risk of missing the start of afternoon lessons.

That day I bumped into a girl from the high school who I had met at one of the formal social events that the two schools collaborated on every now and then. I was awkward around girls. I had been in single-sex education since I was barely able to walk, and I didn't have sisters. It wasn't that I didn't know what to talk to girls about; I didn't know how to talk to them at all.

So while I was browsing the shelves in the newsagents this girl came up, said "hi" and we chatted for a few minutes. Her name was Michelle and I liked her. I can't really remember what I said; it's a bit of a blur. I was just concentrating on not spitting, swearing or belching. But it seemed to go off okay and she smiled as she said goodbye. She was pretty, I was blushing beetroot red, and I dawdled and daydreamed all the way back to school where I cycled straight into Mac, lying in wait at the school gates for waifs and strays.

"What the fuck time do you call this?" he asked.

"Sorry, I just, um..." Nope, no way out, caught bang to rights.

He grabbed the magazine.

"Hey, hey, what's this? SEX?"

"Um, no, it's SFX. It just looks like that 'cause the

picture's covering the bottom of the F."

"So you say. But all I can see is a magazine with a woman in a bikini on the cover and SEX written across the top of it."

"It's Princess Leia."

He rolled up the magazine and whacked me round the head with it as hard as he could.

"I don't care if it's Princess bloody Diana, it's confiscated."

There was no point protesting.

"So you a geek then, eh? Little spoddy sci-fi fan? Wank off over pictures of Daleks do you?"

So many cutting responses came to mind but I wasn't stupid enough to deliver any of them. I just stood there, head down, silent.

His punishment was typically creative. I had to stand in a corridor and hold the magazine against the wall with my nose. Simple enough, you might think. But he made me keep my feet a metre away from the wall, with my hands behind my back. I was leaning forward at an angle of about 45 degrees, and all my weight was pushed down onto my nose. Within a minute the pain was excruciating. He made me stand like that for half an hour. I never crossed him again, and he soon forgot who I was.

I was still in junior school when I learnt the secret to dealing with bullies: hit them as hard as you possibly can and make their noses bleed. Always worked for me. But when the bullies were officially sanctioned, when they were prefects (or teachers, come to think of it), then the more you protested, challenged them, fought back, or answered their rhetorical questions, the worse things got. They had authority on their side and any argument, reason or excuse you offered could just be ignored.

So I learned to swallow my pride, to bite back the retorts, to clench my fists but not let them fly. Keep your head down, don't draw attention to yourself, fly under the radar. Secret to a quiet life; secret to survival.

That instinct was deep ingrained in me by the time The Cull came around. I suppose that's why I didn't challenge Mac at the start, why I motioned to Norton to keep quiet when Hammond needed our help, why I decided to try and bring Mac down by infiltration and subterfuge. A lifetime of learning how to survive institutional bullying had taught me how to be sneaky, but I no longer understood the rules of open confrontation.

Mac still had the authority, although now it came from the muzzle of a gun and a cadre of lackeys rather than a fancy blue blazer braid, and I was still locked into the role of submissive victim, seething with resentment but staying silent, fighting the injustice indirectly, with plots and schemes.

But I still remembered the satisfaction of bloodying a bully's nose, and longed to feel Mac's cartilage crack beneath my fists.

My mouth felt dry and sandy, my eyes were gummed shut, and my leg was just a distant ache. I could hear someone moving around in the room, but I couldn't speak or move for a minute or so. Eventually I was able to manage a croak, and I heard a squeal and what sounded like a glass hitting the floor. I'd made somebody jump.

Then the sound of someone filling a glass of water from a jug, and a hand behind my head lifting it and putting the glass to my lips. I gulped down the liquid gratefully.

"Thanks," I rasped.

"You're welcome." The Dinner Lady.

"What's... where..."

"Don't try and speak, just rest your head a minute."

I heard her dabbing something in water and then a cool flannel wiped my eyes clear of sleep and I cracked them open, wincing at the bright sunlight streaming through the windows. I was still in the San.

"How long?"

"You've been unconscious for a week. We weren't sure you were going to survive, to be honest. Your leg was pretty bad. But your fever broke last night, and the infection seems to have burnt itself out. You are a very, very lucky boy."

I squinted up at her. My head felt like it was full of rocks.

The San door opened and Green poked his head inside.

"He awake?" he asked.

"Just about."

"Great, I'll go get Mac." He closed the door and I heard him walk off down the corridor.

The Dinner Lady leaned in closer, conspiratorially.

"Now listen, before he gets here, I've got a message for you from Matron."

She saw my agitation and shushed me.

"I stayed behind deliberately that night. What, you thought she'd left me behind? Someone needs to be here to keep an eye on you boys and I thought it might as well be me. But we've got a little system and we leave notes for each other. I'm not telling you where; she trusts you but I'm not so sure. Anyway, she's been telling me what drugs to give you, so it's thanks to her that you're still breathing. She wants you to know that she and the girls are all right. They're not too far away but the place they're hiding has already been searched by one of Mac's hunting parties, and they didn't find them. They're unlikely to search it again so we think they're safe for now."

I breathed a sigh of relief, which probably sounded more like the gasp of a dying man, because she offered me more water. I drank thirstily.

"Mac? Bates?"

She hesitated and looked at me with deep suspicion.

"Mr Bates is dead and buried, God rest his soul. Mac's spent most of the time searching the area for the girls, and training the boys in drill. He's had an assault course built down by the river and he makes them do it every day for an hour. You should see the way he treats them. Scandalous. Says he's preparing them for war. Mad fool will get us all killed, mark my words.

"He's been very interested in you, though. Thinks highly of you, he does. Wants you fighting fit. Says he doesn't want to start a fight without you there. So you just take your time getting better. The longer you laze around here feeling sorry for yourself the better off we are."

She fell silent as we heard Mac and Green arriving outside.

"All right, thank you Limpdick, stay on guard, there's a good boy," said Mac, as he entered. He dismissed Mrs Atkins with a glance. She made her exit and Mac took her vacated seat.

"Hi," I said weakly.

"Hi yourself." He sniffed and considered my leg. "How's it feel?"

"Throbbing."

He nodded.

"Well, I'm told you're a lucky laddie and you're gonna be fine. You rest up 'til you're fit, but don't take too long coz I'm gonna need you."

"Why, what's been going on?" I was barely conscious, disorientated, croaking like a frog, and I was being bombarded with information my brain wasn't quite ready to process. But I needed to know how things stood.

"We've got a traitor. Some fucker shot Batesy. Put him out of his misery and spoiled all our fun. I would've had you down for it, but you was semi-conscious and raving here in the San when I came to see where you were. So don't worry, we know it wasn't you. But we dunno who it was and that makes me... jumpy. Either one of my officers is going behind my back, or some junior's got a gun hidden away that we don't know about. I don't like either of those possibilities.

"Anyway, the fat lady'll get you some nosh and we can start sorting you out. I'll fill you in on my plans when you're more with it."

I was grateful; I was having trouble keeping my eyes open.

"You rest up, mate," said Mac. But I was already half asleep.

During my convalescence I had plenty of time to assess the situation.

The school was now a fortified camp. There were patrols of the perimeter twenty-four hours a day, and permanent manned guard posts at the main gate and the school's front door. As a rule there was one officer in each patrol or guard detail, to keep the boys in line.

The day began with parade and inspection at 8am, followed by breakfast, then drill and exercises all morning. The afternoons were taken up with sports and scavenging hunts. Mac had kept the evening movies going for as long as there was fuel, but it was all gone now, so we had to live without electricity. The only technological toys we had left were battery-powered stereos and torches; we'd scavenged enough batteries to keep us going for a while, so we could at least listen to music. When Mac wasn't running a night exercise the evenings were free time. Boys played board games; Green organized a theatre group and started rehearsing a production of *Our Town*; a third-former called Lill started up a band.

Heathcote and Williams had expanded their farm and we now had a few fields of livestock. Petts' market garden was coming along well. Everywhere there was business, activity and purpose.

But there was no disguising the tension that hung in the air at all times. The officers, united by their shared crime, had become a coherent unit, a tight, loyal gang who held absolute power and weren't afraid to use it. We were lucky that only one of them, Wylie, was an outright bastard. The others bossed and bullied and threw their weight around but things never threatened to get as violent as I had feared they would. Mac seemed to be restraining himself a bit, and I didn't know why. I had expected that by now he'd be using thumbscrews on a daily basis, but he mostly just shouted and threw the occasional punch. His punishment of choice was getting miscreants to run laps of the pitches before breakfast.

I think maybe he'd shocked even himself with how he'd behaved towards Bates.

He had stopped searching for Matron and the girls. With all the fuel gone our minibuses were now useless and so our search area was limited to a few miles in every direction. Horses were collected when and wherever they could be found, and a Haycox was running riding classes for the officers. I could already ride but it was not until very late in my healing that I could bear the pain of being bounced up and down on top of a galloping quadraped.

All Mac's efforts seemed to be going into securing our position and training the boys. But training them for what? I asked him and all the cryptic bastard would say was "You'll see". I was supposed to be his second-in-command but he wasn't taking me into his confidence.

And as he made his plans and preparations, so I made mine.

Norton's attitude towards me changed after I shot Bates. Although he was still jokey and conspiratorial I could sense a wariness about him. He didn't quite know what to make of me any more. I think my actions had surprised him almost as much as they'd surprised me. I didn't blame him. I was wary of myself.

My father used to wake screaming at night sometimes. I know something awful happened to him during a tour of duty in Bosnia, but he would never tell me what it was. Now I too was waking up sweating and shouting. In my nightmares Bates would scream into my face from his crucifix and Mac would stand by, applauding, as I carved our old teacher into tiny pieces, all of which grew mouths and joined the chorus of agony.

I had never had nightmares before. All the horror and death I had witnessed during The Cull, all the violence that had been done to me physically and psychologically, had never caused me a single night's sleeplessness. But the violence I had visited upon others was tormenting me. I had always believed that something awful had been done to my father; now I knew it was something awful that he had done to someone else. I realised that I hardly knew my father at all, or what he was capable of.

I was starting to realise what I was capable of, though. And it terrified me.

Nonetheless I remained focused on my objectives – gain Mac's trust, find an opportunity to betray him, find Matron and the girls, make the school the sanctuary it should always have been. I was willing to do almost anything to achieve my goals, but I couldn't do it alone.

"You've got a gun, so why don't you just shoot the bastard?" asked Norton one day as he was wheeling me around the pitches for my morning constitutional.

"What, you mean just walk up and shoot him dead in cold blood?"

"Well, duh. Yeah, that's exactly what I mean. Why not? Seriously, why not?"

"Not exactly ethical, is it?"

He burst out laughing.

"Ethical? Are you fucking joking? This from the man who shot our history teacher, the man who's accepted a position as second-in-command to a psychopath, the man who, in any court of law, would be held an accessory in the murder of those TA men? Ethical? Don't make me laugh. Is it any more ethical to plot his downfall from your hospital bed? At least if you went up and shot him you'd be being honest and direct. There's some ethics there."

"I'm not a cold-blooded murderer," was the only answer I could give him.

"Sorry mate, but you are."

We moved past the assault course. It was a collection of netting, rope and wood constructions, and a little bit of barbed wire. There was climbing, crawling, jumping, swinging and all that sort of stuff. A group of the youngest juniors were racing through it under the supervision of Wylie, who was hounding poor Rowles, throwing clods of earth at him, firing his gun off close to the boy's head to simulate being under fire, screaming at him all the time. The poor boy looked utterly terrified.

"If I shot Mac there's no telling what the other officers would do," I said. "They certainly wouldn't take orders from me. I'm just a fifth-former, remember. I may be second-in-command but I've not given a single order yet and when I do it'll only be because of Mac that they obey it. I need to get to know them, earn their respect and trust before I make a move. Divide and conquer, that's what we have to do here. I'm just trying to get through this with the fewest possible deaths."

He didn't pursue the argument, but I could feel that he and I were on tricky ground. We were still friends and allies, but I'd need to be careful not to alienate him any further. Mac tolerated my friendship with Norton, and I needed him to be my eyes and ears amongst the regular boys.

He wheeled me back to Castle in silence, but despite his reservations the next day we sat down to compare notes.

"Wylie is our biggest problem," Norton explained. "It's like he's trying to out-Mac Mac. The others are mostly content with handing out laps, the occasional slap or chores. But Wylie likes to humiliate people. He made Thackaray do ten rounds of the assault course naked the other day. The kid was a mess of cuts and bruises by the end. And he's got Vaughan sleeping in the cow shed just 'cause he didn't finish his breakfast."

"Okay, so if Mac goes then Wylie is most likely to try and take his place, you think?"

"For sure. The rest of them are much of a muchness except Green, who sits at the other end of the spectrum. He's the whipping boy, the runt of the litter. They've started giving him nicknames."

"Like?"

"Gayboy. Bender. You know the kind of thing. Limpdick is a popular one."

He looked at me significantly until the penny dropped.

"Oh man," I whispered. "You think that..."

He nodded. "Couldn't get it up is my guess."

"And that makes him vulnerable. They'll resent the fact that he's not as guilty as they are and they'll hate him for it. Plus, you know, he is kind of a poof."

"You should see him directing *Our Town*. I think he wants to play Emily himself. He's got Petts doing it. Says if boys dressed as girls were good enough for Shakespeare then it's good enough for us."

I considered this intelligence.

"Right then, we attack on two fronts," I said. "I try and get Mac to see Wylie as a threat, and foster Green's resentment of the others until he's ready to turn."

"And while you're doing that what do I do?"

"You need to sound out the others, but do it subtly. We need to identify those boys who are coming off worst and use that to get them on side. We need officers of our own who can be ready to move when an opportunity presents itself."

Norton grinned. "Finally we have a scheme."

"And a plot."

We shook hands.

"Marvellous," said Norton. "I think we just increased our chances of being crucified by about four hundred per cent."

After three weeks of rest I finally took to my pins and started walking with a stick. I would always have a pronounced limp, but I began a programme of exercise designed to help build the leg back up to strength.

On the day I walked again Mac asked me to join him in his quarters. He had moved into the headmaster's old flat. As I knocked on the door and waited for him to let me in I noticed that he'd added a lot of locks to the door. Just like a leader – caution takes the place of ease and soon, inevitably, paranoia takes the place of caution. I hoped I'd be able to hurry that process along a little.

He opened the door and gestured me inside with a smile.

"Take a seat," he said. I looked around the living room where I'd fought Jonah and was relieved to see that Mac had replaced the furniture; I didn't fancy sitting on the stain of half-dissolved headmaster. I slumped into the plush upholstery gratefully. I couldn't remember when I'd last sat on a sofa; it felt like the height of luxury.

I was expecting to be offered a cup of tea or something, but instead he opened the drinks cabinet and poured a couple of large whiskies. He handed one to me and then sat opposite, regarding me thoughtfully.

"I don't think you like me very much, Lee," he said eventually.

Oh.

Fuck.

Play innocent? He'd never buy it.

Make a joke out of it? He'd see straight through that.

Okay. Play it straight. Be serious but not confrontational.

I met his gaze. "What makes you think that?"

He shrugged. "Instinct and observation."

He sipped his drink. I did the same. I felt like I was playing poker.

I don't know how to play poker.

"I think Bates was right, you see," he continued. "I think you think you're better than this. I catch you, sometimes, looking at me and I think I can see you changing your expression, trying to hide the look of contempt before I notice it."

"Don't be daft." I laughed, all matey. He didn't smile.

"I'm many things, right? But I'm not daft." There was an edge of warning in his voice, but he didn't seem like he was about to get angry. Not unless I said something really stupid. I held up my hands and mimed innocence.

Mac leaned forward. "Thing is, you're right not to like

me. I'm a cunt. A total and utter bastard and I don't care who knows it. I'm a murderer and a rapist, and that's just for starters. I shoot first and ask questions later. I'll fucking slaughter anyone who gets between me and what I want, I don't care who they are. And I enjoy being in control of things. I like bossing people around, giving orders, laying down the law, playing the big man.

"But the thing is, Lee, it's the only thing I'm good at. I have a talent for it, see. Ask me to do maths or English, paint a picture or play the piano and I'm a fucking retard. But give me a situation that needs some muscle, a bit of ruthlessness, and I'm your man.

"And the one thing The Cull did, the one great, beautiful, brilliant thing that The Cull did, is it handed people like me the keys to the fucking world.

"There's no rozzer to haul me in for GBH, no magistrate to hand me an ASBO, no judge to send me to the Scrubs. There's only one law now, and it's not who's got the biggest gun – it's who's bastard enough to use it first. And I am.

"And so are you, I reckon."

All I could manage was "Eh?"

"Oh, don't embarrass yourself by playing innocent. You shot Batesy."

I tried to keep a stoney face, give nothing away. But there was no point.

"Yeah," he said, studying me, "I thought so."

This was not going well.

"Now you might think I'd be angry at you for that. And I was for a bit. But then I got to thinking. You probably did it coz you wanted to put him out of his misery, right?"

I didn't make a sound.

"Right?" There was that note of danger again.

I nodded, never breaking eye contact.

"Merciful. Heroic, even. But that doesn't change the

fact that you killed him. Shot him dead in cold blood. However you dress it up, you're a killer now. Just like me. And I like me, so I like people like me, yeah?"

Again, I nodded.

"The others are just followers, thugs, pussies who feel hard when they're around a big man like me. But I reckon you've got a bit more spine than that. I reckon you've got a bit of backbone. You went behind my back, deliberately did something that undermined what I was trying to do. That took guts, especially with that leg of yours. I like guts. But I do not like people who fuck with me.

"So that leaves me with a choice to make."

We stared at each other.

"Let me guess," I said eventually. "Kill me or promote me."

He inclined his head in agreement, leaned back in his chair and took another sip of whisky. Then he reached out his right hand, placed the drink on the side table and lifted the Browning that had sat there throughout our conversation, a silent threat. He placed the gun in his lap but kept hold of it, his finger resting gently on the trigger.

"What do you think I should do, Lee?"

I said nothing.

He lifted the gun, put it back on the table, and lifted his drink again.

"See, you took a risk and made a difficult decision because you thought it was the right thing to do. If I can convince you that helping me is the right thing to do then I reckon you and I will be quite a team. But I have to convince you, not threaten you into it. If I threaten you then you'll just say what I want to hear and I won't know if I can really trust you.

"So let me give you my sales pitch. After all, I was supposed to be going into advertising. If you don't like it you can walk – sorry, limp – straight out the main gate. I won't stop you."

He leaned back in his chair, took another sip of whisky and settled down to give me the hard sell.

"When I first arrived back here Batesy took me into his office and he gave me a little lecture. All about history, it was, which was his thing. He said to me that if you look at the history of primitive civilisations, then the same patterns keep appearing again and again. Farms clump together into villages. Then these villages get to know other villages and gradually they clump together and you get tribes. But tribes ain't democracies. No-one votes for the leader. The person who's in charge is the hardest bastard around and that's that.

"Now, if you don't like your tribal leader then you can challenge him, and there'll be a fight, and the winner is leader. It's a simple system. Everyone understands the rules. And it works. It works fucking beautifully. That's why it was the same all over the world.

"Democracy is a luxury. You can only manage it if your society is fucking loaded, well off, organised, stable, got a good infrastructure. But until your society has got that stuff, tribalism is the best way to run things coz it gives the most people the best chance of survival. And that is the only thing that matters – survival. The leader is chosen on merit, on strength. People like strength. They understand it.

"Now Batesy reckoned, and I happen to agree with him, that The Cull has left us in situation where we have to go back to tribes. We haven't got electricity, running water, gas. Fuck, we haven't even got much agriculture to speak of. Small, strong groups is the only way for people to rebuild. And strong groups need strong leaders. And that's me.

"You see Batesy's problem is that he convinced me he

was right. And of course once he did that I realised I had to replace him. I knew he wasn't hard enough to lead. A tribe led by him would never be strong enough to keep everyone alive.

"So I replaced him. I crucified the poor sod coz it was the most dramatic thing I could think of. I sent a strong message by doing that:

"I am the leader.

"I am strong and ruthless.

"Fuck with me and I'll kill you.

"And that, Batesy said, is how you establish yourself as the leader of a strong tribe. He knew that was the truth, he knew that kind of demonstration was necessary, but didn't have the stomach for it.

"I did, and I do.

"But it's because I do that I'm the right man to lead this tribe. A tribe led by me has a good chance of survival when it meets other tribes that might want to take us on. I'm these boys' best chance of staying alive. I'm convinced of that.

"Are you?"

Maybe I was.

Dear God, the mad bastard had a point.

It hadn't occurred to me for a second that he'd have anything so evolved as an ideology. I'd just assumed he was a power-mad psychopath. But here he was talking what sounded horribly like sense. Brutal, nasty and dangerous, but logical.

"No," I said. "Not entirely."

He leaned back and took another sip. He gestured with his head for me to continue. I took a deep breath and plunged in.

"Bates may have been right about the tribe thing. I dunno, I was never really into history myself. But it sounds plausible. And if he was right then, yeah, strong leaders are probably a necessary evil, for a while anyway.

"I didn't think much of Bates as a leader. He was bloody useless, frankly. He froze whenever anything difficult happened, and that was dangerous for everyone. He was a liability.

"I don't think crucifying the poor bastard was the answer. But all right, that's done now, and you're leader. Let's ignore what you did to get the job, the question is what are you going to do now you've got it?"

I paused; I needed to phrase this right.

"What I want to know is this," I said. "Do you intend to use the same level of cruelty to hold onto your position as you did to get it?"

"If I need to, yeah," he admitted. "But I don't think I will. I only need to get nasty if there's anyone who looks likely to challenge me. And I don't think there is. I can lay off a bit. Already have done."

"Yeah, I've noticed. I must admit I was expecting things to get really bad when you took control but that's not happened."

It was so weird talking openly to him like this. I was still half sure that this conversation was going to end with a gunshot, but he'd left me with no choice but honesty and I was committed now. Still, I didn't need to be completely honest.

"Look, Lee, I've got the job now," he said. "I'm going to toughen these boys up, and my officers are going to help with that. But I have to get the balance right, make sure I don't piss them off so much that I lose them. I've got their obedience, but I need their loyalty and their respect. And I know that's going to be difficult for me. Not my strong suit.

"With you at my side I reckon I've got a shot at winning them over. I watch you; you get on with the juniors and stuff. They just annoy me, and I fucking terrify them.

Which is good, don't get me wrong, I want them scared of me. But only scared enough. I need a bit of niceness in the mix. Carrot and stick, yeah? And that's why I need you."

"I can see it now," I laughed. "Lee Keegan, the caring face of crucifixion. So what, you want me to be your conscience? To keep you in line?"

"If you wanna put it that way, yeah. Let me know if I'm going too far. Keep your ear to the ground with the boys. Keep me up to date with how they're feeling. Watch the officers and find out which ones might be a problem."

"Wylie," I said briskly.

"Really? I like him. He's cruel," he said with relish.

I gave Mac my best 'well, duh' expression.

"Yeah, okay," he said. "Well, that's my point, innit. You notice this stuff. We make a good team. Plus, I can rely on you in a fight. And that's important. Coz we've got a lot of fighting to do, I reckon."

"So I'm your second-in-command. I can give orders to the officers, and my job is to back you up and let you know when I think you're going too far. And I'm doing this because a strong ruthless leader is our best chance of survival in a tribal world. That about right?"

"Yeah."

I made a show of considering my response and then I leaned forward and held out my hand.

"All right, I'm in."

But as he took my hand in his all I could think about was what he'd done to Matron and Bates, and how badly I could make him suffer before I ended him.

CHAPTER EIGHT

The guard looked us up and down with an expression of distaste.

"What do you want?"

Petts held out a battered Sainsbury's bag.

"We've got vegetables, cheese and milk to trade at the market," he said.

The guard peered into the bag.

"Got any Cheshire?"

"Um, no, sorry. It's just home made stuff. It's kind of soft, like Philadelphia."

The guard sniffed. "Filthy stuff. My wife used to eat that. Shame," he said wistfully. "I did love a bit of Cheshire."

We stood there looking expectant as he drifted away into a soft, crumbly reverie. Williams cleared his throat.

"What? Oh yeah, well, you'd better come in then. Bill will pat you down." He nodded to his colleague, who stepped forward and searched us for weapons. When he was done he pushed the barbed wire and wood barrier aside and nodded for us to go through.

"Curfew's at seven," said Bill. "If you plan on staying you'd best find yourself a bolthole before then. There's rooms at the pub, if you can pay."

Petts, Williams and I walked through the barricade and into Hildenborough.

As far as Mac was concerned this small town, three miles down the road from the school, was our first problem. It was these guys he was preparing us to fight.

To borrow Mac's terminology, their strong tribal leader was George Baker, local magistrate. The man who'd so ruthlessly hanged McCulloch and Fleming was a zero tolerance kind of guy who, like Mac, believed in public demonstrations of authority.

Petts and Williams visited Hildenborough once a week to attend a market at which they would trade the vegetables, meat and cheese they produced. Petts hadn't managed to convince anyone to eat the snails he collected, though.

Markets are a good place for gossip, and Hildenborough boasted what must have been the only working pub for a hundred miles, so it was good place to gather intelligence. The plan was for the others to trade as usual – for some reason Williams was desperate to find a good homebrew kit – while I mingled and got the lie of the land.

The town was well defended. Although it is ringed by open country on three sides, it kind of bleeds into Tonbridge on the fourth, making this the hardest front to defend against attack. To address this they had bulldozed a whole tranche of houses to create an exposed approach, then erected a bloody great fence and put in impressive gun towers. All it needed was a few spotlights and some German Shepherds and it would have been Berlin in the fifties.

Consequently the sides facing open country, where the guards were mostly posted on obvious routes like pathways and roads, were slightly more exposed and would be easier to infiltrate, especially after dark. Knowing this, Baker had imposed a strict curfew. Petts had discovered that the guards patrolled in pairs, with torches, and all wore high visibility jackets to prevent friendly fire incidents.

Before The Cull this part of Kent used to resound with the noise of shotguns blasting away at birds, so the Hildenborough survivors had no shortage of guns and ammunition. But our armoury was far more impressive, so if it came to a shooting match we'd have the advantage. In terms of numbers, Williams thought there were about forty men who acted as guards, and about two hundred residents in total.

Mac wanted me to establish some details about Baker himself, and find out whether he was likely to try and expand his territory.

Petts, Williams and I, all dressed in mufti so as not to attract attention, made our way through town to the market, which was held in front of the large stately home that Baker had adopted as his HQ. It was strange to see streets free of debris and burnt cars. As we approached the big house the cottages increasingly showed signs of occupation; the gardens were well tended, the curtains neatly draped. One thing about the new reality was that everyone who was still alive, no matter what they did before The Cull, got to live in the very best houses in the nicest parts of town. It seemed that in Hildenborough they were proud to show off their newly acquired properties.

Williams told me that the big house used to be some sort of medical centre before The Cull. It had impressive dormitory buildings in the grounds and a big swimming pool. The market, such as it was, was held on the forecourt. A collection of trestle tables had been erected and people were milling about trying to exchange jams, batteries, useless technology, clothes and so forth. There was a barbecue selling burgers and sausages, if you could provide the chef with something he wanted. There was even music from a folkie band, and the pub had laid on a tent and a few barrels of local brew.

The whole thing felt more like a village fete than a post-apocalyptic shambles. A little old lady sat knitting behind a pile of jars containing bramble jam, while a vicar stood proprietorially next to a table piled high with old books. There was an old wooden message board by the entrance to the beer tent and a handwritten note stated that the tug of war would start at two sharp, after the bail tossing and the egg and spoon race, but before the Main Event, whatever that was.

The world may have ended in plague and horror, but Middle England was doing very nicely, thanks for asking, would you like a bun Vicar?

And what could be more Middle England, more 'Outraged of Tunbridge Wells', than stringing people up? Off to one side, clearly visible but mercifully unused at the moment, stood a gallows. I shuddered as I imagined how McCulloch and Fleming must have felt in their final moments, as they stood on the trapdoor waiting for the lever to be pulled.

I let the other two go about their business and made a beeline for the beer tent. I don't like beer much, I'm more a whisky and coke kid, but I had a bagful of leeks to trade so I figured I could swig a few pints and make small talk with some locals. Infiltrate and inebriate, that was the plan.

In the end I didn't need to, because Baker himself was in the tent, jug of beer in hand, holding forth to an appreciative audience. I swapped a handful of leeks for a mug of mild, sat down on a bendy white plastic garden seat, and got an earful of the man himself.

He was tall but round, early fifties, dressed in 'Countryside Alliance' tweeds. His eyebrows were bushy, his cheeks were ruddy and his eyes were piercing blue. His jowls wobbled as he spoke.

"What you've got to understand, John," he said, "is that expansion is our only option."

Wow, ten seconds, job done. I can go home now, thanks. I never knew being a spy was this easy! At least I wouldn't have to drink any more of this foul brew; one sip was more than enough.

"But that doesn't have to mean confrontation," he continued.

Really?

"I see Hildenborough as the centre of an alliance. Some kind of loose affiliation of trading partners. Tribes, villages, maybe even city states, who knows. But we've got a safe, secure position here. We've got all the food we can use thanks to our farming programme, we're well armed and crime is virtually zero."

Interesting.

"Virtually," laughed one of his fellow drinkers. "It'll be zero after you hang that bastard later on." The group of men shared a convivial chuckle. You'd have thought he'd just told a joke about golf or something. That confirmed what the main event was.

"True, true," said Baker. "Anyway, we have stability here and I believe we can export that. Help other communities organise and sort themselves out."

He took a long draught of ale.

"Obviously it won't be easy," he continued. "I dare say we'll have to knock a few heads together along the way, deal with a few thugs and nasties, line some of 'em up against a wall and put them out of our misery. But really, one doesn't have a choice, does one. Got to have rule of law otherwise it'll be back to the bad old days of muggers and rapists and, God help us, niggers with attitude."

Oh no, hang on, I was right to start with – just another racist law and order nut with a passion for execution. Not that I minded anyone stringing Mac up and watching him dangle. But I didn't particularly want to become a citizen of Daily Mailonia. I'd rather take my chances with Mac.

A little alarm bell at the back of my head said 'so who's choosing their strong leader now then? Who's putting faith in the hardest bastard around to protect them? Who's starting to think that maybe Mac is right?'

I ignored it.

I was just about to get up and leave when Baker said

something that brought me up short. One of the others had asked something about local communities.

"The nearest thing to a community in the area is a school up the road," said Baker. "A proper school, mind; fee-paying, uniforms, teachers in gowns, army cadets, pupils from good families. There's a whole collection of boys there playing soldiers."

"So are you going to approach them? Bring them into your alliance?" asked another.

"Hard to say. We've been keeping them under surveillance for a while now..." Shit! "...and there have been some pretty unpleasant goings on there recently. About six weeks ago they actually crucified one of their teachers."

Various exclamations of disbelief.

"No, really. And they're very heavily armed. They raided the armoury of a Territorial Army HQ, so they've got machine guns and grenades. They've not threatened us at all but I have a suspicion that they may be behind my niece's disappearance. She left in pursuit of three looters a few months ago, and two of them were boys, so..."

As he momentarily lost the thread of his conversation in a choke of emotion I had a familiar sinking sensation. Here was the biggest player in the area and Mac had only gone and shot his bloody niece. A confrontation would be inevitable if this ever came to light.

"Anyway," he continued, "I've been considering our first move and I think we have to let them know who's boss. After all, they're only boys, they should fall into line if they're shown a firm enough hand. No need for a shooting war. I think a strong demonstration of authority should sort them out."

This was all starting to sound familiar. Mac's idea of a strong display of authority involved crucifixion. I imagined Baker's would involve some poor sod swinging at the end of a noose. Anxious that it shouldn't be me, I lustily knocked back the remains of my pint, forced myself not to gag, and rose to leave. But as I made for the exit Baker stepped into my path and said:

"My dear Lee, where do you think you're going?"

"I apologise, Lee – it is Lee isn't it?"

I nodded.

"I apologise, Lee, for misleading you back there. I am well aware that your glorious commander-in-chief executed my niece."

Baker was sat at a huge desk in what I took to be his office. I could see the business of market day proceeding normally through the huge arched window behind him. A tall woman had just taken the lead in the egg and spoon race.

I was tied to a chair, facing Baker across the desk and wondering how I'd ended up here.

"My source passed on that tidbit of information a few weeks ago," he said.

"Your source?"

"Steven Williams. I believe he helps run your little farm. He's out there now, trading vegetables. Nice young man. He thought rather highly of Mr Bates and didn't take his death well. He came to us one market day and asked for sanctuary, but we were able to persuade him to return to the school and draw us a few maps, detail your defences, provide us with profiles of the key players, that kind of thing. He's been most helpful."

I took a moment to digest this. Williams had betrayed us. I didn't know how to feel about that. On one hand, I couldn't really blame him; but on the other he'd thrown in his lot with a bunch of tweed-clad fascists who probably thought The Cull was all the fault of immigrants.

"He told us about you, too, Lee. The loyal second-in-command, wounded in action, accessory to at least three murders that we know about."

There was no point explaining that I was planning to betray Mac too. I was going to have to stay in character; play the part I'd created for myself and hope I could find a way out of this.

How ironic if I ended up hanging for Mac's crimes before I had a chance to hang Mac for them myself.

"You killed two boys who were just scavenging for food. Don't you dare talk to me about murder," I spat.

Baker rose from his seat, walked around the desk and backhanded me hard across the face. A large signet ring cut a groove across my cheek and I felt blood begin to trickle down it.

"Don't answer me back, boy," he growled, his façade of civility momentarily stripped away. "I killed looters. Plain and simple. We need law and order, especially now. There can be no exceptions to the rule of law, not for sex or age. Wrongdoing must be punished. Justice must be seen to be done and it must be swift and merciless."

I lifted my head and stared at him.

"What about the right to a fair trial? What about mitigating circumstances?"

"A fair trial? Like the one you gave your teacher before you killed him? Don't be naive."

Dammit, why did all the nutters I found myself talking to always have to keep making such fair bloody points? Anyway we'd killed his niece. There was nothing at all that I could say that would change that. There was no talking myself out of this.

"Okay, I'm your hostage, you've got a plan to take the school and you're probably going to kill me. So let's get it over with. Why don't you tell me what you've got up your sleeve and then I can escape and foil your evil scheme. What do you say?"

Even as I said the words I cringed inwardly; I've seen too many bad movies. Perhaps it was because this was a scenario I'd seen played out so many times that I couldn't quite bring myself to feel I was really in jeopardy. The hero always ends up talking to somebody who's about to kill them, and they always manage a last-minute escape. It's a rule.

"My dear boy," replied Baker, his façade back in place. "I won't have time to explain my plans. Sorry."

Baker was working from the script of a different film.

"Why? Got an appointment to keep?"

"No. But you do."

Only a few months ago I had found it hard to conjure up any real concern when faced with imminent death. Reeling from the carnage of The Cull, emotionally shut down after burying my mother, I was barely interested in my own survival. Now, after being savaged and shot, I was keenly aware of how easy it was to die, and more determined than ever not to do so until I was old, feeble and surrounded by fat grandchildren.

But as I was marched up to the gallows I couldn't see any way to stay alive beyond the next five minutes. My nerve was only barely holding. By the time the rope was slipped around my neck I felt like shitting myself and I wanted to cry.

I stood on the raised wooden platform looking down at the assembled faces of the Hildenborough market crowd, eagerly awaiting the 'Main Event' – my death. Some looked excited, others looked bored. They munched on hot dogs or sipped their beers as if it were just another day. Williams avoided my gaze.

I tried to work out how a simple trip to market and a little light gossip had led so quickly and inescapably to my imminent death. This hadn't been the plan. I wasn't supposed to die here, not now. What about Mac? What about Matron? What about my dad? This was supposed to be an ordinary day, nothing too risky, nothing spectacular. This wasn't supposed to be the second date on my tombstone.

It seemed that death had caught me unawares.

Which, of course, is what it always does.

Baker stood beside me and addressed the throng as I tried to prevent my knees from buckling. The rope itched and scratched at the soft flesh of my neck.

"Citizens of Hildenborough, and honoured guests, today marks a new beginning for this town."

There was a smattering of enthusiastic applause and a few cheers.

"Ever since The Cull descended upon us I have striven to make this town safe – safe for mothers and children; for families and old people. In this town I have made it my business to preserve the values and ideals that made this country great. And I believe I have done so, with your help. Hildenborough is a haven, a sanctuary in a violent and depraved world. But no longer. Today we shall begin to take the message to the country. Today we shall start the process of civilisation anew. From this town, from this very spot upon which I stand, we shall spread peace and safety throughout the land and we, *I*, shall be its saviour.

"And that process begins with an enclave of violence and sickness that sits on our front doorstep. Yes, friends, in a small village not far from here is the school of St Mark's. I know that some of you had children that attended that school, and you remember it as a centre of excellence, fostering values like duty, respect, obedience and independence.

"It is my sad duty to inform you that those values have become perverted. Under the leadership of a cruel, vicious man, the surviving children have armed themselves, overthrown their teachers, and declared themselves an anarchist state.

"Their lawlessness threatens us all. If we allow them to go unchecked then it won't be long before we are overrun by thugs and bullies, muggers and hoodies; feral children who know only the instinct to smash and destroy the homes and lives of their elders and betters.

"I am here to tell you that this shall not be allowed!"

Cheers and applause again. But, I noticed, not from everyone. A group of about fifteen men stood at the rear of the audience and they appeared to be watching not Baker, but the crowd. The hysteria Baker was whipping up with his well judged oratory was not reaching them.

When the cheering had died down Baker gestured to me.

"This young man had a bright future. He's not from a good family, his parents own no land and possess no great wealth. But his father served in Her Majesty's forces and they helped pay for his son's education at one of the finest schools in the land. They offered him an opportunity to better himself, to rise above his humble origins and excel. And what has he done with that chance? He has put on a uniform to which he has no right, picked up a gun, and embarked on a campaign of slaughter that is too horrific to relate to you good people here today."

I wanted to point out that it was Mac he wanted. But that was beside the point. Baker had to demonise me before killing me, only then would his point be made and his lesson handed down.

"One could say that he has simply reverted to type.

That he was never of good stock and had no place at a school such as St Mark's. I leave such judgements up to you. What I can do, however, is dispense justice for the men and women he has slaughtered. One of whom, friends, was my own, dear niece, Lucy."

A gasp from the crowd.

"The execution of this murderous animal signals the start of my campaign to clean up this county, *this* country! Even as we stand here a force of men is taking control of the school that harboured his vile criminal urges. By tonight we shall have expanded our territory to include this great institution for education and civilisation which I shall personally see is restored to its rightful place at the heart of a nation ruled by respect!"

Huge applause. And the group of men at the back of the crowd sloughed off their long coats and stood waiting for... what?

Baker turned to me.

"Lee Keegan, I find you guilty of the crime of murder and I hereby sentence you to hang by the neck until dead."

And he pulled the lever.

CHAPTER NINE

Jon used to have this battered old hardback book called *The Hangman's Art*. He was sick like that. It was the memoirs of an executioner but also a manual for a good hanging. Amongst all the factors the author considered important – a black canvas hood, the binding of hands and feet, the fluid motion of the trapdoor – the most crucial detail was the length of the rope.

If you hang a man with a rope that's too long the drop will decapitate the condemned, and nobody wants that. Conversely, if the rope is too short then the condemned person's neck will not break and they will swing there, choking to death. This outcome was not considered merciful.

The book contained a graph charting the ratio between the weight of the condemned and the correct length of rope required for a clean, clinical snap of the neck and a swift, essentially painless dispatch.

Thank Christ nobody on Baker's staff had a copy.

I don't think there's any shame in admitting that as I fell into space I lost all control of my bodily functions and shat myself. As I reached the full extent of the rope's length it snapped tight and dug hard into my windpipe.

I heard a sharp crack and knew that I was dead.

The brain takes a fairly long time to die once deprived of oxygen. I remember Bates telling us once that during the French Revolution the severed heads of guillotine victims could blink on command for up to four minutes after the chop. I wonder what they were thinking, how conscious they were of their situation. Were they screaming silently or were their final, bodiless minutes strangely serene?

As I swung there, knowing that my neck had snapped and that I was beginning the irreversible process of brain death, my vision swam and my lungs cried out for breath that I couldn't force into them. I didn't feel serene at all. I wanted to kick and fight and bite and scream my way out of the noose. But my hands were tied and my feet kicked helplessly at thin air. All I could see was the sky rotating above me.

I've no idea how long I hung there, it felt like a lifetime. Eventually, just as my vision was starting to fade and the roaring in my ears reached the pitch of a jet plane taking off, I felt someone grab my feet and push upwards. The pressure on my windpipe briefly abated and I gasped down the tiniest of breaths before the grip loosened and I swung free once more.

Then my weight was taken again, but this time it felt like I was standing on someone's shoulders. I was pushed upwards until I flopped onto the wooden platform like a landed fish. I felt hands loosening the noose and I breathed deep. Before I had time to get my bearings, while my hearing and vision were still blurred and faded, I was pulled to my feet and two people took my weight. I staggered between them, powerless to control where I was being led.

My senses began to re-establish themselves as we hurried down off the scaffold and across grass, around the side of the main building and away from the market. I could hear screams and gunshots. After a short run we stopped and my two rescuers started arguing.

"Where?" Petts.

"Um..." Williams.

"Quickly! We won't get far with him like this."

"Okay, inside."

"Are you fucking nuts?"

"Inside!"

They dragged me through a side door into the main building and then up three flights of stairs. When we finally stopped we were inside a tiny attic room, probably an old servants' quarters. A small window looked down onto the square below. There was a bed in the corner and my two schoolmates dropped me onto it. Williams closed the door and pushed a chest of drawers across it before slumping onto the floor.

"Who are they?" asked Petts.

"How the fuck should I know?" shouted Williams, on the edge of hysteria.

Resting on the bed I felt the adrenalin surging through me. I was shaking like a leaf but I could breathe!

"My... my neck. I heard it break," I gasped. "Why am I still alive?"

"If your neck was broken you'd be dead. Your neck's fine," said Petts. "I mean, you've got a hell of a bruise, and rope burns and shit, but no broken bones."

"But I heard it! I heard it break!" I protested.

"That wasn't your neck, that was a gunshot," said Williams. "They opened fire the second you dropped."

I levered myself upright and felt the awful slickness in my pants as I did so.

"Who opened fire?"

"Take a look," said Petts, gesturing to the window.

I shuffled sideways on the bed and peered down onto the market square. It was a scene of total chaos. The first thing I noticed was Baker, lying next to the lever, half his head missing, sprayed across the gallows platform.

At least that was one less mad bastard to worry about.

The forecourt was still full of people, but they were surrounded by the men I had seen at the back of the crowd. Some of these men carried guns; all brandished what looked like homemade machetes. There were some bodies lying around the place, a few villagers, and two of the attackers.

I could hear sporadic gunfire in the distance.

"They shot Baker just as he pulled the lever, and the crowd panicked," explained Petts. "There was a stampede but they were ready for it and they herded everyone back towards the building's entrance. Some of the men had guns and there was a fight, and during the confusion we were able to get to you. But it looks like these new guys, whoever they are, have got things under control now. By the way, Lee, you stink."

"Yeah, sorry about that."

At that moment a strange figure appeared, walking down the driveway towards the house. He was tall and lean and dressed in an immaculate three-piece pinstripe suit, complete with stripy tie and bowler hat. He carried an umbrella and his face was daubed with watery brown paint. He was flanked by two huge bodybuilder types, stripped naked and entirely daubed with the same brown stain. Both men carried machine guns.

Obviously an unknown force had stormed the town. I reasoned that one or two of them must have made it over the wire under cover of darkness and hidden a cache of weapons, probably in one of the abandoned houses. Then the main force had arrived one by one, ostensibly for market day, collected the weapons and waited for the appointed time – my execution. The gunshots in the distance indicated that another force had attacked the guard posts once they'd heard the shooting from inside the town. It seemed like a well organised and effective attack. Now here, in his finest suit, came their leader.

Much as I wanted to see what transpired I was conscious that a force of men from Hildenborough was about to storm the school. We couldn't hang around here, we needed to get back and warn them. I turned to Williams.

"When do they attack?"

He looked up at me, wide-eyed. "What?"

"Look, I know you sold us out to Baker so don't waste my fucking time. Do you know when they are planning to attack?"

Williams stared at me like a rabbit in headlights.

"Williams, listen to me. I don't give a damn about what you've done, all right. I just need..."

"I don't know," he muttered. "He didn't tell me."

"Hang on," said Petts. "Are you saying..."

"No time, Petts, not now. Got to get back to school and warn them. Stay here. I'll be back."

I rose to my feet. My knees felt like jelly but I forced myself to walk to the door. I listened but could hear no-one outside, so I shoved the chest aside and pushed the door ajar. No-one. I edged out into the corridor and worked my way along the rooms until I found one with a wardrobe full of clothes. I stripped my lower half and used a towel to clean myself up as best I could. I put on a clean pair of trousers and went back to the room, where I found Petts beating the living crap out of Williams.

I pulled them apart.

"Leave it Petts. Later!"

He was breathing hard and his fists were raw; Williams' nose was broken and his lip was bloodied. He was terrified.

"Oh God, he's going to crucify me. He's going to crucify me," was all he could say.

"I fucking hope so!" said Petts. I glared at him and told him to back off. He reluctantly sat on the bed. I knelt down and looked straight into Williams' eyes.

"Nobody is going to crucify anyone, Williams. I give you my word."

He looked at me for a moment and then nodded.

"Right now I need you to keep it together and help us get out of here without running into any of these guys with the machetes. Can you help us do that?"

He nodded again. "I know a way," he said.

"Good man. Right, we're going to try and get out of town as quickly and as quietly as we can, all right?"

Petts and Williams nodded. I sighed. I had just been bloody hanged. Why, oh why, did I have to take the lead yet again? The shit on my shorts wasn't even dry. All I wanted was a long bath and a stiff drink. And maybe a massage.

I led them out onto the landing and let Williams take point. We descended to the second floor but then we heard voices coming up the stairs from below. They were searching the house. I ushered the boys through the nearest door.

We had taken refuge in a bathroom.

"Dammit," I cursed. "Why couldn't it have been an armoury?"

There was precious little to use in the way of weapons. Petts cracked the door open and peered out while I unscrewed the shower hose and handed it to Williams – at least he could use that to choke someone with. Not that I had any intention of killing anyone, I just wanted to get back to the school as quickly as possible. For all I knew this new group could be the good guys, and I didn't want to go slaughtering them willy-nilly until I at least knew who or what I was dealing with.

I picked up the heavy porcelain slab that sat on top of the toilet cistern and held it ready to use a bludgeon. The only other potential weapon was a bottle of bleach. I pressed it into Petts' hand.

"Only if we need to," I whispered. "And try not to kill anyone, okay?"

They nodded.

The voices came nearer and two young men appeared at the top of the stairs. Both were wearing jeans and T-shirts. Their arms were daubed with the brown stain but their hands and faces were clean; left that way so they could blend in with the normal market crowd without arousing suspicion.

They began to work their way along the corridor towards us, checking the rooms as they went. I steadied myself and got a firm grip on the cistern lid; if I swung it right I should be able to take one of them out of the picture.

Two doors along from us they found someone hiding and both vanished into the room, where a struggle ensued. I was just about to try and use the distraction to slip past them when they dragged an old man of about eighty out into the corridor, threw him to the floor and kicked him hard in the ribs. He lay there, gasping, clutching his chest.

One of the men looked guiltily up and down the corridor, and then said to his mate: "Lets bleed 'im."

His colleague looked uncertain.

"What, here?" he asked.

"Of course here, you berk. Where else?"

"David won't like that."

"David doesn't have to know." He gestured to his face and hands. "I feel naked like this. Don't you? We're not safe, mate. Gotta be safe."

"Yeah, I s'pose."

"So let's bleed the cattle and then we can relax, yeah?"

"Yeah, all right, then. Bleed him."

The old man who was the subject of this banal, macabre exchange, whimpered helplessly. The first man grabbed him by the arms and lifted him upright, while the other advanced towards him with his machete. It was only then that I realised exactly what they were talking about.

The brown stain wasn't paint at all. It was blood.

Human blood.

Right. So. Not the good guys.

I felt a familiar sinking feeling as I realised that I was going to have to get involved. I turned to the others and whispered "Follow my lead". Then I pushed open the door, bellowed as loudly as I could, and ran at the man with the raised machete.

On the whole I try to avoid picking fights with people, especially people who are clearly insane, daubed in blood, and carrying a fucking huge knife, but I was now doing exactly that, armed with only a detachable piece of flushing toilet.

I had surprise on my side and my target had little time to react. I swung the cistern lid with all the momentum of my short run up, and smacked him under the chin as hard as I could. There was a shattering crunch as he was lifted off his feet and his head smacked satisfyingly into the corridor wall. He slumped to the floor, unconscious, his jaw a bloody mess.

His mate shouted out in anger and threw the old man aside, raising his machete and moving towards me menacingly. At which point Williams snuck up behind him, wrapped the shower hose around his neck and tugged him off his feet. They collapsed backwards in a tangle of limbs. Then Petts ran forward and squirted bleach into the man's face.

Williams scrambled clear as the man clawed at his eyes and screamed loud enough to raise the dead. Before I could knock him out with my trusty cistern lid, the old man stood up and drop-kicked his would-be murderer into the middle of next week.

There was a brief moment of calm as all four of us stood there breathing heavily, contemplating the two unconscious men.

"Thanks, lads," said the old guy, cheerily, "but I had it all under control."

We all gaped.

"Know a bit of unarmed combat from my army days," he went on. "I was just waiting for him to get a little closer then I'd have kicked him in the goolies, tossed this chappy over my head and done a runner."

"You were whimpering!" I said.

"All part of my act, dontchaknow."

We didn't have time for this.

"Right," I said. "Good. Fine. Um, we're running away now, if that's okay with you. So you ain't seen us, right?"

He tapped his nose and winked. "You hotfoot it, lads. I'll take care of these two." He bent down and picked up a machete. "Haven't used one of these since Burma," he said with relish.

We legged it.

We made it to the ground floor without encountering anyone else. We could hear someone giving some sort of speech from the forecourt, but I didn't want to hang around so Williams led us through the kitchens to the back door.

"We go out here and around the side of the house," he told us. "Then there's a garden hidden from the driveway by a tall hedge. Then it's over the road, across a field and into woodland. We should be safe from then."

I pushed open the door. No guard. We ran as fast as we could, Williams in the lead, until we came to the sheltered garden that ran alongside the forecourt. Still no sign of anyone. They were all on the other side of the hedge listening to whoever was ranting. We were halfway down the garden when we heard a truly bloodcurdling scream. It was no use; I had to see what was going on. I ran to the end of the garden and peered around the edge of the hedge.

I wish I hadn't.

The men with machetes were still encircling the captured citizens of the town, but all attention was focused on the scaffold. The noose was lying on the platform, the rope slack. A middle-aged woman was struggling in the grip of the two heavyset, naked guards, but she was tied hand and foot and had no chance of escape. One of the naked men looped her feet though the noose and then a third pulled the rope. She swung into the air, suspended upside down.

The man in the pinstripe suit, who was also standing on the platform – I assumed he was this group's leader, David – stepped forward and began to undress, meticulously piling his folded clothes to one side. The last thing he removed was his bowler hat, which he placed on top of the pile. He stood there naked, his body caked in crumbly dried blood. He spread his arms and addressed the crowd.

"In the fountain of life I shall be reborn," he intoned.

All the machete men chanted back in unison: "Make us safe."

From then on it was call and answer, like some kind of Catholic Mass gone horribly wrong.

"With the blood of the lamb I wash myself clean."

"Make us safe."

"From the source of pestilence comes our salvation."

"Make us safe."

"Life for life. Blood for blood."

"Make us safe."

He turned, tenderly cradled the woman's head and kissed her lips.

"I thank you for your gift," he said.

Then she was hauled as high as the rope would go.

David stood directly beneath her. One of his acolytes stepped forward and smoothly, emotionlessly, drew his machete across the trussed woman's neck.

And David showered in her fresh blood as the crowd screamed and his acolytes chanted together:

"Safe now. Safe now. Safe now."

Suddenly Mac didn't seem like such a bad guy after all.

I turned away in disgust to find Petts, white-faced in shock, Williams, throwing up, and a very big man with a machete standing behind me.

Without hesitation I threw a punch, but he rocked backwards and I swung into thin air. He snapped upright and brought his machete scything down at my shoulder. I followed my fist and spun left as the metal blade sliced within a millimetre of my ear. I stumbled, my weak leg momentarily betraying me. I hit the ground and tried to roll with it.

I'm not a martial arts specialist. That's Norton's thing. I can do guns, no problem. I can even do toilets, in a pinch. But straightforward fighting, especially when I'm unarmed and the guy I'm fighting has a piece of metal specifically designed to split me in two, is not something I'm very good at.

My cack-handed attempt at a forward roll probably saved my life. The man brought the machete around with lightning speed and chopped at the space where I would have been had my hand not slipped in some mud, pitching me face first. I scrambled forward on my hands and knees as he raised the knife again.

Petts barrelled into the guy's side, classic rugby tackle. The man staggered sideways but didn't fall, and he brought the machete handle down on the back of Petts' neck, hard. He went down like a sack of spuds.

I had regained my feet by now, and the man and I

circled each other warily. I caught a glimpse of Williams, running for the safety of the trees in the distance. Cowardly bastard. Maybe I would crucify him, if I ever saw him again.

I considered letting myself be captured, escaping later. But after what I'd just witnessed I didn't want to spend any more time in the company of these lunatics than I had to. No point taking a chance of being bled. But I was hopelessly outmatched here. This guy was faster, older, stronger and armed. I was limping, breathless and my neck hurt like hell.

He lunged forward, sweeping the machete sideways, trying to gut me. I sucked in my stomach and bent myself like a bow. The knife missed its mark. He then stepped towards me, and in one fluid movement the knife swept up and across, slicing down at my neck. I took a single step forward, ducked under the swing, and raised both hands to grab his forearm. I spun and shoved my back into his belly, tried to use his weight against him, throw him off balance. But, dammit, he was too solid on his legs and I hadn't practised this move before; I was just aping what I'd seen on TV, and he obviously knew what he was doing. He pulled in his arms, kept me cradled to him and squeezed, lifting me off my feet and tossing me aside.

I got to my feet and ran. Of course I say 'ran', I was still limping so there was no point my making for the tree-line; I'd just never make it. Instead I ran back to the house, making it inside just seconds before my pursuer. I flung myself through the kitchen door and scanned left and right for some kind of weapon with which to defend myself.

When the man came pelting through the door in pursuit, his face met the business end of a frying pan and his feet went out from under him. He crashed down onto the hard tiled floor with a rush of expelled breath. But still he kept a tight grip on his machete. I aimed a kick at his nuts but he rolled away. Nonetheless I connected with his thigh and he grunted. Finally a stroke of luck – I'd given him a dead leg.

He pulled himself up on a table as I swung at his head with the frying pan again. He swatted it away with the machete and it went flying from my grip, clattering to the floor. His nose was bleeding freely and one side of his face was vivid red where the pan had caught him on the cheekbone.

He snarled at me, wiped his hand in the blood from his nose, licked it, smacked his lips, and then smeared the fresh blood all over his face, mixing the new blood with the old.

"Safer now," he chuckled as he advanced, limping, towards me.

Jesus, was this guy for real?

I backed away, looking all the time for another means of defence. There was a rack of knives to my left, and I snatched a short one which I brandished menacingly. A voice in my head mocked: "Call that a knife? That's not a knife. That thing he's got, *that's* a knife!"

I continued backing away, trod on my discarded flying pan, and went flying like a character in a bad slapstick comedy. To add insult to injury I somehow contrived to land on my own knife, stabbing myself in the side. I yelled in pain as I pulled the blade out and felt hot blood seep down my hip. I looked up and there he was, looming over me, grinning.

"Good cattle. Bleed yourself. Save me the trouble."

"Oh, fuck off," I said wearily. And then I sat up, leaned forward and buried the knife hilt-deep into his thigh. Now it was his turn to yell. I flung myself backwards to avoid the answering swipe of his machete. I scrambled to my feet again and staggered away from him.

He resumed his advance without even pausing to remove the knife. I started grabbing things off the work surfaces and hurling them at him without taking time to see what they were. A colander, a kettle, a bottle of oil, a box of teabags; nothing slowed him down. This was futile.

I turned and scurried to the door.

It was locked. I looked left and right frantically. This wasn't the door Williams, Petts and I had entered from, that was on the other side of the room. This was – oh fuck, it was the door to a walk-in freezer.

I was trapped.

Long metal work surfaces stretched forward on either side of me, hemming me in. Behind me was a locked door, and in front of me stood some kind of Home Counties Jason Voorhees, dripping with blood, and grinning.

"Time to bleed, boy."

There was nowhere to run, nothing to hand offered any chance of defence or offence. It was just me, him and a very big knife.

Fuck it.

I put my head down, and charged the bastard. I slammed into his midriff and this time, with both legs damaged, he lost his balance and fell backwards. We tumbled to the floor and slid across the tiles and – hallelujah! – I saw his machete go sliding away underneath the tables. We wrestled, each trying to gain some purchase, but both of us were slick with blood and our hands kept slipping off each other. I tried to reach up and grab his throat but he was way too strong for me. He forced my arms down and somehow spun me, taking a firm grip on my clothes and pinioning me, face down on the floor. He folded his arm around my neck, nestling the soft inside of his elbow on my already bruised and battered windpipe, and squeezed.

For the second time in an hour I was being choked to death and I couldn't see any way of escape. I writhed and kicked, tried a reverse head butt, scratched and gasped and thrashed, but he was solid as stone, bearing down on me. I couldn't move him an inch.

Again my vision began to cloud, my ears began to roar.

And then my thrashing hands brushed against something hard. The knife – it was still in his thigh! I grasped it, twisted and pulled. He grunted and tightened his grip. I couldn't move my arm up to hit anything vital so I resorted to stabbing him in the thigh again.

And then again.

And again.

And again.

I kept the knife pumping in and out of his thigh with all the force I could muster, but as my body failed, my thrusts got weaker and weaker.

Eventually the blade fell out of my blood-slicked hands and I felt myself blacking out.

I regained consciousness what must have been a minute or two later. The dead weight of my assailant was still on top of me, but his grip on my neck had loosened. I lay there for a second as my head cleared. He wasn't breathing. I roared with the exertion of throwing him off of me, and I slipped and slid in the blood pool that surrounded us both before finally standing upright. Pausing only to pick up the machete, I staggered away, back towards the garden.

My windpipe was so badly swollen that I could only breathe in short ragged bursts. My side was on fire where the knife had speared me. I was a mass of bruises, my head felt light, my hearing was muffled and I was covered, absolutely covered from head to toe, in blood – both mine and that of the man I had killed.

No, don't think about that. Don't think about the killing, about the intimacy of it, the penetration and the spurting and the tactile slickness of his dead skin. Don't think about his breath on my neck, his hands on my throat, his knee in my back. Don't think about how awfully, sickeningly different it was to the clinical dissociation of a gunshot. Don't think about it. Save it for later. There's time for the nightmares later. Things to do.

I limped outside into the sunlight and listened. The chanting had stopped but I could still hear the noises of a large group of people. My route to freedom was still the same, so I started walking towards where Petts should have been lying unconscious. But he wasn't there. Had he regained consciousness and fled, or had he been found and captured? I peered around the corner of the hedge again and saw the machete men herding the townspeople into canvas-topped troop trucks, which had pulled up at the edge of the forecourt. They were shipping them off, presumably to their base of operations.

One man carried the dead body of the woman from the scaffold and tossed it into a truck amongst the living cattle.

Oh God, they had a use for corpses as well. Could they be cannibals too?

With a jolt I saw Petts, holding his head, clearly disorientated, being shoved into one of the trucks. There was no hope of a rescue. He'd have to take his chances.

There was nothing I could do here. I had to get back to the school and warn them about the imminent attack by all that was left of Hildenborough's militia, assuming it hadn't already taken place.

I made my way as fast as I could across the small section

of exposed ground and then back into cover on the road, behind the hedgerows and up to a stile. Even the simple act of climbing over a stile felt like an achievement given what I'd been through. And then into the field and safe to the trees.

Apart from the young woman, daubed in blood, carrying a gun, barring my way and looking at me quizzically.

We stood and stared at each other for a moment, and then I smiled and said:

"Safe now."

She regarded my blood-soaked self and nodded.

"Safe now," she replied.

And I was free to go.

CHAPTER TEN

I had no idea what awaited me back at the school, but that three-mile journey felt like one of the longest of my life. I wanted to run but I just wasn't capable. A shambling half-jog was the best I could muster.

I wondered how good David's intelligence had been. Had he chosen this afternoon to attack Hildenborough because he'd known that some of their forces would be busy elsewhere? And if so, did that mean he knew about the school? Could we be his next target? All this, of course, assuming the school wasn't already occupied.

I decided my best approach was to head along the river and come at the school from the rear, through the woods. That way I could get a sense of what had happened before showing myself.

The River Medway was part of the Ironside Line, the premier inland line of defence against the expected German invasion during the Second World War. As a result there are pillboxes all along the river, five of which mark the rear border of the school grounds. Under Mac's defence plan only two were manned at any one time, and never the same two on consecutive days.

I approached the first, but it was empty, as was the second. But the third had finally seen combat, many decades after its construction. There were four men, all of whom had been carrying shotguns, lying spread-eagled on the ground; victims of the General Purpose Machine Gun that had been housed in the pillbox. When I entered the pillbox I found one of our boys – a third-former called Guerrier, who I don't think I'd ever even spoken to – dead from a shotgun blast to the face. There was no sign of the GPMG, so I assumed the remainder of the Hildenborough attackers had commandeered it to use against further resistance. That would have evened the odds slightly.

I picked up one of the shotguns, emptied the cartridges from the pockets of the dead men, loaded the gun and moved on.

The fourth pillbox was empty but the fifth was pebble-dashed with shotgun pellets, and there was an abandoned GPMG inside, surrounded by spent casings. There were no bodies anywhere. Whoever had been manning this pillbox must have done a runner.

I moved cautiously through the woods to the edge of the playing fields and the assault course, which provided me with cover. I crawled through the netting and under the barbed wire and took up position by a wooden climbing structure.

There was no-one to be seen and no gunshots or screams to be heard; the school was silent and still. The fields offered no cover, but I had to keep going. I ran to the edge of the playing fields and made my way towards the school keeping myself close to the hedge. I made it to the outbuildings, where the walls were freshly chipped by what looked like GPMG rounds. One of the minibuses was aflame. The GPMG that had been taken from the pillbox was beside it, still resting upright on its tripod. There'd been a hell of a fight here, but it had moved on. There were two more Hildenborough attackers lying dead on the gravel path at the back of the building. All the windows on the ground floor were broken and one had a dead boy lying across it, half in and half out. I walked over and lifted his head. It was a junior called Belcher. I'd known him; nice kid, cried himself to sleep at night because he missed his mum.

Then I heard shots. But they weren't the sporadic shoot and return of a fire-fight; it was a series of measured single shots, about ten in all. I had a horrible suspicion I knew what that meant.

I made my way carefully through the corridors of Castle, passing bodies and bullet casings, splintered wood panelling and blood-soaked floorboards, until I came to the front door. I looked out across the driveway and lawn.

The guard post at the front gate was smoking and I could see the body of a boy lying across the sandbags; it was Zayn.

One less officer to worry about.

One less rapist for me to deal with.

The fight at the front didn't look like it had been as fierce as the one out back, which had obviously ended in a running battle indoors. I figured they'd sent a small force to the gate as a distraction, while the main force had attacked from the river. It's probably what I would have done. Fat lot of good it did them. Because standing in front of the school, before the assembled body of surviving pupils, stood Mac, smoking Browning still in hand. To his left lay a row of eleven men, all with their hands tied behind their backs, all with neat bullet holes in their heads. Six more men were kneeling to his right.

As I watched, Mac popped the clip out of his Browning. Empty. He nodded to Wylie, who raised his rifle and executed the next man. Then Wolf-Barry, Pugh, Speight and Patel each took a life. Green protested but he had a gun forced into his hands by Wylie. Mac barked an order and stood beside him, menacingly. Given no choice, Green closed his eyes, turned his head, and pulled the trigger. Mac patted him on the back.

One more team-building exercise.

One more crime to unite them.

I pushed open the front door and walked outside. The gasps of the boys alerted the officers, who turned, guns raised, and then stood there, amazed. Mac came running up to me, his face a mask of astonishment. He looked me up and down and said:

"What the hell happened to you?"

I told him.

"So what you're saying is that I've just executed a whole bunch of potential allies who could have helped us take on a far nastier bunch of heavily armed psychotic fuckers who like bathing in human blood and are probably cannibals?"

"That about covers it, yeah."

"Fuck."

Mac ordered the officers to hang the corpses from the lamp-posts that lined the school drive in the hope that they'd deter any attackers for a while.

After filling Mac in on my escapades I went to the San and attended to my own wounds, dosing myself with antibiotics and rubbing antiseptic and arnica on bruise after bruise. The wound in my side was excruciatingly painful, but I'd managed to miss all my vital organs and I didn't think I'd punctured my guts. I stitched it up and hoped for the best; it would make strenuous physical exercise even more awkward and painful for a while. By the time I was done a hot bath had been prepared for me, one of the privileges of rank. Lowering myself into it was sweet agony, but I lay there, boiling myself for about an hour, letting all the tension seep away, trying to work out my next move.

We had been training for a potential war with Hildenborough, but after a brief, bloody skirmish they were out of the picture, replaced by a far more menacing enemy. This new force was highly organised, armed with machine guns and machetes, driven by religious fanaticism and pre-emptively attacking communities in our area. We had no idea what, if any, strategy they were using, where they were based, or when, if at all, they planned to attack. We were vulnerable and uninformed; what we needed more than anything else was good intelligence.

When I was cleaned up I briefed all the officers on the events in Hildenborough. I was relieved to find that there was no sign of the resentment I had been expecting from them; I had been blooded once again and it seemed I had earned their respect without even having to try. Mac made it clear that all information regarding the new threat remained amongst officers only; he didn't want to scare the boys.

"Give 'em a day or so to mourn the dead and celebrate our victory," he said. "We've seen off an attacking army of adults – twenty-eight of them – with only five boys dead. We can use this to increase morale a bit, coz if what Lee is telling us is correct then this was just a warm-up. I won't leave one of my men in enemy hands so we've got to go and rescue Petts. That means picking a serious fight."

Once the briefing was over the officers went back to the grisly task of hanging out the Hildenborough dead, and burying our own. Mac and I pored over an OS map of the local area and picked out the most likely bases of operation for the group that Wylie had colourfully christened the Blood Hunters. We mainly focused on places that would have good defences, which meant stately homes and old manor houses. There were a lot of them, but we prioritised and drew up a search plan.

While Mac pondered the offence that we would adopt as our best defence, I sent a note to Matron via Mrs Atkins, warning her of the new threat and telling her to be on guard.

"I have never been so bloody scared in my entire life," said Norton. "There were bullets everywhere, the windows were exploding, the minibus blew up. I just closed my eyes and fired blind. Fat lot of use I was. Give me hand to hand and I know what I'm doing, but this was mental. Just fucking mental. And what I don't understand, right, is why they picked a fight with us in the first place? I mean, what've we done?"

"They were watching us," I said. "They saw Bates' crucifixion, thought we were a threat. You can see their point, I suppose."

"Still, couldn't they have just, y'know, knocked on the door and said 'hi, we're the neighbours, we baked you a cake?' I mean, there was no reason to come in guns blazing, no reason at all."

"Look where it got them."

"Look where it got Guerrier, Belcher, Griffiths and Zayn."

I had no answer to that.

"I don't want to die like that," he said eventually.

"If it's choice of being shot or being bled and eaten, then I'll take a bullet every time, thanks. After all, been there, done that."

"Yeah, yeah, stop boasting," he teased, sarcastically. "By my reckoning you've been shot, stabbed, strangled, hanged and savaged by a mad dog since you came back to school, three of those in the last twenty-four hours."

"I also shat myself."

"All right. You win. You are both vastly harder and far more pathetic than any of us."

"And don't you forget it."

"So, oh great unkillable smelly one, do you want to know how I've been doing?"

I nodded eagerly.

"Things in the ranks are confused. Some boys are really pumped up about the fight, gung-ho, ready for more. They reckon Mac's leadership saved our bacon and they're willing to fight for him now."

"Mac's fucking leadership provoked the bloody attack in the first place."

"But they don't know that."

"Which boys are we talking about?"

"Most of the fourth and fifth formers. They're the ones who cop it least from the officers, so they've got a less highly developed sense of grievance. But I've had a quiet natter with Haycox, the horsey one, and filled him in on what happened to Matron, and he's with us. He's trying to spread the word, subtle like."

"And the juniors?"

"They're more interesting. Rowles is a sneaky little sod when he's not sniffling, and he's got pretty much all of them on side. They loved Matron and Bates, and they fucking hate Mac. Plus the officers pick on them all the time and they're feeling pretty pissed off."

"So we've got basically all the seniors led by Mac, against all the juniors, led by us," I said, morosely. "Not going to be much of a fight is it."

"Do we have a better plan?"

I shook my head. "We'll just have to choose our moment carefully, won't we?" I said.

After breakfast the next morning – a surprisingly good Kedgeree made with fish from the river – everyone gathered in the briefing room. Without explicitly detailing the situation, Mac told the boys that there was a new threat abroad and that we were going to be searching for their

HQ. A group of five search teams was assembled, each comprising one officer and two other boys, and they were allocated specific targets to recce. The rest of us were to concentrate on repairing the damage of yesterday's attack and bolstering our defence perimeter.

As walking wounded I was excused any actual work. Instead I spent a quiet day with three boys who had been wounded in the fight. The youngest of these, Jenkins, had been shot in his left hand, which was shattered and unlikely to be fully useable ever again. He was only eleven but he had already made it to grade six on piano; he was having a hard time coming to terms with the fact that he'd never make grade seven. Vaughan had a nasty head wound, although this was from crashing into a table as he dived for cover. He was a bit concussed but he'd be fine. Feschuk had taken a splinter of glass to his left eye, and it was likely that depth perception was a thing of the past for him. We spent the day rummaging through the dusty library for any useful books and sharing stories of life before The Cull.

I casually manoeuvred the conversation around to the subject of Mac and was horrified to learn that, despite the wounds, despite what his actions had cost them, despite how he'd treated Bates and Matron, they were starting to like the bastard.

"If it weren't for him we'd have been captured and hung yesterday," said Feschuk. He related how Mac had taken his place in the defences when he'd been hit and had rallied the boys in the heat of battle to regroup and ambush the attackers inside Castle itself.

"The officers are a pain, but at least we're safe here," said Jenkins. His best mate Griffiths had died in the fight but he seemed detached and unconcerned by this. In shock or just accustomed to losing people?

"I never liked Matron anyways," said Vaughan. Who was a prick.

The next morning I swapped dusty books for damp leaves and beetles, as I crawled through mulchy undergrowth on a reconnaissance mission. My side stung every time I moved, but the stitches held and the painkillers I was taking helped a bit. When I reached the edge of the forest I brought out my binoculars and looked down a long sweeping lawn at the headquarters of the Blood Hunters.

"I don't fancy trying to storm that," said Mac, who was lying beside me.

Neither did I.

Ightham Mote was a solid wood and stone 14th century manor house that sat in the middle of a deep wide moat. This house was specifically designed to withstand siege and attack. The main entrance was a stone bridge that led underneath a tower flanked by stone buildings. The other three sides of the house comprised a half-timbered upper storey sitting on a solid stone lower level. There was another, smaller stone bridge at the rear. There were sandbagged gun emplacements on both bridges. There used to be a wooden bridge on one side, but that had obviously been pulled down by the building's new occupants; the National Trust would have had a fit.

One of the teachers used to take junior boys on trips to Ightham and had produced photocopied floor plans for the lessons he gave before the trip. Earlier we had turned Castle upside down and found a pile of these sheets in a store cupboard. The building was a maze, not somewhere you wanted to get involved in close quarters combat.

"This is suicide," I said. "There is no way we are getting in and out of there without getting shot to pieces."

"What this? Nine Lives Keegan walking away from a fight?"

That was his new nickname for me, Nine Lives. Funny

guy.

"Yes," I replied. "Always. Whenever humanly possible I walk away from a fight. I don't like fights. They hurt."

"Petts is in there. He's one of our boys. We never leave one of our boys behind."

Grief, he was starting to speak 'Tabloid'.

"Mac, mate, we're schoolboys not Royal Marines. He's probably already dead. And I know it's callous, but chances are some, if not all of us, will die getting him out. Surely one dead, however regrettable, is better than twenty?"

Mac favoured me with a look of total disgust.

"You'd really leave him in there?"

"Considering the odds, yes."

"Then you're not the man I thought you were."

Hang on, I wanted to say, since when did the murdering rapist have any claim to the moral high ground?

"Look," I said. "I agree with you in principle, of course I do. But for fuck's sake, look at that place. What good does it do anyone getting ourselves slaughtered?"

He just ignored me and crawled away. Clearly I was beneath his contempt.

The more I thought about attacking that place the less I liked it. I could see Mac's point about rescuing Petts, it was the only honourable sentiment I'd ever heard him utter, but it was going to get us killed. The power base that Norton was trying to build for a coup was just not strong enough yet, so there was no way of seizing power before the attack. And Mac was riding a wave of post-victory loyalty, so even our progress so far was looking wobbly. The boys had seen Mac's strategy win them a battle, and he'd been in the thick of the fighting, leading from the front. He'd proved himself both clever and brave. Which is, let's face it, what you want in a leader.

Not for the first time I wondered if maybe Mac was the

best choice to lead us after all. And not for the first time I recalled Matron's face and Bates' screams, and felt my resolve harden.

Time was of the essence. We needed to devise a plan of attack quickly and efficiently and for that we needed more intelligence. We were clear on the approaches to the house and its internal layout, but we needed to know more about the routines and behaviour of the people who lived there. After all, attacking in force during their daily weapons training drill, the only time of the day when every single person inside is armed to the teeth, would not be a good thing. We needed to know stuff, and the simplest way to find stuff out is to ask. Rather than knock politely on the door and ask the insane cannibals to fill in a survey we decided to wait until someone left and then capture them. We didn't have to wait long.

A group of three young men left the house around midday, armed with machetes and guns, and headed off in the direction of a nearby village. Speight led an ambush in which two of the men were killed, and then rode back to school with the survivor strapped across the back of his horse.

"You'll bleed for this, cattle fucker!"

The man was in his early twenties. His blonde hair was slicked back with dried blood and his face, torso and arms were similarly daubed. He stank like a butcher's shop and his breath reeked. Mac had tied him to a chair in an old classroom and was sitting facing him, turning his hunting knife over and over in his hands, saying nothing.

"David will come for me and when he does you'll pay. You'll all pay." This last directed at me and Speight.

"Let me guess," said Mac, impersonating The Count from

Sesame Street. "We'll pay... in blood! Mwahahaha!"

Speight chuckled. I rolled my eyes.

"You'll help make us safe. We're chosen. You're nothing."

"This whole 'safe' thing, let me see if I've got this straight," said Mac. "You smear yourself in human blood to protect you against what exactly... the plague?"

"The chosen shall bathe in the blood of the cattle, and they shall eat of their flesh, and they shall be spared the pestilence."

"But you've already survived the pestilence, yeah? I mean, you're O-neg, right? David's O-neg, your blood brothers are all O-neg, your victims are O-neg. You're all immune anyway otherwise you'd be dead, wouldn't you? So what's the fucking point?"

"The pestilence was sent by God to cleanse the Earth. It was The Rapture, don't you see? The worthy were taken up to The Lord and we have been left behind. We are the cursed ones and we must prove ourselves worthy in his sight before the Second Coming. We are living through the seven years of The Tribulation. We must not fail the trials before us or we shall burn in hell forever. David is the prophet of the Second Coming and he shall lead the chosen into Heaven. He anoints us with the blood of the unworthy so that when the pestilence returns to carry off those who have failed in the sight of The Lord we shall be protected from the mutation. We shall live forever, don't you see? When David takes the blood of the cattle and blesses it then it becomes the blood of The Christ and we are cleansed. Hallelujah!"

We just stared. None of us really had an answer for that.

"Um, right," said Mac, for once rendered almost speechless. "Okay. Look, mate, I don't want to get into a philosophical discussion with you and stuff. I just want to know the routine in your little manor house, yeah? What times you eat, what time you put the lights out, guard changes, that sort of stuff. Oh yeah, and where you keep the cattle from Hildenborough locked up. You know, just the basics. Think you can help me out?"

The prisoner appeared to think about this for a moment and then replied: "Piss off."

Mac turned to me and Speight, and beamed. "Finally, fucking finally, I get to torture somebody!"

He turned back and brandished the knife. "Right, you smelly little toerag, I am going to cut you into tiny chunks and feed you to the pigs!"

"Mac, a word," I said. I was still in Mac's bad books but he hadn't demoted me or anything, so I figured I was still persona grata.

"What is it Nine Lives? I'm busy." He advanced towards the captive.

"Mac, a moment please," I insisted. "Outside."

He turned to look at me. He did not look happy. "This had better be good."

In the corridor I explained my idea to Mac, who thought about it for a moment and then nodded. Speight scurried off to get the necessary torture implements.

"Does this mean I don't get to cut him?" said Mac, disappointed.

"You can, yeah, but not now, eh? Just let me do this, we'll get the info we need, then you can do what you want with him. Fair?"

"All right. This better work though."

"Trust me."

Speight returned and handed the tools over to me. I re-entered the room, with Mac and Speight behind me, and I advanced on the bound prisoner. I placed the torture devices on the bedside cabinet, pulled up a chair, and leaned forward to whisper conspiratorially in the captive's ear.

I told him what I was going to do.

He begged for mercy, but I refused to relent.

I reached into the bowl, pulled out the wet flannel, wrung it out and began to wash the blood from his face.

He screamed.

Not so safe now.

By the time I reached for the shampoo he was telling us everything we wanted to know.

Everyone assembled in the briefing room later that evening, in full combats, camouflage on their faces. Guns had already been issued. The thirty-eight remaining boys, four remaining officers, myself and Mac gathered together to plan an attack that I felt sure many of us would not survive.

Mac talked us through his plan and I watched as it dawned on the boys exactly how dangerous this night was going to be for them. Rowles looked terrified, Norton was ashen-faced. Defensive fighting is one thing, but to deliberately pick a fight with a heavily armed force entrenched in a near impregnable fortress is quite another. Mac gave it the hard sell, and nobody refused to participate. And to be fair, the plan could work, with a huge truckload of luck.

As the sun fell we marched out the front door and began the three mile yomp to Ightham Mote, determined to rescue our schoolmate and neutralise a threat that could destroy us.

St Mark's school for boys was going to war.

CHAPTER ELEVEN

The main assembly hall in Castle is full of names. On the wall that used to face the massed school each morning are six large black wooden boards, all hand decorated in blue and gold. The first three list, in chronological order, the Head Boys of the school going back 150 years. The next two list those pupils and teachers from St Mark's who died in The Great War, and the final one lists the Second World War dead.

But these aren't the only names in the main hall. The wooden panelling which clads the walls, deep polished and ancient, has been carved on by generations of boys. From the modern graffiti, simple scratches with a compass, to the old, ornate graffiti, with serifed fonts and punctuation, which must have taken hours of patient work with a penknife, boys have left their mark on St Mark's.

These names tell stories, and one name always fascinated me. James B. Grant carved his name into the wood panel beneath the farthest rear window. It's a beautiful piece of work, one of the most elaborate signatures in the hall. It must have taken him ages. It reads 'James B. Grant, 1913'.

His name also appears on the middle board of Head Boys, which tells us that he was Head Boy for the school year 1912-13; he must have carved his name on the wall in his final week at school, unafraid of punishment.

Finally, his is the last name on the board listing the dead of The Great War. He died in 1918.

A whole life story in three names.

There are pictures of the boys St Mark's sent to war, all dressed up in their corps uniforms. The faded, sepia photographs hang in the corridor that leads to the headmaster's study, each one with a list of names beneath, telling us who these boys were. There is one photograph, of the school corps from 1912, in which every single one of those names is to be found on the list of war dead. Every single one. Even given the slaughter of those years that's a remarkable and tragic clean sweep.

James B. Grant sits front and centre in that photograph. He's wearing puttees and a peaked cap, and he's got a swagger stick lying across his lap. He looks confident but not serious; there's a twinkle in his eye and a slight hint of amusement about the lips. He looks like a man who doesn't take himself too seriously, and I like that about him. He was an officer in the school corps and was doubtless an officer at the front.

When I was much younger I told my dad about this boy, whose name recurred through the fabric of my school. I remember asking him if I'd ever have to go to war, and he said no. He promised me there'd never be another war of conscription, not in my lifetime. The only people who'd go soldiering, he said, were those who'd chosen that life for themselves, like him. I was reassured.

When I had to do a special project for my history GCSE I took Grant as my subject, and I researched his war record. What I discovered horrified me and reinforced my determination that I would never become a soldier, like Grant or my father.

Now I was marching to war like so many boys before me and all I could think about was the tragic fate of James B. Grant.

Because Grant wasn't killed in action.

He was executed.

The sun was just edging over the horizon as I ran to cover and peered around the corner of the hedge. The two guards on the west bridge hadn't seen me. I gestured to the others and, one by one, Mac, Norton, Wolf-Barry, Speight and Patel hurried across to join me. If we could make it across the five metres of open space in front of us then we'd be out of the guards' line of sight and safe. One of the Blood Hunters' biggest mistakes was trusting the moat to keep them safe – there were no perimeter patrols at all, just the two sets of guards on the East and West bridges.

Dressed only in a pair of shorts, but daubed all over with shoe polish and carrying a plastic bag with clothes and weapons in it, Mac crawled forward across the lawn until the corner of the building shielded me from the bridge. Then he ran to the stone wall that ringed the moat on the North side. We followed quietly and without incident. There had been a wooden bridge entrance on this side of the house, but it had been knocked down by the Blood Hunters. They thought this side of the house was safe from attack.

Mac clambered over the wall and then climbed down the rough stone. He slid into the moat silently, but we heard him give a tiny gasp at the shock of the cold. He trod water until he was acclimatised and then he turned and swam slowly across the moat to the tiny set of stone steps that led down to the water's edge from a small door. He climbed out of the water and stood in the doorway. Once there he opened the plastic bag he'd been carrying and popped on a dry shirt and trousers. He also pulled out his gun and machete.

We watched him climb the three narrow steps and peer through the leaded window into what had been the house's billiard room. There were no lights on, so we couldn't be sure if anyone was in there or not. He used the machete to force the fragile door until it opened with a splintering crack that I felt sure must have been heard. We all crouched there, frozen, listening for sounds of alarm. Nothing. He pushed the door open and stepped into the room, then turned and waved us across. We were in.

A few minutes later all six of us were assembled inside, each of us armed with a gun and a knife that we were hoping we wouldn't have to use. So far we hadn't heard a single sound. Patel, Wolf-Barry and Speight hurried away. Mac, Norton and I waited but we heard no-one raise the alarm. Two minutes later the old longcase clock behind me whirred and chimed six. We heard footsteps overhead.

The Blood Hunters were waking up. Right on time.

Stage one accomplished.

"First in is me, Nine Lives here, Wolf-Barry, Speight, Patel and Norton, coz I'm told he's good in a fist fight, right Norton?"

"Yes sir."

"The two stone bridges on the east and west sides are guarded, but there's another way in they don't have covered. On the North side, out of the sightline of both sets of guards, there's a door in the billiard room that opens onto some steps down to the moat. Nine Lives reckons that when the posh blokes were smoking pipes and playing snooker then the ladies went out this door to a little boat so they could have a row on the moat. Charming, innit? That's our way in.

"Now, the building is square, with all four sides looking down into a big central courtyard. The Blood Hunters get up at six sharp, so we've got to be inside and in place before then, coz that courtyard won't be safe once they're awake. Once inside we split up. Patel and Speight go through the billiard room to the west bridge. There's two men on guard there but they won't be expecting anyone to come at them from inside. It's got to be a knife kill, quick and silent. Think you can manage that?

"Wolf-Barry you take the east bridge. Same drill, but there's only one man there. Once you've dealt with the guards shove the bodies out of sight behind the sandbags and take their places. In the half light there's a good chance you won't be rumbled. Then signal to Wylie and Pugh in the woods and they'll get to work laying the charges."

The three of us went left through a large oak door into a stone-floored ante-room. At the end of this room was another door, which led to a small passageway. We had to cross this passageway and enter the door directly opposite us, which would take us into a room once used by visiting school groups. Unfortunately the passageway was open to the courtyard. Although we'd be in shadow we'd be visible to anyone in the courtyard as we made our dash from room to room. Norton looked out the window and indicated that there was no-one around, so Mac cracked open the door and jumped across. Norton followed suit and I went last. As I stepped out into the passageway I heard a noise to my right and froze, flattening myself against the wall, trying to force myself into the shadows.

A group of men and women were making their way across the courtyard. All were dressed casually in jeans and t-shirts. They were gossiping sleepily, rubbing their eyes, off to morning worship in the chapel. If it hadn't been for the dried blood in their hair and on their faces you'd have thought they were students. They entered the building on the far side of the courtyard and I hurried after my comrades. We made our way through an old pantry and then we stopped at the far door. Beyond this door lay a small room and beyond that lay the crypt, where the captives were kept. We were expecting at least one guard on the door.

Mac and Norton drew their knives, stood side by side at the door and, on a silent count of three, opened the door and stepped inside. I heard a brief scuffle and a muffled groan, then nothing. Mac's face appeared at the door, grinning.

I followed them, past the dead body of a young woman, slumped in a corner with her eyes staring into space and her throat slit open. Mac was wiping his knife clean on her shirt.

The next door would lead us into the crypt. With luck there'd be no guards inside, only prisoners. My heart was pumping for all it was worth as I turned the handle and pushed open the door. The crypt was a low-ceilinged room of white stone with a brick floor. Huddled together in this space were around forty people, crammed in tightly, most of them asleep, curled up against each other for warmth.

Stage two accomplished.

"Me, Keegan and Norton will make our way to the crypt. There's two doors to the crypt but only one of them locks, so there's a guard on the one that doesn't. Luckily that's the door closest to our entrance point, so we should be able to take out the guard easy.

"By this point the Blood Hunters should all be safely settled into the big chapel for morning worship, which starts at 6:15 and lasts about half an hour. We should have woken the prisoners and taken control of both bridges by half-past. They'll still be singing hymns and getting ready for the morning sacrifice, which happens at half-past, sharp.

"Now, the sacrifice is chosen the night before and spends the night locked up in the bedroom of the cult leader, David. And yes, before you ask, both boys and girls receive his personal attentions. They're drugged and then brought to the chapel for the morning show. They're blessed as part of the ceremony and then the whole shebang moves from the chapel to the top of the main tower above the west bridge. It's the most important ritual of their day, apparently, and they like to do lots of shouting; y'know, 'hallelujah', 'praise be', that sort of cobblers. Point is, they'll be making lots of noise and, apart from the guards on the bridges, who are excused, everyone will be there."

We closed the door behind us and scanned the room for Petts. The few captives who were not asleep sat up to take a look at us. I put my finger to my lips and they nodded, becoming alert as they realised what was going on. I recognised most of them from the market at Hildenborough.

"Very quietly, wake the person next to you," I whispered, and the room gradually came to life in a frenzy of shushing. I tiptoed through the half-asleep bodies to the far door and put my ear to it, but could hear no sound outside. I checked my watch. 6:20. Loads of time.

The chapel was on the north side of the house and one floor up, so there was little chance of us being heard, but there was no point taking risks. All three of us moved through the mass of captives whispering for quiet until everyone was awake. We found Petts, alive and well, huddled up with a young girl in the corner. Held prisoner by a blood cult, with nothing to look forward to but a gruesome death, and he had managed to pull. I was impressed. I don't think anyone has ever been so glad to see me in my life. He hugged me, which made me wince as he pressed on my tender stab wound.

"Williams is here, too," he told me.

Shit. I turned to try and find him but I was too late. Mac had him up against the far wall with a knife to his throat. I tried to push my way through the tightly packed crowd to intervene. Williams' eyes were popping out in terror; he must have thought we'd come all this way for revenge.

"You sold us out," Mac hissed.

Williams couldn't say a thing, he just shook with fear.

"Mac, leave him," I said urgently, fighting my way forward. "We don't have time for this."

"You're right," he said. "We don't."

Before I could reach them he drew his knife across Williams' throat. As the boy slid down the wall with a wet, gargled scream, his hands grasping at the gaping wound, trying to push the raw red gash together, trying to push his blood back in, Mac hissed into his face: "That's what we do to traitors."

Before I could react a woman behind me, half awake, unsure what was going on, saw the blood and began to scream.

"They've come for us, they've come for us! Oh God, oh God, I don't want to die."

The man next to her slapped her hard across the face.

"Shut up you stupid cow, we're being rescued." It was the guard from Hildenborough, Mr Cheshire Cheese. He looked up at me, desperate. "We are being rescued, right?"

"Yeah," said Mac. "Just taking care of a little unfinished business. Nothing for you to worry about."

There was a sad, feeble gasp from Mac's feet as Williams breathed his last.

Norton found my gaze and held it. I saw his jaw clench and his eyes widen. His knuckles went white on the grip of his knife.

Now?

Oh, how I wanted to shoot Mac there and then. But there were too many people around; the plan was going too well. It could derail everything and get us killed if I took him out now.

I gave a single, almost imperceptible shake of the head.

Not yet.

Cheshire Cheese stood up, electing himself spokesman for the prisoners.

"You're from the school right?" he said to me. "I remember you."

"I should hope so," I replied. "My execution was the big draw, after all."

"I suppose I should be grateful you survived, then, huh."

"I suppose you should."

"So what's the plan?"

Mac took his small waterproof backpack off, opened it up and started handing out the guns.

While the ten most capable prisoners were selected and armed, Norton got to work on the locked door. That's when things started to go wrong.

"Once we've armed the prisoners, we get through the locked door, go through one more room, and all we've got to do then is walk out across the east bridge. Then, once we're clear, we blow the bridges, trap the fuckers in their little moated manor house, and burn the place to the ground. Take care of these blood suckers once and for all. Piece of cake."

Plan A – forcing the lock – didn't work.

"I can't pick it. This lock is ancient."

Plan B – shoulder charging it – didn't work.

"It's no use, it's too solid, even three of us charging at once can't budge it."

Plan C – shooting out the lock – didn't work.

"Fuck it, they might have heard that. Time to move."

Plan D – blowing the thing open with a grenade and running like hell before the Blood Hunters had time to mobilise – was abandoned when it was pointed out that the crypt was tiny and the explosion would deafen those it didn't kill.

We'd lost five minutes by now, and time was running out.

"Okay, fuck! We'll have to go out across the West Bridge," said Mac. "The East Bridge is inaccessible. That means we go back the way we came, through the pantry and across the courtyard. We'll be exposed to the chapel, and the top of the tower, so wherever they are by now they'll see us or hear us, but if everyone runs like fuck then we should make it across the courtyard before they can open fire. Once you're across the bridge just run for the tree-line. We've got boys there and you'll get covering fire. Everyone clear?"

People nodded and mumbled nervously.

"Okay, Petts you take point," said Mac, and he opened the door we'd entered through.

Petts went first with Norton, Mac and I ushered the prisoners out after him as swiftly as we could. Not all the prisoners were out of the crypt before we heard gunfire from the courtyard.

Fuck, they weren't wasting any time.

We didn't let the remaining prisoners hesitate, though, we kept pushing them out until the crypt was empty, and then we followed.

About half the prisoners had made it across the courtyard, under the tower and across the bridge. We could see them through the gate, hurrying into the trees. Patel and Speight were stood underneath the tower, at the entrance to the bridge, firing up at the chapel windows directly above us. The Blood Hunters were returning fire.

We stood in the pantry with about twenty terrified people and looked out across the twenty metre space. There were two people lying dead on the cobbles.

One of them was Petts.

"They'll be fanning out across the building," I shouted. "If we don't move now we'll be caught in a crossfire. So run!" I shoved the prisoners as hard as I could and they stumbled out into the courtyard and ran, heads down, for safety. Mac and Norton helped me shove, as did Cheshire Cheese, and eventually they all made the dash across the exposed space. Two more were shot, the rest made it out.

We four followed hard on the heels of the last man out, but the second we set foot outside, the man in front of us shook and jerked under the impact of a stream of bullets from the billiard room door in the corner on the ground floor. The Blood Hunters had cut us off. We'd never make it to the bridge alive.

We were trapped.

"Now if things go tits up and we get stuck in there I want the fucking ninth cavalry to come storming in and sort it out. You'll be split into two teams and you'll wait under cover by the bridges. If we yell for help you are to come pelting across those bridges and shoot anything that moves. Got it?"

"We're trapped! Move in!" shouted Mac at Speight and Patel. But they turned and ran across the bridge to safety.

"Oi!" called Mac, but they kept running.

We had no choice but to turn and run back the way we'd come. We heard a huge explosion behind us as we ran. They'd blown the bridge.

"Bastards! This way," yelled Mac, and we hared back through the pantry to the doorway of the crypt. Mac yanked a grenade from his pocket, pulled the pin and rolled it to the far door. He closed the door in front of us, waited for the crump of the explosion, then ran back into the crypt and through the splintered oak door on the far side. As soon as we ran out of the crypt, bullets began smashing into the thick oak-panelled walls around us. In the time it would have taken us to cross the stairwell we'd have been cut to pieces, so instead of dodging right, past the stairs and into the room that housed the door to the East Bridge, we rode our momentum up the flight of stairs that lay directly in front of us.

This was the worst possible thing we could have done. The East Bridge was our only possible escape route now, plus the enemy were mostly upstairs – we were being herded right towards them. We made it to the first floor without being cut to pieces, but as we gathered on the landing we heard a shout from our left. I ducked behind the balustrade, Cheshire and Norton took cover in the doorway to the left of the stairs, and Mac crouched down on the bottom of a small flight of stairs that led up to the second floor. Almost as one, we opened fire at a gang of men and women who came running towards us. Two of them fell straight away but the remaining three took cover and returned fire.

When you're fighting outside you can hide behind walls, cars, trees and things, all of which will easily stop a bullet. But wattle and daub walls with a bit of lime plaster, doorframes and balustrades made up of wooden struts with great big gaps between them, don't provide the best cover.

The sound was deafening. Bullets were flying everywhere and splinters of wood and chunks of plaster smacked into my face and head. The smoke and dust soon filled the hallway with a fog that made accurate shooting impossible. Everyone was firing blind.

Then I heard a yell from behind me and I turned to find Cheshire and Norton struggling with a pair of men. I grabbed my machete and rose to my feet, heedless of the ordnance whizzing past me. One attacker had Cheshire by the throat and was throttling him. I hacked at the man's head and felt a sickening crunch as the blade embedded itself in his cranium. He fell backwards. Norton bucked and rolled and his attacker was suddenly on the floor. Norton shot him in the face and then twisted in the air as a bullet smashed into his right shoulder. He spun straight into Cheshire's arms.

"Mac," I shouted. "We need to go up!"

There were running footsteps approaching from both left and right, so we legged it up the small flight of stairs to the second floor, Cheshire helping Norton. This was the part of the house that had been closed to the public, devoted to private apartments by the National Trust, so we had no map to guide us. We were running blind, but at least we were above our pursuers. With luck there'd be nobody up here.

We were on a landing with four doors leading off it, so we opened the first door and ran inside. We found ourselves in a living room; plush sofas, deep pile carpet, old TV in the corner. There were three mullioned windows along the far wall and Cheshire dumped Norton on the floor and ran to open one of them. Mac and I pushed the sofa across one door and a sideboard across another. We heard the clatter of pursuit up the stairs and the sound of bullets hitting the door.

"Those doors are solid oak," I said. "Bullet-proof unless they've got a heavy machine gun. They won't blow them either, 'cause this floor is all wood and they won't risk burning the place down."

"Great," said Mac. "So they can't get in, but we can't get out."

"Oi!" Cheshire was shouting out the window, across the moat. "We could use some help here."

Mac and I ran to join him. We could just make out a group of boys and prisoners in the trees, milling around. There seemed to be an argument going on but we couldn't hear. A burst of gunfire came from the floor below us, and they ducked. That obviously made their minds up, because a few seconds later the East Bridge, below us and to the left, exploded in a shower of stone and mortar.

"We are so fucked," said Norton, who had joined us at the window, his shoulder a bloody mess and his face white as a sheet.

He was right, we were fucked. And it was all Mac's fault.

I stood and looked at the man who'd led us to this

place. I thought about Matron and Bates; I remembered the twitching corpses of the TA guys, Dave, Derek and the one whose name I'd never know; I saw Williams clutching his gushing throat.

I felt the weight of the gun in my hand.

On the morning of March 24th 1918, James B. Grant was part of a group of men leading an assault on a copse somewhere in Belgium. There was a German machine gun emplacement in this small group of trees and it was holding up some advance or other. Grant and his men were instructed to remove this obstacle.

Although Grant was a Lieutenant he was not in charge of that particular assault. A new officer, William Snead, fresh from Oxford and Sandhurst, was in command. It was his first week at the front and he was eager to prove himself a hero, keen to win his first medal. His naiveté and reckless enthusiasm made him dangerous.

Grant had been serving with that group of men for years. They had seen terrible things; survived the battle of the Somme, lost friends and comrades by the score, trudged through mud and blood 'til they were more exhausted than I can imagine. But they trusted each other, even loved each other, in the way that men who've risked their lives together do.

So when Snead ordered them to make a frontal assault on an entrenched machine gun nest, a strategy that offered both the greatest chance of glory and the near certainty of pointless death, Grant tried to talk him out of it. They should circle around the gun, he said, approach under cover of darkness, and lob a grenade in. Simple, effective, risk-free.

Snead was having none of it. He accused Grant of

cowardice. A shouting match ensued, the privates got involved and Snead, suddenly fearful, drew his Webley revolver and threatened to execute Grant on the spot for desertion in the face of the enemy. Confronted by the muzzle of an officer's gun, Grant backed down. He apologised, prepared to mount the assault as ordered.

And then, as the men readied themselves to attack, Grant shot Snead in the back.

The German position was taken and Snead was listed as the only casualty of the engagement. Grant had saved the lives of his men in the only way available to him. It was an act of heroism in the face of leadership so stupid that it beggared belief.

But Grant couldn't live with himself and the knowledge of what he'd done. He surrendered to his commanding officer, made a full confession, and was executed at dawn the next morning.

As was the custom for cowards and traitors, Grant's name was left off the roll of honour. He was only added to the list of war dead in St Mark's main hall after one of Grant's surviving men pleaded his case with the headmaster of the time.

I wonder how many other St Mark's boys died in the war whose names were not listed. How many were shot at dawn for cowardice as they twitched and shuddered from shell shock; how many were gunned down where they stood because they refused to go over the top to certain, pointless death; how many were executed for refusing to take orders from upper class idiots who were trying to fight entrenched armies with machine guns as if they were Zulus with spears.

Hammond had tried to commemorate those boys who had died in The Cull, but who would paint and hang a roll of honour for those who had survived? Who would paint Petts' name onto black board, or Belcher's, or Williams', or the rest of those boys killed in yet another pointless war they had little choice but to fight?

Who would paint Mac's name?

Who would paint mine?

As I raised my gun and brought it to bear on the man who had appointed himself my leader, I knew exactly how Grant had felt, nearly a century before me. I knew the anger and resentment of someone forced to follow orders that are cruel, cowardly and wrong. I felt the righteous hatred of a man who believed in justice and honour slaved to a ruler who cared only for power. I felt the despair of a man who longed for peace forced to resort to violence because of the madness of others.

I realised that my days of following orders were done.

So I pulled the trigger and shot the bastard.

CHAPTER TWELVE

He didn't fall down. The bullet hit him in the left forearm. Not where I was aiming, but my hands were shaking so much it's lucky I hit him at all. Why couldn't I be like Grant; cool under pressure, calmly ruthless?

We looked at each other, neither of us knowing what to do next. The hole in his arm started to leak. He raised his gun to fire back so I shot him again. I hit him in the right shoulder. This time he fell down.

"Drop it!" shouted Cheshire, raising his gun to cover me.

I stood there, staring at Mac, who had fallen backwards and was sitting on the floor with his back against the sofa. He'd dropped his gun and was trying to put pressure on the wounds to stop the bleeding, but neither of his arms was working properly.

Norton walked over to Cheshire, reached out and gently pushed the gun down.

"Leave him," he said.

I'd killed three people in the last few months. One I could justify to myself as a mercy killing. The other was kill or be killed. The third had been in the heat of battle. But shooting Mac without warning, without any immediate threat to myself, in cold blood... that was different. I wasn't sure of my own motives any more. Had I shot him to save the school? Was I taking revenge for Matron and Bates? Or was I punishing him for what he'd done to me, what he'd made me into?

I looked down at the smoking Browning in my right hand. I couldn't work out what it was doing there. I used to hate guns, I thought. How is it that this thing feels so natural? When did I become someone who always carries a gun? I relaxed my fingers and it fell to the floor.

Mac was fumbling, trying to find some way of repairing the damage. His arms flapped and spasmed uselessly.

I crouched down so I was on the same level as Mac.

"It doesn't hurt yet, but it will," I said. "At the moment you've got so much adrenalin going through you that your body's not letting you feel the pain. I don't know for sure, but I suppose that if you die you might never feel it. It's only if you survive and heal that it hurts."

He looked up at me. If I was expecting confusion or fear I was disappointed. There was only fury.

"You fucking coward," he said. "You pathetic, weak, stupid fucking coward."

The noise from outside had stopped the instant I'd pulled the trigger. I could hear people running back down the stairs. They must have left a guard on the door, but for now they'd stopped trying to get in.

"What is going on here?" demanded Cheshire.

"Call it a coup," said Norton as he sat down in an armchair. "Can you pass me that tablecloth, please."

Cheshire pulled the cloth off the table and began helping Norton to dress his wound.

"Why now?" asked Mac. "Why wait until we're alone and trapped and probably going to die anyway? What is the fucking point of doing it now?"

I didn't have an answer to that.

"I'll tell you, shall I," he went on. "I reckon..." he broke off as a violent coughing fit seized him. "I reckon you were hoping they'd do your job for you."

"Perhaps," I conceded.

"Coward," he said again. "I told you the rules. I explained how this works. You want me out the way you fucking challenge me like a man."

"Like you challenged Bates?"

"Bates was weak. He didn't understand, didn't deserve

the respect. I thought you understood. I thought you got it."

"I get it, I just don't accept it. If I played it your way, by your rules I'd be buying into your bullshit, accepting this strong tribal leader bollocks," I said. "If I challenged you and proved myself the harder bastard then all I'd be doing was extending an invitation to some other hard fucker to come along and knock me off."

"That's how it works."

"I don't accept that. And you know what, the rest of the boys don't either. You might not have noticed, but they've left us – you – here to die. First chance they got, they cut you loose."

"So what's your alternative, eh?" he sneered. "You gonna run the school as a democracy? Student councils? Tea and scones and cricket on the green? Fucking fantasist."

His face was white as chalk. His ruined shoulder made an awful grinding sound as he tried to lever himself into a more comfortable sitting position.

"I don't know what it'll be like, but it's got to be better than rapes and crucifixions. There won't be executions. Boys won't be bullied and tormented."

"And my officers? You gonna deal with them?"

"If I need to."

He laughed bitterly. "Brilliant. Lee Keegan's brave new world kicks off with a group execution. You fucking hypocrite."

He was right. I knew that. But I was in no mood to argue any more.

"Your problem," I said, "is that you thought you were only vulnerable to someone stronger than you. But you never thought you might be vulnerable to someone smarter."

He gave a bitter laugh, which turned into another fit

of coughing. His left sleeve was soaked with blood. It ran down his fingers and soaked into the carpet.

"The smart thing to do would have been to shoot me before we even attacked."

There was that tone of contempt again. I thought of James B. Grant and I knew that Mac was right.

Norton tried to interrupt but I waved for silence.

"I know that," I said. "But unlike you I try to avoid killing people."

He laughed again. "Tell that to the guy at the foot of the stairs with half a head. You're a killer, kid. Stone cold. You just don't want to admit it. Your problem, Nine Lives, is that you never want to do anything. You wanted to leave Petts here to die..."

"He's dead anyway."

"Not the fucking point and you know it," he shouted. "You want me out of the way but you can't pluck up the courage to challenge me like a man so you wait for someone else to take me out of the picture. And when that doesn't happen you figure, screw it, what've I got to lose, and you just fucking shoot me. And then, to add insult to fucking injury, you shoot me in the bloody arms! What's the matter, bullet to the head too fucking easy?"

"Don't tempt me."

"Oh piss off. Like you've got the guts to finish me off." He leaned forward. "Come on then," he whispered. "Pick up the gun. It's right there. Still loaded. One bullet and it's all over. Come on. Finish what you started. Show me you've got the backbone to be leader. Prove it to me. Come on. Look me in the eye when you pull the trigger. Come on!"

Without thinking about it I reached behind me, picked up the gun and pressed the muzzle against his forehead. I pressed hard. God, I wanted to kill him. I mean really, *really* wanted to kill him. I wanted to watch him die screaming. I wanted to laugh in his dying eyes and spit on his corpse. I actually smiled as I began to squeeze the trigger.

And then I saw the look of triumph in his eyes.

"Maybe you're right," I said. "Maybe I am a coward, maybe I was afraid. But I wasn't afraid of you, Mac. Not really. I was afraid of becoming like you."

I threw the gun aside. Mac laughed in my face, soundlessly.

"Face it Lee, you'll never be like me. You haven't got the balls."

I heard a tiny metallic ping.

"Lee!" shouted Norton in alarm.

I felt something pressing itself against my stomach. I looked down and saw Mac's left hand holding a grenade. The pin was on the floor beside us.

I looked up. Mac was smiling.

"I'm holding down the lever, Lee. When I let go the chemical fuse starts and then nothing can stop it exploding seven seconds later. Reckon you can wrestle the grenade off me and throw it out the window in that time?"

I stared into his eyes as I reached down and wrapped my hand around his. There was little strength in his fingers; his shattered shoulder saw to that. As long as I kept squeezing he couldn't release the lever. We were at an impasse.

"You don't have to die here, you know," I said. "We can still get out of this, take you back to school, try and patch you up."

"And then what?"

"You leave. Just go."

Again with the laughing.

"Spineless wanker. You shot me in cold blood and there's no fixing that. At least have the integrity to live with it. I'm never leaving this room and you know it. But I can make sure you never do either."

I don't know how long we'd have sat there if Cheshire hadn't intervened.

He walked over to us, casual as can be, and then rammed his rifle butt into Mac's shoulder wound. He screamed and jerked in agony, and I slipped the grenade from his grasp. I picked up the pin and re-inserted it.

I think I'd been hyperventilating because I had a huge head rush as I stood up. Cheshire reached out to steady me until the world stopped spinning.

When Mac stopped screaming he looked up at me and sneered.

"What did I ever do to you, Nine Lives? What do you hate me so fucking much?"

"You made me a killer, Mac."

"Oh, I see. So basically, I shot myself, yeah?" He shook his head in disbelief. "Jesus, you are fucked in the head."

"Can we focus, please," said Norton, who had tied his arm tight into a sling and appeared to have stopped the bleeding. "Does anyone actually have a plan to get us out of here?"

"Maybe," I replied. "But the silence is bothering me. What can you see out the window?

Cheshire poked his head outside and leapt backwards as bullets ripped into the glass.

"Missed!" he shouted. He turned to me. "They're covering the window from the tower."

I walked to the door and knocked on it.

"Anyone out there?" I asked.

There was a pause.

"Um, yeah. Hi," came the tentative reply. It was a young man's voice.

Norton sniggered and started me giggling. Borderline

hysteria.

"Hi yourself. So, you guarding this door to stop us escaping then, yeah?"

"There's three of us and we've got guns."

"Good to know. The others gone off to the morning sacrifice have they?"

"Got to purify the moat."

"Great." I turned back to Norton and Cheshire. "They're all going to be on the tower for a while, so we've got some time to prepare."

"Any chance of a cuppa while I'm waiting to die?" said Mac, witheringly.

The morning sacrifice was one of the Blood Hunters' more disturbing rituals. The selected victim was brought to morning worship and blessed by David, then everybody processed up to the tower. David then slit the victim's throat and two acolytes dangled the poor sod over the battlements so they bled into the moat. Fresh blood in the water every morning kept them safe, they reckoned.

Serenaded by singing and screams from the tower I opened Mac's backpack and we got to work. It took about ten minutes or so, but by the time the ritual was finished we were ready. Cheshire had picked Mac up and put him on the sofa. He was still conscious.

"You haven't got a cat in hell's chance," he said.

I ignored him.

"Hey, Norton," he went on. "How long you been planning this little takeover?"

"Since day one."

"Traitor."

"What you gonna do, slit my throat, like you did to Williams?"

"Come over here and I'll show you."

"Enough, already," I said. "Does everyone know what they're doing?"

Norton and Cheshire nodded.

"What shall I do, Nine Lives?" gasped Mac, sarcastically.

"Fuck off and die."

We heard footsteps on the stairs. A group of people coming to talk. Then a voice I recognised.

"Hello in there." It was their leader, David.

"Morning," I replied, cheerily. "Lovely day for a blood sacrifice."

"Are any of you hurt?"

"Why do you care?"

"We have first class medical facilities. If you open the door I give you my word your wounded will be given the proper treatment."

"What, no bleeding?"

He laughed. "Of course there'll be bleeding. Got to be made safe. But we need fresh, clean, healthy blood. So we'll make you better first. While there's life there's hope, isn't that what they say?"

"I've got a better idea. We want to convert. We want you to make us safe."

"Sorry. No initiations today."

"They've got a bomb," yelled Mac. I punched him in the face as hard as I could. I felt the cartilage in his nose shatter. Felt good.

"One more word and I'll finish you now," I hissed.

"Like you've got the guts," he replied, and spat in my face.

So I took my Browning and I smashed him over the back of the head, knocking him out.

"Everything all right in there?"

"Fine. We're just, um, conferring."

I gathered up the strings we had taken from the window blinds and backed towards the open windows, where Norton and Cheshire were already waiting.

"Ready?"

They nodded.

"All right, we agree. Come and get us," I shouted. Then we all three turned and leapt out through the windows.

The gunmen on the tower opened fire. As I fell I took the string with me. I felt a slight resistance at the other end and then it came free and sailed out the window after me, with the pins of all our remaining grenades attached to it.

We hit the bloodied water before any of the bullets could find their mark, and the room above us exploded while we were still submerged. Stone, glass, wood and furniture crashed into the water all around us as we swam for safety.

The fire, smoke and confusion that reigned in the building behind us masked our clumsy emergence from the water, using the rubble from the exploded bridge as a ramp. We made it to the tree-line safely. The other boys and the Hildenborough captives were long gone. I stood in the shadow of the trees and watched the conflagration take hold of the fragile wooden house.

Mac was in there. The explosion had probably killed him, and if he'd miraculously survived the blast then his wounds would probably finish him off. Either way, he was gone for good. Everything had gone according to plan. I'd gained his trust, lulled him into a false sense of security, and betrayed him. I was a traitor, pure and simple. I hated myself for it. Mac had been right, I was a coward. I'd opposed him because I'd never accepted that the ends justified the means, and yet look at what I'd done. In order to get rid of Mac I'd betrayed every principle I'd ever held dear. I'd lied and cheated, betrayed trust and committed murder.

But the school was free of him now, and with the Blood Hunters burning in front of me, and Hildenborough ravaged and leaderless, there was no-one around to threaten us. At least for a while.

The means had been despicable, but the end had been achieved. Still, I wondered whether I hadn't failed in one crucial thing: preventing myself from becoming the thing I hated. After everything I'd done I couldn't help but feel that I was that little bit more like Mac than I'd ever wanted to be. I didn't know how I was ever going to come to terms with any of this.

I'd killed two people today and seen many more die. As I watched the fire I prayed that this was the last I would see of killing.

Should've known better, really.

LESSON THREE:
How To Be A Leader

CHAPTER THIRTEEN

"Wasn't my fault. They were bigger than we were."

Wylie was making excuses, but his heart wasn't in it. Like all the best bullies he was a coward at heart. It turns out the boys hadn't blown the bridges to get rid of Mac and me. The adults from Hildenborough, scared out of their wits, some of them armed (by us), had demanded that the boys blow the bridges immediately. Wylie, who'd been in charge of that part of the operation, had agreed.

I was wet through, cold, tired and very, very pissed off.

"You left us to die," I said, through gritted teeth.

"You look fine to me." Cocky little shit.

I raised the Browning and pointed it at his face. He hadn't expected that.

"Give me your gun," I said.

"You what?"

I twitched the gun sideways an inch and fired a shot past his right ear. He jumped, yelled and backed away.

"What the fuck are you doing, man?"

"I won't ask again."

He threw the rifle at me. I let it fall to the floor.

"Here, have it you fucking psycho." His shout was half whine, like a spoiled brat being told to give back the car keys.

I didn't lower my gun.

"How old are you, Wylie?"

He glanced left and right looking for support or a way of escape. I had him cornered.

"Seventeen. Why?" he said. Half petulance, half defiance.

"And how many men have you killed?"

His eyes widened as he felt a jolt of genuine fear.

"Just the one."

"One kneeling man with his hands tied. What, you didn't off a few more when the Hildenborough men attacked?"

"My... my gun jammed."

I laughed.

"Not what I heard."

Rowles had found him cowering in the art room. He hadn't told anyone but me because he was too afraid of what Wylie would do to him if he blabbed.

"Fuck you! I'm a sixth-former! And a prefect!" He was starting to cry.

"That's right. And I'm only fifteen. But I've killed four people, two of them this morning. So who do you think is the scariest person in this room?"

He sniffled.

I chambered another round.

"Who do you think is the scariest person in this room?"

I fired a shot past his left ear.

"You. You are, all right. You." His lower lip was trembling.

I nodded.

"Right again. I am. I am the scariest person in this room."

I was having fun. I'd have been worried by that if I'd stopped to think about it. But I didn't. I was enjoying myself too much.

"You're a bully, Wylie. And a coward. I don't like cowards much. But I hate bullies."

His nose started to run.

"But do you know what I hate even more than bullies, Wylie? Do you?"

He shook his head. Mingled snot and tears dripped off

his wobbling chin.

I walked right up to him and pressed the gun against his temple. He let out a low moan of fear.

"The one thing I hate more than bullies," I said. "Is anyone who was in the room when Matron was raped."

He looked like he was about to shit himself.

"It... it... it wasn't my idea. It was Mac... he made us... he had a gun and everything."

"Don't. Care."

"I had to! I didn't enjoy it. Honest. I didn't enjoy it all. Really."

"Not an excuse."

"What... what are you going to do to me?"

"Haven't decided yet. I reckon it's a choice between shooting you in the back of the head or crucifying you. Do you have a preference?"

His knees buckled and he fell to the floor, snivelling and moaning.

I knelt down beside him and whispered in his ear.

"I'm inclined to crucify you myself, but it's time-consuming and a bit of a drag. Probably easier to just shoot you. What do you think?"

"I'm sorry, all right?" he cried. "I'm sorry, I'm sorry!"

I yelled into his ear as loud as I could: "I don't care!"

He cowered against the wall.

"Choose!"

"Oh God."

"Choose!"

"Please, no, I'm sorry, please." He buried his face in his hands and curled up into a foetal ball, wracked with sobs.

"Fine," I said. "A bullet it is."

I grabbed him by the shoulder and hauled him to his feet. He made a half-hearted attempt to resist, so I kneed him in the balls. Then I herded him down the corridor and out the front door. He could barely walk for pain and terror.

I kicked him down the steps and he sprawled in the gravel, clawing for purchase. He tried to get up, but the best he could manage was to crawl away on all fours. I sauntered after him. When he reached the grass I planted a foot in the small of his back and he collapsed onto the turf.

"Kneel," I said.

He let out a cry of anguish and scratched at the dirt.

"Kneel!"

I bent down and grabbed him, pulling him up until he was kneeling in front of me. The second I let go he toppled sideways. I kicked him in the ribs as hard as I could.

"Kneel, you pathetic little shit."

I pulled him up again and this time he stayed in position. He shuddered and shook, gasped and wept.

"This is pretty much the spot where you executed that helpless, unarmed man, isn't it? Kind of fitting you should die here too."

He started to beg.

"Please, oh, God please don't. Please don't."

"Is that what she said, huh? Is that what Matron said?"

I pressed the hot muzzle of the gun against the nape of his neck. He screamed.

"Is it?"

I let him sweat for a good minute or two before I pulled the trigger.

After all, he didn't know I'd used all my bullets.

"Was that necessary?" asked Norton, as we watched Wylie limp out of the school gates. I gestured to the faces pressed against the windows of the school behind us.

"Yes."

I looked at the faces of the boys before me. They looked so tired. They hadn't slept all night and they'd marched three miles expecting to go into battle. In the end they'd only been shot at from a distance before being threatened by a bunch of fear-crazed adults, but it must have been terrifying for them, especially the little ones.

It wasn't just the events of the past twenty-four hours, though. These were boys whose lives had been calm and orderly before The Cull. They'd lived every day according to a rigid timetable set down for them by distant, unapproachable grown-ups. They'd played games and sat in lessons, pretended to be soldiers on Fridays and occasional weekends. They'd eaten set meals at set times and known months in advance exactly what they'd be doing at any given day and time.

Of course there had been bullies, beatings and detentions, but unless Mac was the bully in question it never went too far. And Matron had always been there to give them a hug and put a plaster on whatever cut or bruise they'd received.

But for the past few months things had been very different. They'd seen their parents die and had run back to the one refuge they could think of. They'd hoped to find safety in the familiar routine of St Mark's. Instead they'd killed men in combat, seen their teachers and friends die before them, been bullied and abused, subject to the whims of a gang of armed thugs who'd ordered them about day and night. They'd been trained for war and had learnt to live with the expectation of their own imminent deaths.

I was looking at an entire room of young boys with post-traumatic stress disorder. And I was supposed to lead them.

I didn't have a clue where to begin.

"Mac's dead," I told them. I had expected some response; a few cheers, perhaps. But all I could see were dead eyes and dull faces.

"As his second-in-command I'm in charge and things are going to be different around here. Right now I want you all to get some sleep. Leave your guns at the door and go to bed. There'll be cold food available in the dining room for anyone who wants it, but your time is your own until tomorrow morning. Just... relax, yeah?"

I waited for them to leave, but they just sat there. I looked at Norton, confused.

"Dismissed," he said.

"Sorry. Dismissed."

As the boys got up I added: "Oh, and no more army kit, all right? You can wear your own clothes from now on. We'll collect the uniforms tomorrow and they can go back in the stores."

The boys shuffled out in silence.

When they'd gone I was left alone with Norton, Mrs Atkins and the remaining officers: Wolf-Barry, Pugh, Speight, Patel and Green.

"Gather round everyone," I said.

They all came and took chairs at the front. I sat down too.

"You all saw what happened to Wylie earlier, yes?"

The officers nodded.

"Good. You were meant to. Mac would have shot him, but I let him go. That's the difference between me and Mac; I'm not so keen on killing. But I want to make it perfectly clear to you that I will see you dead and buried if you disobey a direct order from me. Understood?"

The boys mumbled and nodded.

"In which case I want you all to pile your guns in the corner and sit back down."

They did so.

"Good. Rowles!"

The door opened and Rowles entered, holding a rifle. The officers flashed me confused glances.

"What's going on?" asked Wolf-Barry, suddenly nervous.

"You're leaving," I said. "All of you. Right now."

"You what?" said Patel.

"I said you are leaving. *Now*. Out the gate and don't look back. I don't ever want to see any of your faces on these grounds again. *Ever*. 'Cause if I or any of the other boys see you inside these walls again we will shoot to kill without hesitation. Understand? And count yourselves lucky. I've fantasised about killing each and every one of you in all sorts of creative ways. But there's been enough death for one day, I don't think I could stomach any more."

"Now look here..." Speight rose to protest.

There was the unmistakable sound of a gun being shouldered ready for firing. He turned and saw Rowles taking aim.

"Permission to shoot, sir?" asked the junior boy.

Speight froze as I made a play of considering the request.

"Escort these men from the grounds, Rowles. If any of them resist you have permission to shoot."

Nobody moved. The officers looked confused and scared.

"But where will we go?" said Pugh.

"Somewhere else. Anywhere else. Just not here," I replied.

"You're not going to fire that gun are you, Rowles?" said Patel. He rose to his feet and started walking towards the boy, his hand outstretched. Rowles smiled one of the scariest smiles I've ever seen. I wondered what had happened to the quiet, scared little boy who'd hung on Bates' every word.

"Try me," he said.

Patel, wisely, thought again.

"Enough," I barked. "I want you all out of here immediately. You are expelled."

I was relieved when they made to leave. I hadn't wanted any more violence today.

"Green, stay behind a minute," I said, as he reached the door. The other officers made their way outside. I gestured for Green to sit down. He looked petrified as he did so. I regarded him for a moment before asking: "Why do they call you Limpdick, Green?"

"I don't know, sir," he mumbled.

"Please don't waste my time. I'm tired and I want to have a cup of tea and go to bed. The sooner I can finish here the sooner I can relax. So, I ask you again, why do they call you Limpdick?"

He stared at his feet and mumbled a reply.

"'Cause of Matron."

"You were there when she was attacked?"

He nodded.

I swallowed hard. I didn't want to know the details, but I had to ask.

"Did they all take a turn?"

He nodded.

"But you couldn't, yes?"

He nodded again.

"Are you gay, Green, or just a fucking wimp?"

That got a reaction.

"Fuck you!" he shouted, suddenly defiant. "Just 'cause I don't get off on raping somebody doesn't make me gay, all right?! I liked Matron. What happened in that room wasn't right. It just... wasn't right. I told Mac I wouldn't do it, I argued with him, but they teased me and... they had guns. They made me take off my trousers and lie on top of her. And she was just staring at the ceiling. I kept apologising to her but she wouldn't look at me. I couldn't do it. I just couldn't do it."

Tears welled in his eyes.

"And the man you killed?"

He broke down.

"Mac said he'd shoot me," he sobbed.

I sighed heavily. Good.

"Okay. That's what I thought. I just needed to be sure."

I got up and went to sit next to him. I put my hand on his shoulder. He shrugged it off resentfully and stared back down at his shoes.

"Will you stay here, with us?" I asked.

He looked up at me, confused, and wiped away the tears.

"But I thought..."

"We're going to get Matron tomorrow. If she corroborates your story, and I'm sure she will, then we'd be glad to have you. We need people like you here. Petts is dead, so you'll have to recast, but God knows we could use some entertainment to take our minds off everything. So stay, put on your play. Yeah?"

I held out my hand. He took it and we shook.

When he was gone Mrs Atkins smiled at me.

"Not a bad start," said Norton. "Not bad at all. Now can I please go and sort out this fucking bullet wound before my arm falls off."

While Norton got himself patched up I went to my room and changed out of my wet clothes. Peeling off the muddy, half-dried uniform was like uncovering a map of my recent escapades.

I had a scar on my left calf where Jonah had bitten me; a puckered red hole in my right thigh where I'd been shot; a bandage around my waist where I'd stabbed myself; a deep purple welt across my throat where the rope had cut into me; my torso and arms were covered in bruises; my right eye was blackened, my left cheekbone was blue and I had long scab on my cheek from Baker's signet ring, which would probably scar as well.

I was a complete mess.

I collapsed onto my bed. I was so tired I felt like I could sleep for a week, but my mind was racing. I had done it. Mac was gone, our enemies were defeated. Before Cheshire (his name, it turned out, was Bob) had gone back to Hildenborough he'd assured me that the two communities would be allies from now on. My job now was to find a way to mend the school. Tomorrow I'd go to the farm where Matron and the girls had sought refuge and see about bringing them back to Castle. Mrs Atkins had told me that there were twenty girls there now, under Matron's protection. We could use the fresh blood; this place was altogether too male.

Not that I wanted to do away with everything Mac had achieved. The school had withstood an attack from a force that had been well prepared for our defences, and in all the time he'd been in charge there'd been very little dissent or division. I had to try and use community building and reconstruction to maintain the unity that he had achieved through fear and force.

I would need my own officers, but I wasn't going to keep the military structure. There would have to be guard patrols and so forth, and they'd have to wear combats and carry guns, but for everyone else we'd go back to normal clothes and activities. We'd start lessons again, organise some round robin sports tournaments, foster a sense of structure and order that didn't come from a strict military outlook. St Mark's should start to feel like a school again, not an army camp.

Norton would be my right hand man, and Rowles would be the spokesman for the junior boys. I'd divvy up jobs to those boys that wanted them, delegate responsibilities. The deaths of Petts and Williams had left the garden and livestock with only Heathcote to tend them; he would need help. Riding was going to be our main form of transport now, so we needed to try and round up some more horses for Haycox to look after. We should try and find some glass to re-glaze the windows broken in the attack, too. Couldn't have the rain getting into the building.

And there was the Blood Hunter we'd taken prisoner. By the time I'd finished washing him he was gibbering and hysterical. He was still locked in a store cupboard, raving about the Second Coming.

There was so much to do.

Maybe, if I kept myself busy enough, I could prevent myself dwelling on the things I'd seen and done. Maybe I'd go to bed so tired each night that I'd be able to sleep without nightmares.

Maybe.

The next morning I put on a pair of old Levis and a t-shirt. It felt odd to be back in normal clothes. Comforting, though. I ignored my tough leather boots and put on a battered old pair of trainers. Luxury.

I went downstairs to the refectory and helped myself to some water and a slice of fresh bread. We hadn't got any yeast, so it was flat bread, but it was still warm and delicious. I walked across the courtyard to the old kitchen, where Mrs Atkins was already baking the second batch of the day.

"Mrs Atkins that smells wonderful and you are a marvel," I said. I cleared away a pile of cookbooks and perched on the work surface.

"You sound chipper," she said.

"I can't remember the last time I woke up feeling good about the day," I replied. "But the sun's shining, we've got fresh bread and eggs for breakfast, and as far as I can tell nobody's trying to kill us. There'll be no drill today, no weapons training or marching, no assault course ordeals, gun battles, executions or fights. I think tomorrow I may spend the whole day just sitting in the sun reading a book. Can you imagine? Actually sitting and reading a book in the sun. In jeans! Today is going to be a good day, mark my words, Mrs Atkins. It's a new start. I warn you, I may even get down off this table and give you a hug."

"Don't you dare," she said, but she was laughing in spite of herself. "If you leave me alone to finish this batch of bread and get the breakfast done I'll see you later and tell you where Matron and the girls are. Deal?"

"Done!"

I jumped down, ran over and gave her a big kiss on the cheek. She threw a wooden spoon at me so I left. I might have been whistling.

The boys wandered down to breakfast in ones and twos over the course of the next hour. With everyone dressed in normal clothes again the refectory looked welcoming and normal. Mrs Atkins' scrambled eggs, collected from our chicken enclosure, were delicious. With no drill scheduled or battles to fight, the boys were all at a loose end, and they hung around the refectory when they'd finished eating, waiting to see what would happen.

I stood on the table at the top of the room and cleared my throat.

"Morning everyone. Looks a lot nicer in here without

all the camouflage gear! Now, I know we should have
a timetable and stuff, and I'll be sorting one out soon,
but I think we should have a day off, yeah? I don't want
anyone leaving the school grounds, and Norton is going
to organise a few of you into guard patrols, but for today
let's just relax and enjoy ourselves. Go play football, swim
in the river, go fishing, read a book, whatever you want
to do is fine. Dinner and supper will be at the usual time
and I'd like everyone to gather here at six this evening.
We should have Matron back by then and I'm sure she'll
want to say hello to you all. But until then bugger off and
have some fun. You've earned it."

"You should have been a red coat," muttered Norton
when I sat down again. "Let's go have tea and scones
on the lawn and play croquet. And maybe we can have
lashings of ginger beer and get into some scrapes."

"Piss off."

"Yes sir, three bags full sir."

"How's your arm?"

"Unbelievably painful, but I don't think there's any
major damage. I've stitched and sterilised it. Not going to
be playing rugby any time soon, though."

"Fancy coming with me to get Matron?"

"Nah. Bouncing up and down on a horse doesn't
really appeal. I'll be here, taking many, many painkillers
and bestowing the gift of my withering sarcasm on the
juniors."

"Just be careful Rowles doesn't shoot you."

"I know! When did he get scary?"

"I think he killed someone in the fight with
Hildenborough. I have a horrible feeling he kind of
enjoyed it."

That grim thought stopped our banter dead.

As I walked out to the paddock there was a football
match kicking off on the rear playing field; one boy was

walking off to the river carrying a fishing rod; and the third formers had a beatbox on, using up precious battery power playing music as loud as they possibly could. It was just like an ordinary Saturday in term-time. But with fewer children, and no teachers to spoil the fun.

Haycox was tending the horses. We had five now, all of which were happy to be ridden. He'd had converted one of the old stables back to its original use, and all the animals had warm quarters for when the weather changed. Each had its own saddle and bridle set, too, which Haycox polished and oiled. As long as he was left alone to look after the horses he was a very contented boy indeed. I'd been riding since I was ten, it was one of the extra activities the school offered on weekends, but with my wounded side and tender leg I found it hard going. The ride to Ightham and back for reconnaissance the day before yesterday had been agony; I'd been happier when we'd walked there *en masse.*

Nonetheless, I asked Haycox to saddle three of the horses for a short trip. He gathered up their reins and led them back to the courtyard.

There was one task I'd been putting off all morning, and I couldn't delay it any longer. I walked across Castle to the headmaster's old quarters. The door was locked. I suddenly saw an image of the keys, in Mac's pocket, burnt into the dead flesh of his thigh in the smouldering ruins of Ightham Mote.

It's surprising the different and creative ways your imagination can find to torment you when you've got a guilty conscience.

I kicked the door open.

Mac hadn't tidied up before leaving, and the flat revealed details about his private life I didn't really want to know. A half-finished whisky bottle sat on the coffee table, next to a tatty copy of *Barely Legal* and a box of mansize tissues. There was a CD player on the sideboard, and the bookcase had a huge pile of batteries on it. The kitchen was a stinking mess. There was a small calor gas ring with a saucepan on it and a collection of tinned food sitting next to it; baked beans and macaroni cheese, mostly. A huge pile of empty tins and Pot Noodles lay in a pile in the corner, a beacon for rats and 'roaches.

In the bedroom the quilt lay half-off the bed, exposing crumpled, stained sheets. We hadn't got the best laundry system worked out. I made a mental note to prioritise that.

Above the bed was a collage of photographs, blu-tacked to the wall. There must have been a hundred pictures. Most were of his family, but some were of friends, and there was one corner reserved for pictures of a pretty blonde girl I didn't recognise. It'd never occurred to me that he'd had a girlfriend.

I didn't want to linger here, to look at his pictures and see his crumpled bed sheets. I didn't want these things making me think of him as an ordinary person, giving my imagination any more details to torture me with. But it was already too late for that. I knew that somewhere in my nightmares that blonde girl would appear, accusing me of murder, weeping over Mac's chargrilled corpse.

Angrily I flung open every drawer and cupboard I could find. I rummaged through underwear and socks, spot cream, CDs, books and t-shirts until I found what I was looking for: the spare set of keys to the cellar. I left that room as quickly as I could and slammed the door behind me. I didn't look back.

Rowles was already waiting for me when I got to the armoury. The small door that led down to the cellar was underneath the rear staircase in what had originally been the servant's quarters. Mac had kept it padlocked and guarded at all times; I didn't think we needed the guard.

I opened the door and switched on the light. The cellar smelt damp and musty. We went down the stone steps and found ourselves in a corridor with vaulted rooms lying off it to the left and right. There were six chambers down here; all but two were full of guns, ammunition and explosives.

Without being asked, Rowles selected a rifle for himself, picked up a magazine, and snapped it into place. He seemed completely at ease, as if operating a semi-automatic machine gun was the most normal thing in the world. I reminded myself that he was only ten and wondered if I'd be able to restrict guns to older boys. Would that weaken our defences too much? One more thing to worry about.

I was appalled by how comfortable I'd become with guns, how naturally the Browning nestled into my palm like an extension of my hand, as it was designed to. I didn't want to be someone who always carried a weapon. I worried that I would come to rely on it to solve all my problems. After all, as Mac had pointed out, there was no-one to haul me off to prison for murder. The only thing stopping me ruling at the muzzle of a gun was my own determination not to let it happen.

But we were riding out of the school into unknown territory. Who knew what we'd encounter? Reluctantly I picked up the cold metal pistol and checked that it was loaded.

I promised myself that I'd return it to the cellar as soon as I got back.

We saw the smoke long before we saw the farm.

Rowles, Haycox and I approached on horseback from the west, but we tethered the horses to a fence and made our final approach more stealthily. At first I thought it was probably a domestic fire, maybe someone burning rubbish or leaves, but as we got closer I could see that it was the dying embers of a much larger blaze.

Panicking, I started to run. My reluctance to carry a gun was forgotten as I drew my weapon, but I knew before I arrived at the farmhouse that there was nobody to shoot or save. This place was abandoned.

The main building was a shell. It could have been smouldering for days. There was a discarded petrol canister on the grass in front of the house. Someone had deliberately burnt this place down. Dispatching the others to check the outbuildings and oast houses, I peered in through the front door.

The floorboards had been burnt through and all that remained of the crossbeams were thin charcoal sticks. The ground floor was gone and the cellar was exposed to the sunlight for the first time in two-hundred years. There was no way in here. I circled the building, looking in through the empty, warped window frames. All I could see was blackened furniture and collapsed walls. I didn't see any bodies.

Rowles reported that the oast houses were empty, but we heard Haycox yell and we hurried to the stables. When I first saw the body of the young boy lying there, half his chest blown away by a shotgun, I didn't realise the significance of it; after all, there was a lot of blood. It told me was that there'd been a fight, and the body was long cold. I reckoned he'd been dead about three or four days, which must have been when the farm was atacked. But then my stomach lurched as I saw that his hair was matted with blood. It wasn't his own.

Matron and the girls had been taken by the Blood Hunters.

CHAPTER FOURTEEN

We had ridden to the farm at a gentle canter, but we left galloping as fast as our horses could carry us. I felt the stitches in my side split. I ignored it.

Rowles rode back to the school to let Norton know what was happening. Haycox and I made straight for Ightham. The farm had been attacked three days ago, which meant the Blood Hunters had taken Matron and the girls captive before we'd stormed their HQ. My imagination started finding new ways to torture me. Perhaps they'd been held prisoner in a different part of the building and they'd burnt to death as a result of our attack.

I remembered the screams of the morning sacrifice. I'd been so grateful for the respite that had offered us. But maybe it had been Matron hanging from those battlements bleeding out in the moat. Maybe I'd swum to safety through her diluted blood.

I kicked the horse hard. Faster. Must go faster.

It took about an hour to reach Ightham. My horse and I were exhausted by that point. Haycox looked like he'd enjoyed the ride. We couldn't just go storming in; the surviving Blood Hunters could still be here. We tethered the horses in the woods and approached through the trees, weapons drawn, on the lookout for sentries or stragglers. There was nobody around.

The building was still on fire. All the wooden parts of the house had collapsed into the stone ground floor, where they were burning up all the remaining fuel. The house was a shell, completely abandoned, but there were about twenty bodies in the moat. I really didn't want to do this, but I had to be sure, so I found the wheel that controlled the level of water and turned it all the way.

The water slowly began to drain away through the sluice gate. When it was down to knee height we jumped in and began to work our way around the building, turning over the bodies. Most were badly burnt. It was a tiring and grisly task, one of the most distressing things I've ever had to do. None of the dead were Mac or David, but the final body I turned over was Unwin's little sister.

So they'd been here all the time we were rescuing the people from Hildenborough. I looked up at the burning building. They might still be inside, charred and lifeless. I could be directly responsible for their deaths. There was no way of knowing.

Haycox and I climbed out of the moat and searched the grounds for evidence of escape. The canvas-covered trucks I'd seen them driving at Hildenborough were nowhere to be found, but there were fresh tyre tracks in the gravel of the car park. At least some of them had escaped the fire and moved on.

They could be miles away by now.

But had they retired to lick their wounds and start again somewhere else, or were they planning their revenge?

When we got back to the school we were met by guards at the gate. Norton had beefed up security upon Rowles' return. I left Haycox to tend to our exhausted steeds and I went straight to the store cupboard and flung open the door. Our captured Blood Hunter was curled up into a little ball, rocking back and forth muttering in the dark. I grabbed him and hauled him out.

"The other prisoners," I yelled. "Why didn't you tell us about the other prisoners?" I shook him and kicked him, slapped him round the head and yelled into his face but I could get no reaction. He was oblivious.

An hour later, after we'd given him some food and something to drink, he started to talk.

"But you only asked about the prisoners from

Hildenborough," he said. And there was that urge again, the one I was trying to resist. The urge to shoot someone in the head.

When the girls and Matron had been captured the crypt had been full so they'd been imprisoned in the library, on the south side of the house. As far as he knew they were still there when we attacked. There was nothing more he could tell us, so we escorted him to the main gate and turned him loose.

Then I went to find Unwin. I had to tell him that his sister was dead.

In the months that followed we searched far and wide. We collected six more horses, Haycox trained all the boys in riding, and we sent out three-man search parties every day. After a month we'd searched everywhere within a day's ride and we had to start sending out teams that slept under canvas. Two-day searches gradually evolved into three-day searches, and still no sign of the Blood Hunters.

Eventually we had to abandon the hunt. It was likely that Matron and the girls were dead, that David died in the explosion, and that the trucks were taken by the remnants of a leaderless cult which had now scattered far and wide. We were probably searching for a group that no longer even existed. It was a hard reality to accept but eventually we had to move on.

As spring turned into summer the school slowly started to become what it should always have been. We cultivated a huge vegetable garden, and erected a couple of polytunnels for fruit and salad. The herds of sheep, pigs and cows grew steadily, and all the boys helped when it was time for lambing and calfing. Heathcote's careful husbandry made sure we never went without meat, milk, butter or cheese. The river gave us plenty of fish, and the re-established Hildenborough market grew to the point where we could trade for sauces, jams and cakes.

Hildenborough elected Bob as their new leader. We developed close ties with them, and even played them at cricket once a month. A few of their adults came to live with us, mostly those with surviving children. I made it clear to the parents that I was in charge and any adults were here strictly by the permission of the children.

One market day Mrs Atkins came back to school with a tubby, red faced, middle-aged man, and she moved him into her room without ceremony or hesitation. His name was Justin, and the two of them made the kitchen into the hub of the school. They were always in there cooking something up, and all the boys loved to hang out there. It felt homely, which was something none of us had felt for a long, long time.

Our searches had found no trace of the Blood Hunters, but they had allowed us to compile a very good map of the area's settlements and farms. We made contact with as many as would allow us to approach, and although it was early days I could sense the beginning of a trading network.

Once I was sure that the school was secure and running smoothly, we began to look for new recruits. There were plenty of orphaned kids in the area, running in packs, or living with surrogate families. Seventeen new children joined us, ten of whom were girls. A few tentative romances blossomed. Two women from Hildenborough volunteered to teach classes, and so each morning for two hours there were lessons. We didn't have a curriculum to follow, so they just taught whatever took their fancy. Both of them were naturals, so although attendance wasn't compulsory they always had a full house.

Green's theatre troupe was a roaring success, too. They abandoned *Our Town* in the end, and produced a revue that they took to Hildenborough and some other nearby settlements. They were our finest ambassadors.

In spite of the sunshine and goodwill we didn't neglect the military side of things. We maintained a strict defence plan, with patrols and guard posts, and every Friday we did weapons training and exercises. I devised a series of defensive postures for possible attacks, and we drilled the boys thoroughly in all the permutations; if someone came looking for a fight they'd find us ready and waiting.

Every now and then we'd catch a whiff of something happening in the wider world, rumours of television broadcasts and an Abbot performing miracles, but our fuel was long gone so we couldn't tune in. Whatever was brewing in the cities couldn't reach us out here in the countryside. Not yet, anyway. So we carried on building our little haven and prepared for the day when either madness or order would come knocking on our door again.

I flatter myself that I was a pretty good leader. The boys would come and talk to me when things were bothering them, and I did my best to resolve disputes and sort out any issues. I think I was approachable and fair. You could hear laughter in the corridors of Castle again, something I never heard when Mac was in charge. I relied on Norton and Rowles to let me know when and if I got things wrong, and they weren't shy about knocking me down a peg or two when necessary.

As my wounds healed I continued exercising my leg and found that my limp became much less marked. My cheek did scar slightly from Baker's ring, and Norton joked that it made me look like an Action Man. Within a couple of months I felt as fit and healthy as I'd ever done.

None of this stopped the nightly visitations of the dead keeping me awake, of course.

And there was still no sign of my dad.

I went three whole months without picking up a gun.

Felt good.

Couldn't last.

The Woodhams farm was about two miles south-west of the school. A collection of outbuildings and oast houses around a Georgian farmhouse, it was inhabited by ten people who'd moved down from London after The Cull. They'd found the place empty, moved in and started running the farm, which boasted a huge orchard and fields devoted to fruit production, including grapes and strawberries. Mrs Atkins met them at Hildenborough market and they'd extended an invitation for Green and the theatre group to visit their farm for the weekend. The boys would put on their show and in return they would put the boys up, feed them, and let them bring back some fruit for the rest of us. Lovely. What could possibly go wrong?

Jones was one of our new recruits. His parents were dead but he'd been living in Hildenborough ever since The Cull. He was a good pianist, so Green had recruited him for the revue, and he'd fitted in well. Green's troupe had left for the Woodhams place in a horse-drawn cart, so when Jones came staggering through the front gate after midnight the duty guards raised the alarm.

"I'd just played the opening chords of After Fallout when there was a knock on the door," he told us. "Ben

Woodhams got up to answer it, we heard a struggle at the door and then a gang of men burst in wearing balaclavas and waving guns around. Green put up a fight and he got hurt pretty badly. I managed to slip out in the confusion and I've been running ever since. It's about two hours or so now. You need to hurry!"

Me, Norton, Jones, Rowles, Haycox and a new kid called Neate, who fancied himself a soldier boy, were dressed, armed and saddled up within ten minutes. There was no moon and we rode blind to the edge of the farm, but we could see flickering candle light around the edges of the curtains.

"There are seven boys and ten adults in there," I said. "Jones reckons there were four or five gunmen, that right Jones?"

He nodded.

"We've got no idea what's going on in there," I continued. "They might just be looting the place, they might have decided they like the look of it and want to move in, they might be doing any number of things. Our advantage is that they don't know we're coming, so we should have surprise on our side. The hostiles are dressed all in black and had balaclavas on."

"Why?" asked Norton.

"What?"

"Why were they wearing balaclavas? Were they afraid of CCTV or what? Doesn't make sense."

"I don't know. Probably just for effect."

Norton didn't look convinced.

"Haycox and Neate, you cover the front door," I said. "I don't want you to shoot any of the hostiles unless necessary. If they make a run for it let them go. But if they try to leave with hostages I want you to fire off some warning shots and force them back indoors. We need to try and contain them.

"The rest of you are coming with me. Everyone was in the living room when they were attacked, and that's at the front of the house so we're going in the kitchen door at the back. We go in quietly and cleanly, and we keep an eye out for sentries. We use knives until such time as they become aware of us, after that you can fire at will. Don't take any chances, but only kill if you have to. Jones knows the house so he and I will take point. Questions?"

"Just... be careful everyone, all right?" said Norton. "I don't like this at all. Something doesn't feel right to me."

I smirked. "Corny line!"

"I'm serious."

We left the horses a safe distance away and approached on foot, knives drawn. There were candles burning in the kitchen but there was no-one inside. The door wasn't locked and it didn't creak. So far so good. The room still smelt of roast beef. I looked greedily at the pile of dirty plates as I tiptoed around the large wooden table. The interior door was open a crack. It led into a corridor that ran to the front door. A number of rooms opened out of it to the left and right, and at the far end there was a staircase on the left.

I couldn't hear any voices and I couldn't see anyone. Gesturing for the others to stay in the kitchen I pushed the door gently and got lucky again: no creak. The hallway was carpeted so I took a chance and walked to the living room door, which was ajar. I leaned in and listened. Total silence. I was just about to try the other doors when I heard a small cough from inside and then someone shushing the cougher.

They were in a remote farmhouse, after dark, no-one expected or likely to arrive. Why would they be trying to keep so quiet?

I heard a small creak behind me and to the left. There was someone on the stairs. Suddenly I felt the world shift around me and I realised that I wasn't the hunter at all. I was the prey.

This was a trap.

There was a slim chance whoever was waiting on the stairs hadn't seen me. Without looking up at them I backed away towards the kitchen as slowly and quietly as I could.

And then another noise, this time behind me. Someone opened a door between me and the kitchen and stepped out into the hallway. I spun to see a black-clad man looking straight at me. He was wearing a balaclava and carrying a sawn-off shotgun.

He opened his mouth to shout a warning as I lunged forward. Normally I would have drawn my gun, told him to freeze. But something odd was going on here and I felt cornered and threatened. I wasn't inclined to take any chances. I led with my knife. I slapped my left hand over his mouth and shoved the blade up between his ribs as hard as I could, lifting him onto his toes with the force of the thrust.

I felt hot blood spurt out across my hand as I stared into the eyes of the man I was in the process of killing.

It wasn't a man, it was a boy. I recognised him. It was Wolf-Barry.

There was no wall behind him and he toppled backwards. I tried to follow him down, to maintain the silence, but I was overbalanced. We fell backwards together and as we hit the floor his shotgun went off, blowing two big holes in the plaster ceiling.

Dammit, this always looked so easy in the movies. I felt reassured that I wasn't a practised and professional killer – I didn't ever want to be that – but *fucking hell*, it would have been nice not to screw it up just this once.

I saw the eyes of the boy I had just killed begin to glaze over. I had a sudden memory of the first time I'd met him, in IT lab three years earlier. I remembered he'd made some joke about the headmaster, but I couldn't recall what it was. It was funny, though. I thought he was funny. And now I'd stabbed him through the heart without a second's hesitation.

I felt everything I'd achieved in the last three months evaporate in an instant. Who had I been kidding? This was my life now. Not cricket and plays and lessons, but killing and bleeding and dying. I was a fool to ever hope otherwise.

With both barrels fired and a knife in his chest, Wolf-Barry was no longer a threat, and since our cover was well and truly blown there was no longer any need for stealth. I rolled off him, trying to draw my gun as I did so, but I was tangled up and couldn't pull it free. A man came down the stairs swearing loudly, and as he turned the corner into the hallway someone behind me fired twice. Both bullets found their mark and he jerked backwards, two holes in his chest.

There were shouts from the living room; Green shouting "In here!" and a woman screaming. But no-one came out of the door.

Without rising to my feet I crabbed backwards towards the kitchen door and safety. The door was wide open and Norton and Rowles were stood there, smoking guns aimed down the corridor over my head, covering my retreat.

"You were right, it's a trap!" I shouted.

I reached the door and sprang upright. As I did so there was gunfire from outside, at the front of the house. Someone was attacking Haycox and Neate, someone who'd been waiting for us to get inside the house before revealing their presence.

I pointed to the boy on the floor in front of me, the one

with the pink froth bubbling out of his mouth.

"That's Wolf-Barry," I said.

"I fucking knew it," replied Norton.

"And I think that's Patel," I said, indicating the corpse at the foot of the stairs.

"Green," I shouted. "Are you alone in there?"

"What do you fucking think?" came the reply. It was Wylie.

This was not good. Not good at all.

"I've got a gun to Limpdick's head, Keegan. If any of your men offer the slightest resistance I'll splash his brains all over the walls, got me?"

"What do you want, Wylie?"

"Want? I've got what I want: you. You're surrounded. My men were waiting outside in the dark. There's ten of us, how many of you?"

Fuck fuck fuck.

I heard the sound of a gun hitting the floor behind me and I turned to see Jones standing stock still at the back door, his eyes wide as saucers. Pugh had a knife to his throat.

"Drop the guns," he said.

Nobody moved.

"I said, drop the guns!"

Pugh pressed the knife into Jones' throat and a small trickle of blood escaped.

We dropped our guns.

"Now on the floor," he shouted. "Hands behind your heads."

We complied. The kitchen tiles were hard and cold.

"All right, chief, we've got them," he said.

Ten minutes later I was tied to a chair in the dining room. The other prisoners were being kept next door. I'd caught a glimpse of them through the door when I was being trussed up; Green had a huge purple bruise on his forehead, and Neate had been shot and killed out front, but everyone else was okay. All ten of the farm family were there, as were the six kids from Green's troupe, Norton, Jones and Rowles.

I'd obviously been set aside for special treatment. I didn't want to dwell on what Wylie was likely to do to me. My hands and feet were firmly bound, and there was no give in the ropes at all. I wasn't going anywhere.

Wylie pulled over a chair, reversed it, and sat facing me, resting his arms on the seat back. He had removed his balaclava, no need for it now. He looked very pleased with himself. And so he should. I'd walked obediently into his trap like the amateur I was. I would've kicked myself if my feet hadn't been tied. I figured that the best I could hope for was a bloody good kicking and I saw no reason to prolong the agony.

"Patel and Wolf-Barry are dead," I said. "That just leaves you, Pugh and Speight. So who are the other guys, Wylie?"

"They're old friends of yours, Lee," he said. "Wanted a chance for a bit of payback. Actually I'm working for them, sort of sub-contracting. They wanted me to deliver you to them. Piece of piss, really."

"Wolf-Barry didn't look like he thought much of your plan as I shoved a knife into his heart."

Wylie looked annoyed. "He shouldn't have broken cover. He was supposed to stay in there 'til I gave the signal. Prick."

"No wonder you command such loyalty, you're just so compassionate."

He smiled the smile of a man who knew he was in total

control. "No point trying to piss me off, Lee. I've got my orders and I'm going to stick to them. You're not going to annoy me into making mistakes. I'm supposed to deliver you in one piece and that's what I'm going to do."

He stood up and walked over to me, leaning down so we were face to face.

"Doesn't mean I can't hurt you just a little bit first though, does it?"

He leaned back, raised his right leg and stamped on my balls.

There's no point describing the pain. If you're a woman you've got no idea, and if you're a guy you know only too well. Suffice to say I screamed for a bit, whimpered for a while, and then passed out.

Unconsciousness passed into sleep. Wylie woke me in the morning by kicking me in both shins. The first thing I heard, apart from my own curses, was a chorus of screams from outside the house. He untied my feet and led me out the front door, where a familiar canvas-top truck was parked. The engine was running and the rest of the captives were already in the back. All except Mr Woodhams, who was lying on the grass, sliced open from pubis to throat, with a group of young men stood around him, dabbling their hands in the gore and wiping it all over themselves.

Blood Hunters.

Pugh and Speight were standing at the back of the truck, machine guns slung across their chests. They were trying not to watch the gruesome ritual occurring right in front of them. Pugh looked sick.

Wylie forced me into the truck, and then the six Blood Hunters climbed in and sat at the back. They sat silently, staring into space. Each carried a machete and a gun. They stank like an abattoir. Pugh closed the tailgate, the three sixth-formers went to sit in the cab, and we pulled out of the driveway onto the road.

The nine remaining residents of the Woodhams farm were cowering in the far end of the truck, in various states of hysteria. The eleven St Mark's boys were all there too, hands bound, all looking to me for ideas or hope as we were bounced about by potholed roads. I shrugged helplessly. But Norton found my gaze and winked. Good to know somebody had a plan.

We rumbled along for about five minutes until I felt a nudge from Jones, who was sitting next to me. I felt something cold touch my fingers. A knife! Where the hell had he got a bloody knife? I glanced up and saw Norton grinning at me. He nodded subtly downwards and wiggled his right foot. He'd had a knife in his boot. I could have kissed him. I scanned the faces of all the other boys. All of them still had their hands behind their backs as if still tied up, but they all looked at me, excited and nervous. Christ. They were all free!

I grabbed the knife and set about cutting the rope that bound me. It didn't take long; it was razor sharp. I felt my hands come free and I squeezed the knife handle firmly in my right hand. I looked up. All eleven boys were looking at me.

I mouthed silently: "One, two, three."

As one, we leapt up from our seats and shoved towards the six Blood Hunters. One of them went over the tailgate and smacked onto the road before he even knew what was happening. I buried the knife in the eye socket of another, and grabbed his machete as he tumbled backwards towards the tarmac. The other four were no match for the combined shoving weight of twelve boys, but the tailgate was still closed, and they braced themselves against it. One of them tried to grab his gun, but the crush of bodies was so tight that he couldn't bring it to bear, and his hands got stuck down on his chest so he couldn't defend himself. Rowles hit him repeatedly, over and over again, both hands working the man's face like a punchbag. Jones wrestled for control of another man's machete, which was suspended over his head. But he was too weak to prevent it coming down and splitting him open. As the Blood Hunter tried to wrench the blade free, Haycox, who had somehow got hold of a machete in the struggle, returned the favour, striking his head from his shoulders with one powerful swipe. Norton grabbed the decapitated man's feet and tipped him over the tailgate onto the road.

The Blood Hunter being hit by Rowles was unconscious by this point, and only remaining upright because of the mêlée surrounding him. Rowles kept punching him anyway. The other two Blood Hunters were backed right up against the tailgate now. One was hacking and slashing wildly, and as I watched he sliced open the throat of a young boy called Russell, who sang comic songs in Green's revue. The boy tumbled backwards with a terrible screech. The other Blood Hunter was struggling with Norton for possession of his gun until his mate's wild swinging blade smacked into the side of his head with a soft crunch. Norton shoved him back over the tailgate and onto the road, the machete still embedded in his head.

The one remaining Blood Hunter, bladeless, tried to reach for this gun. But suddenly he jerked and wretched as his eyes went wide and a torrent of blood gushed from his mouth. Haycox pulled his dripping machete free of the man's ribcage and pushed him back over the tailgate.

Job done.

I reached down past Rowles, who was still punching, and grabbed the machine gun from the unconscious Blood Hunter beneath him. I pushed my way through the crowd to the front of the truck.

"Everyone brace yourselves," I shouted.

"Lee, hang on, do you think..." said Norton.

But I didn't let him finish. I popped the catch and emptied the entire clip through the canvas in front of me, riddling the driver's cab with bullets and killing Wylie, Pugh and Speight instantly.

"Should have done that in the first place," I said, as the lorry swerved violently off the road. I was flung off my feet in a tumbled tangle of limbs as the lorry hit a ditch and rolled over onto its side. There was a monstrous crash, a chorus of cries and then stillness and silence.

I'd come to rest under a pile of bodies, my nose buried in somebody's armpit. It took a few minutes for everyone to untangle themselves and climb out of the lorry onto the road. We took stock.

Russell and Jones were dead, and a young girl from the Woodhams farm had broken her neck in the crash. Otherwise it was all just scrapes and strains. I pulled the clip out of the machine gun. It was taped to another, which was still full, so I reversed it and slammed it home.

Norton was incandescent.

"What the fuck was that, Lee?" he yelled. "Why the fuck did you shoot them up? That was the most insane thing I've ever seen you do."

I grasped the gun tightly, my finger itching at the trigger.

Calm down. Things to do.

"Look at where we are," I said patiently.

Norton glanced down the road.

"So?" he said, confused.

"The school is about a mile down the road. We'd have been there in two minutes. They were taking us to the school."

"Oh." He realised what I was getting at. "Oh shit."

I turned to address the other boys, who were sitting in

the road, catching their breath. "Listen everyone. Wylie was taking orders from the Blood Hunters. His job was to lure me away from the school and then deliver me to them. But they were taking us back to the school."

"So?" said Rowles. "They were going to let us go?"

"Don't you see? While we've been gone the Blood Hunters have attacked St Mark's."

CHAPTER FIFTEEN

I gave a machine gun to the Woodhams party, so they had some means of defence on their journey home, and they carried away the dead girl. One of them, a young man, had to be restrained from attacking me. He was still shouting after me as he was pulled away: "Murderer! Psychopath!" I couldn't blame him. I'd caused the crash that killed her. But what choice did I have? I could have shot above the officers' heads and told them to pull over, but in moments we'd have been within earshot of the school. If I'd had to fire again then the Blood Hunters would probably have heard the shots and come running. Assuming I was right, and they were at St Mark's.

It was one more death on my conscience, but I could worry about it later. Things to do.

I walked around to the front of the crashed truck and peered into the shattered cab. I could see that there were three bodies inside, but I didn't look too closely. They weren't moving, so I was satisfied they were dead. (When had I started taking satisfaction in killing?)

I was starting to appreciate Mac's point of view; perhaps I wasn't ruthless enough to be a leader. My decision to let the officers go had led directly to four deaths. Wouldn't executing them have been better?

Three months ago I was unable to contemplate such a thing, but now I found that I could. Perhaps it was because of what we'd achieved in the last three months. When I was planning to topple Mac and take control it was in the hope of building something good, but my aims had been intangible and distant. Now it was a reality. We'd achieved so much, built something so valuable. I felt as if I was willing to go to any lengths to protect it.

I dispatched Haycox and Rowles back down the road to collect the guns from the bodies of the dead Blood Hunters. When they returned we had five machine guns and six machetes, and enough ammunition to pick a fight. Green, Norton, Haycox and Rowles each took a gun; we shared the big knives out amongst the remaining members of Green's troupe.

"We have to assume they've taken control of the school," I said. "And they probably have lookouts and sentries posted. We need to know what's going on inside, and we can't approach mob-handed. So Norton you're with me. We'll cut across country and come at the school from the river. Haycox and Green, I want you to get behind these hedgerows and follow the road, out of sight, until you can see the school gates. Only approach if you're absolutely certain there's nothing wrong. This is just a recce, right? We don't get involved, we don't show our faces. Rowles, take the rest of the boys to Hildenborough and wait for us. We'll rendezvous back there when we're done. Everyone clear?"

Nods all round.

"Good luck everyone."

It took thirty minutes to reach the edge of the school grounds, but the sight that greeted us was not what we expected at all. We crawled through the undergrowth until we could just make out the first pillbox. We could see the muzzle of the GPMG poking out, but it was trained towards the school. I couldn't work out why that would be. We needed a closer look.

Leaving Norton to cover the pillbox, I crawled back out of sight and stripped to my boxers. I discarded my gun but kept the machete, then I ran to the river's edge and slipped into the water. I let the current take me slowly downstream, along the edge of the school grounds. As I drifted past the first pillbox I could see the body of a boy lying against one wall. He'd had his throat slit. I was right, the Blood Hunters had attacked, and they'd taken this pillbox. But why train the gun on the school... unless they hadn't succeeded in capturing it!

I drifted further. I couldn't see anything at the second pillbox, but two Blood Hunters were sitting outside the third, looking towards the school, smoking. There was no sign of a corpse anywhere, but their hair shone slick with fresh blood. I grabbed the bank of the river and hung there for a moment, considering my options: sneaky or direct? I could return to Norton, head to Hildenborough with what I'd learned; or I could choose to kill without mercy. Three months ago I wouldn't even have had to think about it. But I thought again about where my reluctance to kill had brought us and my resolve hardened. There was no longer any point pretending that I wasn't a stone cold killer.

Time to start acting like one.

I climbed out of the water as quietly as I could, and crept towards them, knife in hand. The secret to stealth in woodland is to tread straight down, not to roll your feet with each step as you do normally. That way you avoid snapping any twigs you stand on. Barefoot, I stalked my prey.

As I approached I could hear them gossiping. They were trying to decide whether a girl called Carol fancied the one on the left. He thought she didn't, but his mate was sure she did, and was urging him to 'get in there'. Murderous religious fanatics, coated in human blood, wittering about dating. They were so engrossed in their debate that they didn't become aware of me until I pressed my cold wet blade against the throat of the one on the right.

"Hi," I whispered in his ear, as he stiffened in fear.

His mate exclaimed loudly and jumped up. He brought his gun to bear on both of us.

"Now, now," I said conversationally. "Don't be hasty. Pull that trigger and your friend dies." *Plus, every Blood Hunter in the area comes running.* "So put it down, eh?"

He hesitated, unsure what to do. I pressed the knife harder into the throat of the man in front of me, and he moaned. His mate cocked his gun, chambering a round. "So?" he said, trying to sound more confident than he was. "He gets his eternal reward a little early. He'll thank me when I see him again."

"Um, Rob," said the man in front of me. "He's gonna slit my throat, man."

"He's right, you know," I said. "I am. So if you don't want to break poor Carol's heart, best drop the weapon."

Rob stared at me, trying to maintain his cool. But eventually he bent down and placed the gun on the ground.

"Thanks," I said, and smiled at him. "Now kick it away." He did so.

A minute later I had them both on the ground, face down, hands behind their heads. It didn't take much to persuade them to talk, but it took me a lot longer to believe what they were telling me. When I'd learned all I could, I had a choice to make. I'd been quite prepared to kill one of them to make the other one tell me what I needed to know, but to kill them now would be murder, plain and simple.

Nonetheless, the best course of action was clear. Kill them, bleed them, cover myself in their blood, dump the bodies in the river, then saunter up to the next pillbox and kill the occupants before they realise I'm not really a Blood Hunter. Repeat for all remaining pillboxes. Even the odds while I had the chance. It was the safest thing to do.

I tightened my grip on the knife, gritted my teeth and prepared to strike, but I had a sudden flash of the confusion and fear in Wolf-Barry's eyes as I'd plunged my knife into his chest. I choked. I couldn't do it. Even now, after everything I'd done, I couldn't conceive of embarking on that kind of killing spree, no matter how necessary it was.

I felt like I'd failed some kind of test.

I made them undress, cut their clothes into strips, and bound them tight. Then I swam upstream and rejoined Norton.

I had a lot to tell him.

I couldn't sleep at all that night. In the pub at Hildenborough we'd talked ourselves hoarse trying to come up with a plan of action that didn't leave us all hanging upside down with our throats slit. By the time we finally agreed on a plan of attack it was dark and everyone was exhausted. Norton accepted his role without complaint and walked out into the night to do his part. Bob had prepared beds for us in the big house where three months ago I'd fought for my life. Strange to be sleeping there as a guest of honour.

But of course I couldn't sleep. I ran the day over and over again in my mind. Killing Wolf-Barry, shooting the others, the head of the dead woman hanging limp as she was carried away, the stench of the Blood Hunters, the sense that I should have killed them there and then, the nagging feeling that I still wasn't as ruthless as I needed to be. The knowledge that, had Mac been in charge of us, things would have been a lot simpler. Not to mention my anxieties about the coming day, the probability of battle, the anticipation of more killing, the possibility of my own imminent death and those of my friends. I was afraid of the nightmares sleep would bring.

Plus, it felt wrong to be sleeping safe and sound while Norton was risking his life out there in the darkness.

So I lay there, listening to the owls and the foxes, wishing that my father were here to take charge on my behalf. I wished I could go back to being a boy again, that I could retreat to a world where my only worries were acne, BO and whether that girl from the high school would laugh at me if I asked her to meet me at lunchtime for a bag of chips at the bus stop. That was what my life should be like. I was fifteen, for God's sake. Whoever heard of a fifteen year-old general? Well, Alexander the Great, perhaps. Whatever happened, things would be settled once and for all by the end of the day. Either I'd be dead and the school would be destroyed, or the Blood Hunters would be wiped from the face of the earth like the plague they were. When dawn finally broke I greeted it with a kind of relief; waiting to fight is far worse than actually fighting.

Breakfast was a sombre affair. Green hadn't spoken a word since we'd rescued him, and he sat at the end of the table, picking at his bacon and eggs. Haycox was in shock, coming to terms with the fact that yesterday his life had changed from horse grooming to disembowelling and decapitation. I hardly knew any of the boys who made up Green's theatre troupe, but they were artsy types, uncomfortable in a fight, reeling from the deaths of their friends Russell and Jones. Bob was subdued because he'd had a very hard time convincing some of the men in Hildenborough to provide support for our plans; after all, they'd lost friends in an attack on the school once before. But the opportunity to revenge themselves on the Blood Hunters was enough to sway them in the end.

The only person who ate well was Rowles. He cleaned his plate, and then went back for more. He didn't seem worried at all. But if you looked closely you could see that he was dead behind the eyes. I worried about that boy.

When we were finished we washed up and got dressed. Rowles, Haycox and I had our combats, the others had to make do with green and brown clothes that Bob had begged and borrowed the day before. We met the new Hildenborough militia on the forecourt of the house and went over the plan once again. Weapons were distributed and goodbyes said. Then we walked down the drive towards the rising sun.

We were going to pick a fight.

There's something mediaeval about pitching a tent outside a fortified castle and laying siege to it. But since the Blood Hunters had to do without smart bombs, air strikes or fuel, it seemed logical to re-adopt the neglected arts of war.

The marquee sat to one side of the school's main gate, outside the walls, on the grass between the road and the school wall. The gate itself lay on the ground in pieces, run down by a truck. The truck in question lay on its side about twenty metres inside the gates. There was a corpse hanging out of the driver's side window. The sandbagged machine gun emplacement at the main gate had been scattered by the impact, I had no idea of the fate of the boys who'd been manning it. The Blood Hunters had collected the sandbags and rebuilt it, remounting the GPMG and pointing it down the drive at the school.

With the drive covered, and the pillboxes manned at the rear, all approaches to the school were pinned down.

But the long driveway in front, the playing fields at the back, and the paddocks and gardens on either side provided no cover for attackers who made it over the wall, which meant that a straightforward attack would be suicide. Stalemate.

The Blood Hunters were going to have to starve the school into submission. And I wasn't going to allow them that much time.

I turned my binoculars towards Castle and was relieved to see a Union Jack flag dangling from a window. That was the signal; Norton had made it past the guards and was inside. There was nothing left to do now. Time to begin.

I broke cover about half a mile down the road and strolled as nonchalantly as I could towards the school. I tried whistling but my mouth was too dry. It took them a minute to spot me. Three of the biggest guys I've ever seen ran towards me, weapons raised for firing.

I grinned at them. I was going for confidence but I probably looked unhinged.

"Take me to your leader," I said. So they did.

There was a crowd milling around outside the entrance to the marquee as we approached. A whole tribe of people in jeans and t-shirts, wearing flip flops and trainers, carrying machetes and guns, their faces, arms and hair soaked in human blood. The meeting of mundane and surreal was hard to accept. So was the smell.

I've never been religious. It just never made any sense to me. But I sang the hymns and intoned the prayers at school assemblies and the compulsory Sunday morning service in the chapel. The kind of religion I was exposed to always seemed harmless enough. Either the vicars were pompous bores or young men who tried to be cool by playing guitar or something embarrassing like that. One of the boys in my dorm had attended a thing called the Alpha Course one summer holiday, and the subsequent term he'd stopped smoking and joined the school's Christian Fellowship. But that was about as sinister as it got. And I sort of got it. It was about feeling part of a community, taking comfort in a belief that there was some point to everything. I didn't feel the need of it myself, but I kind of understood why some people did.

But this... I couldn't begin to wrap my head around this. How fucked in the head did you have to be to think that human sacrifice was going to save your immortal soul? How desperate for certainty did you need to be to imagine that smearing yourself in human blood was a good idea? I wondered whether the Blood Hunters were just a collection of weak, scared people in thrall to a charismatic nutter, or were they some expression of something deeper, more fundamental? The Aztec part of us, if you like.

I might as well have been walking through a crowd of Martians. I couldn't comprehend these people on any level. And suddenly I realised I'd made a terrible mistake strolling in here. Because how can you talk to someone when you don't even know their language?

The tent flap was held open for me and I walked into the marquee. The air inside was fetid and humid, and smelt of grass, sweat and blood. Blankets lay on the floor, surrounded by bags and collections of random objects and piles of clothes; lots of little Blood Hunter nests. Running down the middle of the tent was a long red carpet, and at the far end, raised on a wooden dais, was a throne. I say throne, but it was really just a big wooden chair with a gold lame blanket tossed over it and a red velvet cushion. Sat on this throne was David, wearing his immaculate pinstripe suit and bowler hat. His umbrella rested on one of the arms. Two armed guards stood either side of the throne.

I was shoved onto the red carpet and marched down it to meet the Blood Hunters' leader. I had no idea what to expect. I certainly didn't expect him to get up, walk down to meet me, shake my hand and offer me a cup of tea and a slice of cake.

But that's what he did.

"We've spoken before, haven't we?" he asked as he poured Earl Grey into a china cup.

"Yes, we have." He handed me the cup and saucer and I thanked him. "At Ightham."

"I thought so. You were one of the boys who attacked us."

I took a sip. "Yeah."

We sat on canvas chairs facing each other across a wrought iron table. There was a plate on the table with lemon drizzle cake on it. I didn't ask where they'd managed to find lemons, I just helped myself. It was delicious.

Imagine a clown performing for children, his face covered in make-up. Then try to imagine what he looks like when all the slap's taken away. Is he old or young? Ugly or attractive? It's impossible to say. All you can see is the clown face. It was the same with David. I found it very hard to get a sense of what he looked like, because all I could see was the cracked and crumbling patina of blood that caked his face. It made him difficult to read.

Obviously I was taking tea with a madman. But was he personally dangerous? Was he likely to kill me himself, with no warning, on a whim or because of something I might say? Or did his threat lie solely in his power over others? I could find no clue at all in his expression or his cold grey eyes.

"So what can I do for you this fine sunny day, young man?" he said. "Do you wish to join us, perhaps? We always have room for penitent souls." He smiled insincerely.

"I've come to ask you to leave." Even though I'd been rehearsing this in my head all night I still couldn't believe I'd just said that.

"I'm sorry?"

"I want you to leave St Mark's alone. Just leave. Please."

He put down his tea carefully, then he placed his elbows on the table and rested his face in his hands.

"Why would I want to do that? There are young, innocent souls in there, in need of salvation. I can provide them with that. I'm only here to help."

"And if they don't want your salvation?"

"Then they can aid in the salvation of others."

"As bleeders."

"Or food. Or both. Their blood and flesh is a holy sacrament."

"Is that all they are to you, a resource?"

"If they will not accept the word of God then yes." He leaned back and shrugged as if to say 'what can you do?'

I decided to try a different tack.

"When we blew up that room you were outside the door," I said. "How did you survive?"

"I am watched over," he replied.

I thought: *you ran down the stairs when you heard the window break, more like.* "But if your little cult is so blessed, why were we able to burn your house to the ground?"

He laughed, as if indulging a child who's just asked a particularly stupid question. "You were merely the messenger of God's wrath. He wishes me to bring His word to the world. I was betraying my calling by situating myself in one location." He gestured around him, at the marquee. "Now, you see, we are mobile! And we save more souls every day of our never ending journey. All thanks to you."

"You're welcome. So why not move on. Why lay siege to a school when there are so many other places to save?"

"I may be a holy man, but I am not above a little vengeance. You killed my disciples, you oppose me and my followers. That cannot go unpunished."

"People are going to die here today. Lots of people. Yours and mine. Men, women, boys, girls. And there's no need for it all. You can just walk away."

"Shan't."

Strike One.

"All right then, let the people in the school leave and take the building as your new base. Rent free. All yours."

"Didn't you listen to what I said? We are mobile now. That is how it is meant to be."

Strike Two.

"Then take me."

"Excuse me?"

"Take me. Bleed me, eat me, do whatever you want. I won't resist. But leave the school alone."

"My dear young man, I have you already. Where's my incentive to make a deal?"

Strike Three.

Okay then. I'd given him every chance; done everything I could to avoid bloodshed. No choice now but to fight. Only problem was that my plan relied on my being outside. And I was stuck in this bloody great tent. I needed to be creative.

"How many men and guns have you got here anyway?" I asked.

He smiled. It was not pleasant. "Lots and lots."

I made a play of considering this.

"Can I, perhaps, join you, then?"

Finally, I'd managed to surprise him. "You wish to join

the flock of the saved?"

"I don't want to die, so on balance, yeah. Please."

"Do you understand what joining the ranks of the saved entails?"

"I've heard about the ritual blood letting. Correct me if I make a mistake. A victim is selected from amongst the prisoners or, if the person joining is considered particularly valuable, from the ranks of the already saved. The victim is held down by two men, and the supplicant, who has been stripped naked, slits the victim's throat and collects the blood in a bowl. When the bowl is full they drink the blood. Then the body is turned over and sliced open. You then dab your hands in the gore and make the sign of the cross, in blood, on the supplicant's chest. The supplicant takes the knife, cuts their palm, and drips their blood into your outstretched hands, and you wash your face with it. That about right?"

"And you'd be happy to take the ritual of salvation?"

"If it means staying alive, then yes, I would."

"Can I tell you a secret?"

"Please."

He leaned forward and whispered conspiratorially: "You're not a very good liar."

"I'm not lying. I swear I'll join you if you let me."

"If you wish to join us why did you kill the acolytes I dispatched to bring you to me? We found their bodies on the road yesterday. And why attack and tie up the two men by the river? No, I think it's more likely that you've developed some kind of plan and this conversation is the start of it. Did you really think we would just leave if you asked me nicely?"

He spat the word 'nicely' at me like a curse, and there was a sudden flash of furious madness in his eyes.

"I hoped so. I had to try, didn't I?"

The fury was replaced by contempt.

"You believe yourself to be in a story, don't you?" he sneered. "I think you imagine yourself as the hero who strolls into the enemy camp, baits the villain and then runs away to fight another day. Yes? But you're so wrong. My crusade is holy and righteous and you are nothing but a clueless heathen. I have bound my followers together in faith and blood through the power of my will. I lead them to glory and salvation. You have no idea the trials I have undergone, the opposition I have overcome, the demons I have banished. I am the hero of this tale, boy, not you. You're just a footnote. Nothing more."

He was impressive when he got going.

"I don't know what you and your boy scouts have planned, but I can assure you it's utterly futile," he ranted. "You have no forces to call upon. We have the school surrounded and all your boys and their weapons are contained inside. They can't attack us for the same reason we can't attack them – they'd be cut down before they reached the walls. And even if it does come to a fight, which I think unlikely, my men outnumber you two to one and are not afraid to die. You should see them fight. It's a glorious thing. They fling themselves into danger without a second thought. They are magnificent!"

David's messianic fervour was impressive but I wasn't completely convinced by it. I thought about the two men I'd interrogated on the river bank the day before. Magnificent wasn't the word I'd use to describe them; they were just scared idiots happy to have a tribe to belong to. Obviously there would be a hard core of men, like the one I'd killed in Hildenborough, who'd fight to the last, but I was sure that if David were taken out of the equation then the majority of Blood Hunters would fall apart. I hoped so, anyway. My whole plan relied upon it.

"You're... you're right," I said, trying not to overplay it. "I know we don't stand a chance. I was bluffing. There's no way we can fight you, not like this."

"Don't believe a word he says, David," said a familiar voice behind me. "He's got a plan, all right."

I turned to face the new arrival. The guys I'd interrogated at the pillbox had told me Mac was here, so I'd expected to come face to face with him again. But nothing could have prepared me for how he looked. I recoiled involuntarily at the sight of him.

His hair was all burnt away, his bald head blackened and scarred. The left side of his face was also a mass of scar tissue, and it sagged downwards, indicating that he had no muscle control there. The left side of his lips had been burnt away too, leaving half his teeth exposed and giving him a permanent sneer of loathing and contempt. His left ear was a ragged tatter and his left eye socket gaped, black and empty. His left arm ended abruptly just above what used to be his elbow, but the right hand held a machine gun with measured confidence. He looked like some kind of zombie.

But it wasn't the sight of Mac that froze my blood and stopped my heart.

Because standing next to him was Matron.

And her face and hair were smeared with human blood.

CHAPTER SIXTEEN

"Look," I said, "It's a pretty simple plan."

"Too simple if you ask me," said Bob.

"Can your man shoot as well as you say... yes or no?" I asked.

"He's bloody brilliant," he replied.

"And does he have a problem with shooting people?"

"No," he replied darkly.

"Then I reckon it's our best shot. Um, sorry. Not intended."

"But are you sure it'll work?" asked Rowles.

"The Blood Hunters are a cult of personality. It stands to reason that if we eliminate their leader then they won't know what to do. There's every chance they may just wander off."

"I can't believe this is our best plan. Hope they wander off. Jesus," muttered Norton.

"You said he never comes out of the tent, so how are you going to get him out in the open?" asked Bob.

"I'll improvise. Just make sure your man's ready. The second David steps outside, I want him dead. Then while they're running around flapping their hands and wailing you lot come out onto the road and line up, weapons raised. But don't fire unless you have to. And Norton, you lead the boys out of the school and do the same. With their leader dead, and us sandwiching them between two rows of guns and making a show of force, I think there's the possibility of a surrender."

"And Mac?" said Norton. "We don't expect him to just walk away, do we?"

"No. I don't really know what he's going to do. He's the wild card."

Matron held a gun on me as Mac and David walked to one side and talked quietly, glancing over at me every now and then. I stayed seated. I looked up at Matron, trying to get some indication that she was under duress. Nothing.

Eventually David returned to the table. Mac stood behind him, his twisted mouth lolling into a dangerous smile. His face was as hard to read as David's, probably because half of it wasn't really there. But he was up to something, and I didn't like it.

"At the urgings of Brother Sean, I have reconsidered your request to join us," said David.

What the fuck?

"Oh. Um... thanks."

"If you wish to retire to prepare yourself, Sister Jane will sit vigil with you in seclusion until the appointed hour."

"Great, thank you," I said, confused and suspicious. "I promise you won't regret this."

And so Matron and I found ourselves sitting on the grass in a corner of the tent, shielded from view by an improvised partition made of blankets draped over wooden stands.

I had so much I wanted to say. Jane Crowther was funny and vivacious; she stood up for herself and didn't take any shit from anyone. Could this blank-eyed acolyte really be her?

"I'm sorry," I said eventually.

She looked up at me. It was hard to tell, but I thought she looked confused.

"If I'd just got rid of Mac earlier then I could have brought you back to the school sooner. They'd never have found you."

"Thank heaven they did," she replied. "For I am saved!"

Please, God, no. I felt tears starting to well up.

"Nah," she said eventually. "Only kidding."

I had never been so relieved in my life. Except for that time when I didn't die on the scaffold. On reflection, that probably trumps it. But I was pretty bloody relieved. I went to hug her but she pushed me away.

"Better not. I kind of stink. The blood, y'know," she whispered, careful that we shouldn't be overheard by anyone lurking on the other side of the blanket.

"Yeah, about that. I meant to ask, why exactly are you covered in blood, carrying a gun and hanging out with psychotic religious cannibals?

"I'm a loyal disciple now, Lee. Have to be."

"Why?"

"They have the girls. There are about a hundred people travelling with David now, and many of them have medical conditions that need to be managed. They need a doctor, so they need me alive. But I made it clear when they took me that if they harmed any of my girls I'd kill myself. The girls stay alive and untouched as long as I co-operate. They keep them in a caravan but they park it about a mile away from the main tent each night, just so I'm not tempted to try and find them."

"But you're not a doctor."

"You don't know everything about me, Lee," she snapped impatiently. I'd touched a nerve. "I went to medical school for three years."

"So why..."

She interrupted me. "Not important right now. That was another life."

I looked at her blood-caked face.

"You had to convert?"

"Yes. It was a condition."

"So you performed the ritual?"

She nodded. "They chose a Blood Hunter as the victim. Made it a little bit easier. I couldn't have done it to a prisoner. God knows what would have happened to us then, but I couldn't have done it. Even so, it was..." she broke off, unable to continue.

"So the girls are safe and you're the cult doctor, yeah?"

"Yeah."

"I don't really want to ask this, but Mac...?"

"Yes, I patched him up. Not the prettiest job, and he died on the table twice, but I managed it in the end. I think it was sheer force of will that kept him alive. He's very, very angry at you, Lee."

"No shit, Sherlock. But why the fuck would you help him?"

"It's my job. I save people. It's what I do. I don't... I try not to kill."

"But after what he did, how could you?"

"How could I not?" she replied furiously.

I didn't know what to say to that. "And he's David's right-hand man?"

She groaned. "Yes. After I patched him up he asked to convert and David let him. Said he had brought a message from God and deserved to be saved. They chose a child for his initiation. A young girl, no more than fifteen. He didn't hesitate for a second. And then he started doing it again."

"Doing what?"

"Worming his way in. Showing off, seizing the initiative, getting things done. He brought back more prisoners in the first month than they'd had in the previous three. Their strategist died in the attack on Hildenborough. Mac sussed that there was a vacancy, and filled it. David relies on him a lot now."

"He should watch his back then. He'll be crucified before he knows it."

"Not that easy. Mac doesn't have the same power base here. He's not been able to gather a little gang of followers. Everyone's first loyalty is to David. It was Mac who persuaded David to come here, and he devised the plan of attack. I think he stumbled across the, let's call them officers for want of a better word, a few weeks back, and they hatched the plan together. Lure you away, attack while you're off-site. He was incandescent when the attack on the school failed. He didn't anticipate such an organised resistance. And when he found the bodies of the boys in the truck yesterday evening, my God. Did you do that?"

I explained what had happened to us at the farm and subsequently. As I told her about killing Wolf-Barry she did the strangest thing. She reached out and stroked my hair.

"You poor boy," she said, her voice full of compassion and sorrow.

I suddenly felt very uncomfortable.

"It was necessary," I said awkwardly. "I'm just doing what has to be done."

She nodded, wordlessly. But she left her hand resting on mine.

"So what's with persuading David to let me convert?" I asked.

"I have no idea. Whatever he's got planned it can't be good."

"But the ritual takes place outside, yes?"

"Normally."

"Good. When we get outside things are going to kick off. With any luck there won't be a proper fire-fight, but if the shooting starts I need you to run, as fast as you can, across the road. There's a stile in the hedgerow a few metres to the left of the school gate. They'll be waiting for you and they'll give you covering fire if need be."

She nodded.

At that moment a blanket was flung aside and Mac leered down at us.

"How's the reunion going?" he croaked.

"Sorry?" I replied. "Couldn't quite catch that. Could you enunciate a little better, please."

He looked down at me, furious. It's hard to talk when your lips have been partially burnt away.

I stood up and held out my hand.

"Hey Mac, you look great. No hard feelings, yeah?" I glanced down and pretended to be surprised that there was no hand for me to shake. "Oh. Sorry." Mock embarrassed.

"Come with me," he said, with what looked like an attempt at a smile.

A crowd had gathered outside the tent, and Matron and I were led through them to a clear space in the centre where David was standing. This crowd was no good at all. The sniper wouldn't be able to get a good shot at David in amongst all these people. I was thinking as fast as I could but I had nothing. I might have to go through with this foul ritual after all.

"Have you selected a victim for today, David?" asked Mac. And something in his tone of voice made me even more uneasy.

"I have decided to take your advice, Brother Sean," David replied.

The crowd parted and two men walked forwards, herding a boy between them. It was Heathcote. So now I knew what had happened to the boy manning the GPMG at the school gates. His face was streaked with tears and snot, and he was snivelling. He looked utterly petrified. He saw me and a moment of hope flashed across his face, but he swiftly realised what was going on, and he let out a low moan of animal terror. He started muttering: "Oh God, oh God, oh God no, please God no."

His escorts walked him into the centre of the space and forced him onto his knees. Once he was kneeling I could see that his hands were tied behind his back. One man grabbed his hair and pulled his head back, exposing the soft flesh of his throat. Heathcote fell silent, too terrified to even whimper. He knew he was about to die. As he looked over at me I saw the mingled pleading and fear in his eyes and I felt like I wanted to be sick.

I was so transfixed that I didn't even notice Mac walk up beside me. I only registered his presence when he whispered in my ear.

"You weren't there when we taught this bitch a lesson. You weren't there when we executed the men from Hildenborough. I made you my second-in-command but you never really earned it, did you? You never got your hands wet. Or your dick, for that matter."

I clenched my fists. Mustn't let him provoke me. I had to think of a way out of this.

"It was too easy for you," he continued. "I wonder, would you have shot one of the prisoners that day if you'd been there?"

I turned to face him, defiant and angry.

"No, I wouldn't have. I'm not a murderer."

He chuckled. "You keep saying that, Lee. Who are you trying to convince? I should warn you, I'm a hard sell. I'm the one you betrayed, shot in cold blood and left to die, remember. Bates might disagree with you too. And I imagine you killed at least one of my officers yesterday. So what's the difference between a killer and a murderer, hmm? Coz you're definitely a killer."

I just stared into his eye.

"No answer to that? Well, let's put it to the test. You

have a choice. If you want to live you have to kill Heathcote. Take a knife, slit his throat, watch him die. And then you have to drink his blood. You want to be in my gang you have to earn it this time. If you refuse I'll put a bullet in both your kneecaps and hang you upside down to bleed."

David was smiling indulgently at the pair of us. He couldn't hear what Mac was hissing in my ear, but he was allowing his favourite acolyte a little fun.

"And what's this lesson supposed to teach me?" I asked.

"That you aren't capable of doing what needs to be done," replied Mac. "If you kill Heathcote and join us, then I won't be able to touch you. You'll be protected as one of the brethren. Then you can plot and scheme to your heart's content. Try and bring him down the way you did me. You may even pull it off. God knows you're a devious little fuck. There's a chance that you might be able to save the school. And Matron, and the girls. But only if you stay alive. And you only stay alive if you kill Heathcote. Sacrifice him to save the others, or sacrifice yourself to save your conscience. Your choice."

He pressed a hunting knife into my hand.

"You've cheated your way into leadership without ever having to make the tough choices. This is what leadership is, Lee: the willingness to send men to their deaths when necessary, the ability to kill without compunction or hesitation when you need to. Show me what you're made of."

He stepped back, his hand resting on the butt of his holstered pistol.

The knife felt heavy as lead in my hand. I stared at Heathcote's wide, terrified eyes as he shook his head imperceptibly, in denial of what was happening. I looked around me, at a sea of blood-smeared faces, expectant and excited. And David, amused but curious at my hesitation.

"Come, come young man," he said briskly. "If you wish to join us you know what you must do. Bleed the cattle. Earn your salvation. Make yourself safe."

I thought of the two men at the pillbox who I had spared. If I'd killed them and taken care of the river defences, we'd have been able to evacuate the school unseen by the forces at the gate.

I thought of the officers I had released. If I hadn't let them go then Ben Woodhams, that young woman, Russell and Jones would all still be alive.

I thought of Mac. If I'd killed him before he'd seized power then Matron would have been spared her ordeal, and countless lives would have been saved.

If I had done what was necessary, so many people need not have died.

Every time I'd spared a life I'd made things worse. Mac was right. And Heathcote was a dead man anyway.

So I stepped forward, bent over the quivering boy, leant into him, whispered 'I'm so sorry' into his ear, and slit his throat open. All the while, looking straight into Mac's face. Even half ravaged as it was, his look of triumph was unmistakeable. It was the most terrible thing I have ever seen.

He mimed applause as the crowd began shouting hallelujahs.

As I stood up I saw Matron standing in the crowd. She was crying. Her tears ran red as they streamed down her cheeks. It was only then that I realised I was crying too.

The two men held Heathcote as he writhed and kicked his way to death, collecting the blood that flowed from his throat in an ordinary breakfast bowl. When his feeble struggles finally ceased, and the bowl was brimming with fresh blood, David stepped forward, lifted the bowl and brought it to me. He raised it to my lips. My nostrils filled with the metallic tang of slaughter.

"Drink of the blood of the lamb, and be transformed to your very soul," he said.

He didn't realise that I was transformed already.

I took two short, deep breaths, and leaned forward to take a sip.

As I did so I gripped the knife tightly, and brought it up as hard as I could into David's chest, aiming for his heart.

The blade bounced off the bullet proof vest that David was wearing beneath his jacket, and fell to the grass.

And all hell broke loose.

CHAPTER SEVENTEEN

I didn't expect to survive. If it had been a straight choice – kill Heathcote or die – I like to think I would have chosen death.

Thing is, I had a knife, but David was ten feet away. If I moved towards him I'd be shot down before I got halfway. The only way to kill him was to get him to come to me. And the only way to do that was to kill Heathcote and continue with the ritual. I knew, when I slit that poor boy's throat, that his death was buying me the chance to kill David. That was the deal. I also expected to be shot in the head a second after the knife slid into the bastard's heart. I was fine with that.

But he didn't die. Nor did I. And so I have to live with the knowledge that I killed a friend in cold blood. The other nightmares keep me awake, but Heatcote's hopeless pleadings whisper in my ears every waking second.

"Oops," said David, grinning. Then he kneed me in the balls. I doubled over and he brought his knee up again, into my face, smashing my nose and sending me reeling backwards. I stumbled and fell to the ground. A huge cry went up from the crowd, and they fell upon me. Everything was a blur of kicks and punches, shouts and screams. Boots slammed into every inch of my body, I managed to raise my arms to try and protect my head, but it was of little use.

I heard a dreadful crack as my left arm snapped in two. I screamed in agony, and my head began to swim. It felt like I'd come adrift from the ground, weightless. I was starting to pass out.

Then the shooting started. The beating stopped almost instantly and I heard the screams of bloodlust change to cries of fear. I heard feet running left and right, the loud, insistent stutter of machine gun fire, and shouted orders from Mac and David. I lay there, unable to move. Every part of my body hurt, and my arm was agony. My head felt twice its normal size. I tried to calm my breathing. Couldn't lie here in the open like this. Then I felt hands reaching underneath my arms and lifting me. I opened my eyes but all I could see was swirls of colour; nothing made sense. I'd taken so many blows to the head it felt like my brain was bouncing back and forth inside my skull. Whoever was helping me managed to get me upright and I took a few shuffling steps.

"Down!" Matron.

She pushed me forwards and I sprawled back onto the grass. I landed on my broken arm and passed out.

When I came round I was moving again, staggering forward with Matron holding me up. I could hear the sounds of battle but I couldn't tell where they were coming from. Were we in the thick of the fighting or had we left it behind? Then I felt canvas on my face as we pushed through the flap into the tent. My vision started to clear slightly, and I could make out vague shapes and colours.

"Sit here," she said as she lowered me onto a chair.

My vision and hearing continued to improve. There was a hell of a battle going on outside. Matron came running up with a medical kit.

"You're holding your arm, is it broken?" She was breathless, and kept glancing over her shoulder at the tent door.

"Think so."

"This is going to hurt," she warned, and then she took

hold of the arm and wiggled it a bit, trying to find the break and set the bone.

I passed out again.

When my senses returned my arm was in a sling, bound tight across my chest. I looked up and saw Matron struggling with an attacker. My vision was still blurred, and I couldn't make out the details, but I could see she was being overpowered. I looked around for a weapon and saw the med kit case lying at my feet. I leant down and picked it up with my good right arm. I tried to stand but my legs were like jelly. I managed to rise off the chair and then I toppled sideways and crashed to the ground. Luckily I fell onto my good arm this time.

Deep breaths. Focus. Things to do.

This time I managed to get upright and I lurched towards the struggling couple. I brought the corner of the med kit case down as hard as I could on the head of the man who had his hands around Matron's throat. He grunted and slumped to the ground. Hang on, he wasn't a Blood Hunter. Fuck.

Matron greedily sucked in some air with a hoarse yelp.

"Thank you," she gasped.

"We need to get out of here," I said. "Our guys are going to think you're the enemy, and any Blood Hunters who see you helping me will cut you down. You need to go."

"I know. Need to find the girls. One last thing, though."

She grabbed the med kit, opened it, pulled out a syringe and bottle. She filled the syringe and jabbed it into my good arm before I had a chance to ask what she was doing.

"What the fuck is that?" I asked.

"Home brew," she said. "Should help you stay on your

feet for a bit. Take this." She pressed a machine gun into my good hand. Then she leaned forward and kissed me hard on the lips. "Good luck!" And she was gone, machine gun held ready, out the rear tent flap.

The spot where she'd injected me felt red hot. The heat spread out from my arm, creeping through my veins until my entire body felt like it was full of lava.

It felt fantastic!

A stream of bullets ripped through the tent fabric right in front of me, cutting a horizontal line. I dived for cover. The bullets stopped for an instant, hitting something between shooter and tent, and then continued. A body slammed into the canvas, and slid down to the grass. Then a Blood Hunter backed into the tent, firing wildly. Once inside he turned and made to run for the other exit, but he saw me. He screamed furiously and raised his gun. I was quicker. Two bullets to the chest took care of him.

The man lying beside me groaned and rubbed his head, coming around. I vaguely recognised him as one of the men from Hildenborough.

"Wake up," I yelled at him. He looked up at me, shaking his head to clear his vision.

"You all right?" he asked.

"Will be. You?" He nodded.

We got to our feet.

"Come on then," I said. And we ran out of the tent into the battle.

I'd never seen anything like it. It was a free for all. Everywhere I looked there were people fighting hand-to-hand; everywhere the glint of sunlight on machete blades, the smell of blood and cordite. People were being stabbed and shot, strangled and beaten. It was a mêlée and it was impossible to get a sense of who was winning. The force we had brought from Hildenborough was only forty strong, so they were hopelessly outnumbered.

I raised my gun and took a few potshots, killing two Blood Hunters outright and wounding at least one more. I was shooting one-handed, from the hip, with my other arm useless on my chest, but I was still shooting better than I'd ever done before. All my senses felt crystal clear. Whatever it was Matron had injected me with, it made me feel invincible.

The guy next to me staggered backwards as his head exploded in two, cleaved by a machete. I spun, firing, and the stream of bullets ripped into a Blood Hunter who jerked backwards and collapsed like a puppet with its strings cut. Suddenly I was in the thick of the fighting.

People crashed into me, locked in life and death struggles. Bullets whistled past my head. One Blood Hunter came for me, machete raised. I tried to bring my gun to bear, but it was grabbed by another Blood Hunter. I wrestled for control of the weapon, saw the raised machete out of the corner of my eye and let go of the gun. The Blood Hunter who'd grabbed it fell backwards with a shout of surprise and let off a burst of bullets, which cut down the one with the blade. As he fell I grabbed the blade and whipped around, throwing it as accurately as I could. It found its mark in the chest of the man who'd shot its owner. I grabbed my gun back from the lifeless hands of the Blood Hunter and tried to get some sense of what was going on around me. I couldn't see any boys. Where the hell was Norton?

Through the mass of fighting I caught a glimpse of the sandbagged machine gun nest at the gate. Inside, a Blood Hunter was firing the GPMG down the drive towards the school. A group of Blood Hunters were kneeling next to him, firing back into the mêlée, picking off Hildenborough fighters. If nothing changed it was only a matter of time before the Blood Hunters got the upper hand. We had to shut that gun down, allow Norton to bring re-enforcements. Someone crashed into me from behind, knocking me to my knees. I turned to find a young blood-daubed woman staring at me, a neat hole above her left eye. She fell sideways revealing Rowles, smoking pistol in one hand, machete dripping blood in the other.

"Orders, sir?" he shouted above the din.

"We need to..." He raised his gun and I ducked. A bullet whipped over my head and I heard a strangled cry. I looked up at him again.

Definitely the scariest ten year-old I've ever met. I was glad he was on my side.

"GPMG!" I shouted, pointing towards the gate. He leant down and helped me to my feet. I was only halfway up when I had to shoot through his legs, kneecapping a woman who was coming at him with a machete. He turned and finished her off with a single shot.

Once I was upright I took the lead. We shoved our way through the fight, firing and hacking our way to the edge of the scrum. Then we skirted around the outside, collecting two Hildenborough men on the way. We found a clear space near the wall, and Rowles said "Let me, sir." He raised his gun and took careful aim.

As he took shots at the men behind the sandbags we stood guard around him, picking off any Blood Hunters we could get a clear shot at. The man next to me took a bullet to the thigh and then, as he bent down to put pressure on the wound, another round took him in the top of the head. He collapsed in a heap, instantly dead.

Rowles took a step forward each time he fired and the remaining man and I paced him, keeping him covered. He'd picked two of them off before they worked out who was shooting at them. By that point we were within a couple of metres of the sandbags. Edward's gun clicked empty and he tossed it aside without a second's hesitation.

I dropped to my knees and sprayed the sandbags with bullets as he ran towards them, machete raised, shouting some sort of battle cry. My bullets took one Blood Hunter across the chest and he fell backwards out of sight. The other fired wildly at Rowles but somehow the bullets kept missing, and soon the shooter was missing his left arm.

I heard a fleshy impact above me and the head of the man who'd been fighting beside me dropped at my feet. I dived forward and spun so I landed on my back, firing as I did so. But the gun didn't fire. Empty.

I rolled sideways to avoid the blade that curved down towards my head. In doing so I rolled over my broken arm. Didn't hurt a bit. The blade slammed into the grass next to my ear. I reached across with my good arm, grabbing the Blood Hunter's wrist, but it was drenched in fresh blood from the battle, and my hand slid off as he pulled the blade free of the ground. He raised the machete again as I lay there on the ground, nowhere to go. Then a blur above my head as someone literally dived over the top of me, their shoulder hitting the Blood Hunter in the stomach and taking him down. Haycox.

Even over the din of battle I heard the dreadful crunch as they hit the ground. Haycox sprang backwards, his opponent's neck snapped. He turned and reached down to offer me a hand up. But before I could take it his head snapped sideways as it shattered in a spray of blood and brain matter. Bullet to the head. He fell, stone dead. I scrambled backwards and tried to get to my feet. I was spending far too much of this fight flat on my bloody back. I saw two Blood Hunters come running towards me, lowering their guns as they came. Then they lurched backwards as an arc of heavy GPMG rounds picked them up and flung them, lifeless, to the grass. I looked across at the sandbags and there was Rowles, God love him, unleashing the GPMG at any Blood Hunter foolish enough to offer him a target.

I got to my feet and ran, crouching as I weaved through the fight, to the sandbags. I dived over them, landing smack on the fresh corpse of one of Rowles' victims. I pulled his gun free and took my place at Rowles' side, sheltering behind the wall of sandbags, picking off Blood Hunters.

A quick glance to my right revealed a stream of armed boys, running down the drive towards us; Norton and re-enforcements. But looking at the scene in front of me I realised that it was already too late. The Blood Hunters were overwhelming the opposition. We were losing.

The heavy machine gun next to me chattered once more and then fell silent.

"All gone," said Rowles simply. "What now?"

"Back to Castle. Run!"

As Rowles legged it down the drive, waving for Norton and his troops to fall back, I stood and yelled into the mêlée as loud as I could: "Retreat! Back to the school! Retreat!"

Bullets from a host of Blood Hunters smacked into the sandbags, and I dived for cover again. This time I crawled across corpses and flung myself behind the school wall, out of the line of fire. Then I got up and ran for Castle as fast as I possibly could.

I could hear the sounds of pursuit behind me, cries and crashes and weapon fire. Running is bloody difficult with only one arm; you get unbalanced and wobble all over the place. I got halfway to the school, with bullets whistling past me all the way, and then my torso somehow outpaced my legs. I ploughed, head-first, into the grass. I tried to roll with it, and get back up on my feet, but my useless arm threw me again and I ended up in a heap.

I regained my feet and chanced a look behind me. Twenty or so Hildenborough men, Green, and a few of his surviving actors, were racing towards me, a horde of screaming Blood Hunters in their wake. Mac was leading the pursuit. He was bellowing encouragement to his cohorts, waving a bloodied machete above his head.

As the human tide caught up with me I turned and was swept along with them. Ahead of us I could see Norton lining the boys up into ranks. They shouldered arms and took careful aim right at us. What the bloody hell was he doing?

When we were within ten metres of him he shouted: "Get down!"

We didn't need telling twice. All of us dived to the ground. There was the most tremendous noise as all the boys fired at once, sending a wall of lead into the massed Blood Hunters.

"Positions!" yelled Norton.

We scrambled to our feet and ran forward. Then Norton shouted: "Down!" We dived again. A second volley thundered over our heads.

"Inside!"

We leapt up and piled in through the large double doors. As I stood at the doorway, herding people inside, I could see the results of Norton's volleys. They had wiped out the first rank of approaching Blood Hunters, maybe thirty or more, who lay twitching and groaning on the blood-soaked grass. Once those behind them had realised no third volley was likely, they'd kept running, trampling their dead and wounded underfoot in their eagerness to slice us open. They were nearly upon us. I couldn't see Mac. Had he fallen?

I ushered the last man through the doors and then followed him inside. Norton was there amongst the boys, manhandling an enormous barricade. Constructed from bookcases and table tops, it sat on two wheeled trolleys. They pushed this up against the flimsy main doors. A group of boys at each side took the strain, the trolleys were whipped away, and then the edifice was lowered to the floor. It was buttressed with thick wooden beams at 45 degrees, and once it was down it covered the main doors entirely. Almost the instant it hit the ground a huge body of men slammed into the doors and began pushing. The barricade didn't move an inch.

"Positions!" yelled Norton. Two groups of boys ran left and right out of the entrance hall and into the rooms that faced the lawn on the ground floor. These each boasted huge windows through which the Blood Hunters could pour. But each had thick wooden shutters inside, with metal crossbars to secure them. Through the doors I could see that these were all closed, and had been buttressed and reinforced with anything the boys could lay their hands on. Norton had done his job well. Another group ran upstairs to take up sniping positions at the windows on the first floor. A few moments later I heard the first shots from above as they rained fire down on the attackers. The final group ran backwards to take up defensive positions at the rear of the house.

The group of men and boys who'd survived the battle at the gate milled around, tending their wounds and catching their breath. Mrs Atkins moved amongst them, selecting those who needed the most urgent care.

Norton came running up to me and pressed a Browning into my hand.

"What happened?" he asked

"The wild card got creative," I replied. "Are all the defences in place as discussed?"

"Yeah, we're ready for them."

I turned and shouted at the people in the hall with us. "All those of you too wounded to fight make your way to the top floor. We've collected all the medicines and stuff in a dorm up there. Go patch yourselves up."

Mrs Atkins led about ten wounded men and boys up the stairs.

Green was standing right in front of me. He had a nasty gash across his forehead and his hair was matted with blood. He was gripping his machine gun tightly, but his lower lip was trembling. He looked like he was about to curl up in a ball and start weeping.

"Green, take these guys to the armoury and issue them with new weapons and ammunition."

He nodded wordlessly, and ran back into Castle, towards the cellar. The others followed.

Suddenly the banging on the door stopped, and the Blood Hunters' guns fell silent. Norton and I exchanged worried looks and ran up the stairs and into one of the rooms overlooking the lawn.

"What's going on?" I shouted.

"Dunno sir," replied one of the boys who'd been shooting down at them. "They all just ran around the side of the building."

At that moment there was a terrible scream in the distance.

"That came from the back," said Norton, and we ran out of the room and across the landing. We pushed through double doors and ran across the main hall balcony to the rear stairs. Norton was in the lead as we crashed through the door and jumped down the stairs three at a time. We came out next to the cellar entrance, and found ourselves in the middle of a pitched battle. Green and the men he'd been arming were fighting hand-to-hand with a group of about ten Blood Hunters, but I could see more pouring into the courtyard outside.

How the hell had they gotten in?

Norton and I opened fire from the stairs. I could see Green, both hands raised, trying to slow the descent of a machete that a big muscled Blood Hunter was forcing down towards his head. The Blood Hunter was grinning as his biceps flexed and the blade inched down. I couldn't get a clear shot through the crowd, so I lowered my head and shoulder charged the fighting men, barrelling through them until I was next to Green. I shoved my pistol into the Blood Hunter's perfectly sculpted six pack and squeezed the trigger twice. The man staggered back and slid down the wall, clutching his guts.

Green fell backwards too, into a corner. He curled up, buried his head in his hands and began to sob. I couldn't worry about him now. Someone banged into my left side and sent me staggering against a door. Which was open. I tottered for a moment in the doorway but I couldn't regain my balance. I reached out with my left arm to steady myself. But my left arm was in a sling. I fell headfirst down the hard stone steps into the musty cellar.

While I sprawled on the damp brick I heard someone slam the door against the wall and come running down the stairs behind me. Still on the ground I turned and saw a Blood Hunter woman charging towards me. I shot her twice but her momentum carried her forward and she collapsed on top of me. Her lolling head cracked into mine and the force smashed the back of my skull against the brick floor.

Bright spots danced in front of my eyes, and felt myself starting to pass out. I closed my eyes, steadied my breathing and tried to focus, but it was hard. God knows how many blows to the head I'd taken in the last twenty minutes. I was pretty sure the only thing keeping me conscious was Matron's home brew. I wasn't looking forward to the come down.

I managed to stave off unconsciousness, and rolled the wounded woman off me. She was still alive, but she was out for the count. I decided the time for taking prisoners had long passed. I put one in her head to finish her off.

I had just got to my feet when I heard a tremendous explosion and a sustained volley of gunfire. It sounded like it came from the front of the school.

They'd blown the doors.

The sounds of battle overhead grew more intense. We were being overrun. I turned and ran into one of the side chambers. I picked up a box of grenades and a kit bag. I shoved as many of the bombs inside as I could, then I nipped into the next chamber along. I strapped two machine guns across my shoulders, put another pistol in my belt, and shoved as many clips of ammunition as I could carry into my pockets. I was carrying more hardware than Rambo.

A Rambo with bugger all muscle tone, gangly arms – one of which was useless – a mild case of acne, a broken nose, a head that felt like a punching bag and a system full of unknown drugs. Still, I had lots and lots of guns.

"Rock n' Roll!" I yelled, cocked my machine gun, and went running up the stairs. Straight into somebody's fist. My nose cracked once more and I went tumbling back down the stairs to the bricks.

"This," I said wearily as I lay there, "is getting repetitive."

"Don't worry," said a familiar voice. "It'll all be over soon." Mac was standing at the top of the stairs, shaking the fingers of his good hand. At least hitting me had hurt. He looked down at me and sneered.

I tried to bring my gun to bear but Mac was too fast for me. He was down the stairs before I could gather myself and he kicked the pistol from my grip. Then he stamped on my good hand. Even above the sound of the battle overhead, and my own shout of anger, I heard yet another bone crack.

Didn't feel it though. Really, *really* good drugs.

There was a stutter of machine gun fire from the top

of the stairs. A Blood Hunter stood there, shooting back into the corridor, guarding the cellar door. At all costs I had to stop them taking possession of the armoury. I wanted to reach for a grenade, but even if my free hand had been working and I could pull a pin I'd only succeed in blowing the entire school sky high, taking everyone with it. Not an option.

Mac stood above me, gun pointed straight at my face.

"I really want to shoot you in the head, Nine Lives," he snarled. "You have no idea how much I want to shoot you in the fucking head."

"Be my guest." I screwed my eyes closed, waiting for the impact.

"But that would be no fun," he said. "I mean, orgasms are great, but they're so much better after a little foreplay, don't you think?"

"Shoot me or shag me, Mac... make your mind up."

He ground his foot on my hand. I could feel jagged edges of bone scraping against each other in my little finger.

The screams and gunfire from above were intense now. I imagined the Blood Hunters pouring through the front door, slicing and shooting the boys, smearing themselves in fresh blood and bellowing their victory.

"It's all over, Lee. There are too many of us. I'll be back in charge of the school within the hour. Maybe I'll celebrate with another crucifixion. What do you think?"

"Not very original," I replied. "You want to supersize it. How about a flaying, perhaps? Or maybe a dismemberment? Surprise me."

He squatted down on top of me, and leaned forward until my broken nose was almost touching his stubby little burnt wreck of one.

"I will, Lee. I promise you that. Now get up and dump the hardware."

He stood up and let me rise, keeping his gun on me as I let the weapons and ammunition drop to the floor.

"Now we wait for the commotion to die down so I can go claim my prize," he said.

"What about David?" I asked. "Won't he have something to say about you taking control?"

"David's my problem. Let me worry about him. You worry about me, Lee. Worry about what I'm going to do to you, Norton and that little shit Rowles, and anyone else who survives the fight. There's gonna be a bleeding tonight."

There was something different about Mac, and it wasn't just the injuries and the missing hand. He was taking real joy in the destruction happening above. He seemed more feral, less in control. His one good eye sparkled with barely concealed madness, very different from the power hungry thug I'd known before. He used to be unpredictable; now he was just plain scary.

"Mind if I sit while we wait?"

Mac opened his mouth to reply, but a burst of gunfire from the doorway silenced him. I saw the Blood Hunter by the door struggling with someone, heard a bone-crunching snap, and a man's lifeless body tumbled down the stairs to land at our feet.

"Yeah, why not," said Mac, ignoring the corpse. "Pull up a box of grenades. Let's bond."

I turned into one of the side rooms, looking for something to sit on.

"On second thoughts," said Mac. "Let's not and say we did."

Something hit me on the back of the neck, hard, and the world went black.

As I lost my grip on my senses the last thing I heard was Mac laughing. It was the insane cackle of a triumphant madman.

CHAPTER EIGHTEEN

I spluttered as the water poured down my face. Ice cold, it brought me round instantly. I was lying flat on my back on wooden boards. I wiped my eyes and looked up to see Mac standing above me. I could see cloths and pulleys suspended high above him; I was lying on the stage in the school assembly hall. I could hear lots of other people moving around, the hall sounded full.

"Wakey, wakey, Nine Lives," he said. "Shake a leg. Rise and shine."

I put my hand to the floorboards to lift myself and found that my little finger was twice its normal size. It had a sharp point of bone sticking out of it above the knuckle. The drugs were wearing off, so when I put pressure on that hand it hurt. A lot. I gasped and gritted my teeth. Wouldn't give him the satisfaction of seeing how much pain I was in. I suspected the drugs were still dulling a great deal of it; my broken arm still felt okay. As long as I didn't do anything stupid, like throw a punch, I'd be fine for a while. I used my elbow to lever myself up into a sitting position.

The hall was to my left. Along one side all the surviving boys and girls, and the men who'd been fighting with us, were lined up. They were kneeling with their hands on their heads. I scanned the crowd and breathed a sigh of relief when I spotted Rowles, Norton and Mrs Atkins, all safe and sound. Green was there too. There were about thirty surviving children and ten men. Bob was not among them, but Mrs Atkins' new man, Justin, was. Guards stood over them with guns and machetes, making sure they didn't try anything. The wooden balcony that ringed the hall on three sides was empty. There were roughly sixty Blood Hunters in the room, each and every one of them glistening with the very freshest blood. They were all staring at the stage. At me. Nobody was speaking.

"Show time," said Mac, with a grin.

I had two options. Stay silent and risk letting them know how terrified I was, or take the piss and try to appear confident.

"Go on then," I replied. "Do us a dance. Show us your jazz hands. Oh, sorry, forgot. Jazz *hand.*"

His grin didn't waver. "Get up."

As I did so I saw that David was sitting behind us on the stage, on his throne. He looked as immaculate and unruffled as ever, apart from where my knife had ripped the fabric of his suit.

"Welcome back, Lee," he said. "As you can see we have taken control of your school. It amused me to organise a little assembly. We might sing a few hymns later, would you like that?"

"Fine by me, as long as we don't have to sing Morning Has Broken. I fucking hate that song."

I was thinking fast, trying to work out the angles. There were guards in the wings at both sides. Behind David the stage stretched back into darkness. There was a fire exit door back there, but I'd never make it. There were three entrances to the hall itself: two sets of double doors on either side of the room and a fire exit at the back. All were guarded. There was no way out of here. Whatever Mac and David had planned I was stuck with it.

"I was going to bleed you in public," David said when I had gained my feet. "Make an example of you to others. But Brother Sean persuaded me otherwise. He has big plans for this place. He wants me to allow him to create a religious retreat here for our brethren. New recruits will be sent here for study and contemplation. Our wounded and old can find shelter here. He would run this endeavour for me. He even wishes to create a blood bank. The children you've watched over would be kept under lock and key, bled regularly but kept alive; a resource for the faithful. I and my chosen acolytes would continue our travels, taking the word to the world outside. I like the idea. What do you think?"

"Sounds lovely," I replied enthusiastically. "You could even have a cricket team, play the locals. Hildenborough are quite good, although you may have just slaughtered their first eleven."

David chuckled indulgently. "I thought you'd like it. But Brother Sean has some strange ideas." *Here we go*, I thought. "Even though we have taken your school by force, subdued your army and seized your weapons he feels bad for you."

"I'm sure his heart bleeds," I said, looking at Mac. His face gave nothing away.

David continued. "He has this quaint notion that he needs to prove he's better suited to run this place than you are. I can't imagine why."

"He's always had inadequacy issues," I said. "It all goes back to his childhood. Bed wetter, you see."

"I see. That explains a lot," said David, winking at Mac.

"I told you how it works, Lee," said Mac. "You want to be boss you've got to challenge the leader and beat him. Prove you're better. You never learned that lesson. But you will now. You're the leader of this place now, so I challenge you."

I laughed incredulously. "What, to a fight? You and me? Are you joking? I've got a broken arm and a broken hand. I fall down if I try to run and I can't even make a fist. What kind of victory would that be? You might as well wrestle a puppy, you fucking idiot."

He stepped forward and hissed furiously in my face:

"Better than stabbing you in the back, you traitorous son of a bitch."

I turned to David and shrugged. "Your boy has issues, Mr David, sir."

"Can I say something?" All heads turned to the crowd of captives. It was Norton.

"No! Shut the fuck up!" yelled Mac, incensed at being interrupted, spittle flying through the gash where half his lips used to be.

"It's just that I remember something you said once about delegating responsibility," continued Norton.

Mac turned to the crowd. "Bring that little fucker up here."

A Blood Hunter walked over to Norton and hauled him to his feet by his hair, then marched him up the steps onto the stage. Mac was on him instantly, holding a gun to his face. "Explain," he growled.

Norton flashed a nervous glance at me and made his pitch.

"Let me see if I understand this. You want to fight Lee for control of the school. Winner takes all, yeah?"

Mac nodded.

"And what happens to the loser?"

"The fight's to the death. If he wants the school he's got to kill me with his own bare hands. He's learned that lesson well. Ask Heathcote."

Norton looked at David. "And you agree to this? If Lee wins then you leave?"

"I'll leave anyway," said David. "It's just a question of who's in charge when I do. Whoever wins, this will be a holy place for us. But I would allow Lee to complete the ritual and take charge for me. He'd have a large group of helpers, of course." David indicated the crowd of Blood Hunters below us, "to keep him on the path of righteousness."

"Okay," said Norton, turning his attention to me. "Lee, you're the leader round here, Mac – sorry, Brother Sean – acknowledges that, don't you?"

Mac nodded, suspicious.

"Then delegate to me, Lee. Let me fight him for you. For all of us."

"No fucking way," snarled Mac.

"Hang on, you're changing your bloody tune," I said. "Only half an hour ago you were telling me that I had to be able to send men to fight and die for me. One of the things real leaders have to do, you said. So why can't I delegate? Norton, you willing to die for me?"

"Sir, yes sir!" barked Norton. He even gave a cheeky salute to go with the grin.

"Good man," I said cheerily. I liked this plan. Norton was a black belt. He'd kick Mac's one-armed arse all the way to next Christmas. "So Mac, this lesson you've been wanting to teach me. Looks like I've learned it. Willing to put your money where your mouth is? Gonna take on my loyal deputy? Or are you only willing to fight if you've got to fight me? I mean, yeah, if I only had a broken arm we'd be evenly matched. But you broke the little finger on my other hand. So unless you're going to give me a gun the best I can do is slap you. Not going to be a very satisfying fight, is it? Your victory won't be worth shit. But beat Norton, well, that'd be something. You'd have earned it then. That's what you said, isn't it... it's all about earning it?"

Silence fell. Everyone in the room was transfixed, waiting to see what Mac would do. If he went for this then we had a chance

I walked up to Mac, who still stood with his gun aimed at Norton. I whispered in his ear.

"All this time you've been pointing out to me the ways in which I'm a failure. The things I can't do that a leader needs to. Not forgetting the rules of challenge and succession you keep banging on about. You want to do this right, yeah? According to the rules? Then here's your chance. Follow your own logic, Mac. Fight the man I delegate to represent me. Prove you're better than the best I can field."

"And what if I delegate too? What if I ask Gareth to fight for me?" He indicated one of David's giant guards.

"Brother Sean, I think you're forgetting who's in charge here," said David, with steel in his voice. "I do the delegating, not you. I'm indulging your whim. Take care that my indulgence doesn't run out. The young man's logic is sound. I suggest you accept the challenge. Otherwise I may decide you're not the man you profess to be. I might decide you're cattle."

Mac looked rattled. But he had no option now. He'd engineered this situation, he'd have to see it through.

"Fine," he snarled as he let the gun fall from his grip, and charged.

Before Norton could react Mac took him in the midriff and barrelled forward, propelling him off the stage. They sailed through the air, crashing five feet to the floor of the main hall. Norton fell flat on his back, with all Mac's weight on top of him. There was a dreadful crack of bone as his spine hit the hard wood floor, then a hollow thump as his skull bounced. Lying on top of Norton, Mac reached his one good arm up, grabbed Norton's hair and slammed the back of his head onto the floor. Once, twice, three times. Then he leaned back, folded his arm and brought the sharp end of his elbow smashing down with all his might on Norton's throat. There was an awful soft crunch as his windpipe collapsed.

The whole fight had lasted about five seconds.

Mac rolled off and got to his feet. Norton lay there, clutching at his collapsed throat, gasping for air. The assembled Blood Hunters roared in triumph.

It's a measure of how used to this kind of thing I'd become that while everyone was watching my best friend die, I took the chance to get to Mac's discarded gun. I dived forward, landing on my broken arm, reaching for the gun with my semi-good hand. Yep, the drugs were wearing off. That hurt.

Gareth the guard stepped forward and kicked me under the chin before I could reach the weapon. I was flung backwards off the stage. I fell hard and lay on the hall floor, winded, next to Norton. We looked into each other's eyes. I could see all the fear and panic and horror in his, as they widened, dilated, and died. The crowd kept cheering.

Mac's leering zombie face appeared over mine.

"Well done," he said, shouting over the din. "One more corpse for the cause. Hope you're proud."

At that moment I finally accepted it. We were finished. We'd lost. I had no clever plan to fall back on, no trap to spring, no argument to put forward. I felt the darkest, blackest despair. I was beyond weeping or begging for mercy. There were no more sarcastic comebacks or flippant put downs. My friends were dead or captured. I was a broken wreck. Everything I'd tried to achieve had been destroyed. I'd failed my friends, my father, myself. All I had to look forward to was a creatively stage-managed death. And I was okay with that. It'd be kind of a relief.

I got my breath back and slowly rose to my feet. Mac faced me across Norton's cooling body, one mad eye gleaming with triumph. I spat in it. He just laughed.

I looked over his shoulder at the kneeling captives. Rowles' face a mask of cold fury, Green weeping, Mrs Atkins staring blankly into space. I wanted to tell them how sorry I was, but it wouldn't have meant a damn.

"Loser," said Mac, taunting me. I didn't reply.

David called for silence and the noise died away. The cult leader rose to his feet and addressed us.

"Brother Sean has brought great credit to our crusade. He led us out of our hermitage and set us on the true path. And now, brothers and sisters, he has brought us to a place of refuge and sanctuary, where the chosen can abide in peace through the Tribulation. This place, once a school, will become a beacon of hope for all the world. Children will study here under our guidance, learning of the one true faith. Here we shall train acolytes and pilgrims, preachers and reapers. The good word shall spill from this hallowed place like a flood and it shall sweep away all the cattle from our lands and make us safe. Hallelujah!"

The Blood Hunters howled their hallelujahs in response. David pointed at me. "Bring that child to me." I didn't wait to be grabbed and herded. I walked to the steps and mounted the stage again.

"No!" shouted Mac. "You promised me! You said I could do it!"

David silenced Mac with a look before turning to me.

"Young man," said David. "You were given an opportunity to join us, but you rejected it. Instead you tried to silence my holy voice. This cannot go unpunished." He gestured to the men in the wings. "Fetch rope," he said. They didn't even have to move, they just reached out and grabbed a rope that dangled from the gods. One of the guards walked out onto the stage holding the rope, which came easily, because it was only anchored to a wheeled pulley way up high. David took the rope and bent down, tying it around my feet.

He motioned to the guard, who walked back into the wings and unlaced the other end of the rope from the metal peg that secured it. Then he hauled on it, and my feet went out from under me. I crashed to the stage, face first. I felt one of my front teeth shatter. I was pulled upwards until I dangled in the air, suspended so my head was level with David's.

I could see Mac in the crowd. He looked agitated.

Slowly, meticulously, David stripped naked. Then he took a knife from one of the guards and walked centre stage. He spread his arms and addressed the crowd.

"In the fountain of life I shall be reborn," he intoned.

The Blood Hunters replied: "Make us safe."

"With the blood of the lamb I wash myself clean."

"Make us safe."

"From the source of pestilence comes our salvation."

"Make us safe."

"Life for life. Blood for blood."

"Make us safe."

He turned towards me, cradled my head and moved to kiss me.

"I'll bite your fucking lips off," I growled. He backed away.

"I thank you for your gift," he said.

Then, suddenly, the right side of his head wasn't there anymore. He reached up to feel his face, as if he were confused at what was trickling down his cheek. Someone in the crowd started to scream. David's hand came away from the gaping wound and he held the bloodied fingers up in front of his face, trying to focus on them. He emitted a bark of laughter and said: "As if by magic!" Then he collapsed in a heap.

Mac stood on the right side of the stage, smoking pistol in his hand.

"You promised!" he shouted at David's crumpled form. "You fucking promised! He's *mine*. I told you that and you promised."

The fallen cult leader craned his head to look at Mac.

He gave a sick, gargling laugh and blood bubbled up out of his mouth. "Safe now," he gasped. And then his head fell backwards, lifeless.

While all this was going on my eye caught a flash of movement as the door to the balcony swung open. I couldn't see anybody emerge. It didn't swing shut, but it was pushed further open, as if someone else was entering. Then again and again it swung a little shut but was pushed back open. There were people crawling onto the walkway overlooking the hall, hidden from view by the waist-high wooden guard rail. Who the hell was up there?

The crack of David's head on the wood jolted the guards out of their shock and they ran at Mac, machetes raised. He gunned them down. While they were still falling, he turned to the screaming crowd and fired over their heads. "Shut the fuck up!" he yelled. Silence fell. "I'm in charge now, right? You!" He pointed at one of the Blood Hunters in the wings. "Cut him down." The Blood Hunter didn't move. Mac waved the gun at him. "Now!" Still he didn't move. Mac paused, seemingly unsure what to do in the face of this refusal to comply.

It was as if his head suddenly cleared and he realised the position his unthinking rage had placed him in. He'd just killed the religious leader of a group of insane cannibals, all of whom were armed. And they were all looking at him.

"Nice one, Mac," I said. "Good move."

There was a collective roar, a guttural explosion of fury from every Blood Hunter in the hall. Then they rushed him. They could have shot him, but I guess there was something about wanting to inflict the pain personally, needing to feel the kicks and punches landing. Some of them even threw their guns aside as they ran. Like a tide, the cultists swept left and right to the stairs and streamed up them onto the stage. I was ignored, forgotten. Mac fired, mowing some of them down as they approached, but it was no use. They fell upon him and he screamed as he vanished beneath a flurry of fists.

Two things happened at once. The boys and men who'd been held prisoner ran forward and grabbed all the discarded weapons they could; and an army of girls appeared on the balcony above us.

Matron stood directly opposite and above me on the balcony, machine gun pointed down. To her left and right, flanking the room on all three sides, were fifteen young girls, all similarly armed.

I saw Rowles look up in astonishment. Then he looked at the stage and he smiled broadly.

"Fire!" he yelled.

All the girls opened up at once, pouring fire down into the throng of Blood Hunters. Those boys and men who'd grabbed discarded guns did the same.

The Blood Hunters didn't stand a chance. It was a massacre. Some of them realised what had happened and tried to bring their weapons to bear, but the onslaught was too fierce, the fire too concentrated. The gunfire seemed to go on forever, a cacophony of stuttering weapons with a staccato accompaniment of spent cartridges hitting the floor. The noise reached a crescendo and then gradually died away as magazine after magazine clicked empty and the guns fell silent. As the smoke rose, and the smell of cordite swamped everything, silence fell.

The stage was piled head-high with twitching, bleeding Blood Hunters; dead, dying and wounded. And me, upside down, swinging gently above the slaughter, splashed with blood and gore, laughing hysterically.

Matron was appalled at what had occurred, but she took control with assured, businesslike calm. She sorted out the youngest children, both boys and girls, and sent them outside to collect weapons from the battlefield. The men and older boys set to work pulling the Blood Hunters off the stage and sorting them into three piles: dead, mortally wounded, and those who could perhaps be saved. Matron co-ordinated the triage.

There was a brief argument between Rowles and Matron, with Rowles arguing that they should all be shot in the head. Matron wouldn't hear of it. Rowles surprised me by accepting her authority.

After I was cut down I sat at the far end of the hall and nursed my wounds, unable to believe that I was still alive. After a while Matron came and sat next to me, resting her hand on my knee.

"You all right?" she asked. I didn't need to answer that. "No, of course you're not. Sorry. Stupid question."

I smiled to indicate I didn't mind and she grimaced. "Ouch," she said, as she leant forward, took hold of my jaw and opened my mouth to reveal my missing front tooth. It had snapped in two, leaving a jagged, serrated edge that I couldn't stop probing with my tongue. "That must really hurt."

"Not yet," I lisped. "Your drugs are still taking the edge off. But I wouldn't mind another hit before you pull the root out."

"No problem. Hold still." She took hold of my re-broken nose and wrenched it into place again, making me yell. "You need a splint on that. I'm not sure it'll set quite right, though."

"Great," I laughed. "I'm a limping, lisping, gap-toothed scarface with a broken nose. What a catch."

She placed her hand on my cheek. "Oh, I don't know." She flashed me a cheeky, girlish grin that made me feel all sorts of interesting things. I actually blushed.

"Are all the girls okay?" I asked, changing the subject.

She nodded. "David kept his side of the bargain. They didn't touch them. Which isn't to say they enjoyed being locked in a caravan for so long." She surveyed the makeshift morgue in front of her. "I was hoping they wouldn't have to open fire; that just the threat would be enough to get the Blood Hunters to disarm. It seems that these days everyone has to end up killing somebody."

I looked at her and suddenly I realised where we'd gone wrong, all those months ago.

"It should have been you," I said to her.

"Sorry?"

"In charge. It should have been you, not Bates."

"Don't be ridiculous," she scoffed.

"Think about it. Every time things went wrong you were the one who did the right thing. You stood up to that woman on the drive; you stood up to Bates and Mac when Hammond was killed. While I was making plots, pretending to be something I wasn't, you were always the honest one. Of all the lessons Mac was trying to teach me about leadership, that's the one he never understood: you can only be a proper leader if you're willing to stand up for what you believe in and be counted when it matters. I never was. You always were. It should have been you, Jane. Not Bates, not Mac, not me. You. Maybe then none of this would have happened."

"Oh fuck off, Nine Lives" said a voice from the stage. There was Mac, fished out from the very bottom of the pile of bodies. He was covered in cuts and bruises, but not a single bullet had made its way through the crowd to him, curled up on the floor at the epicentre of the lynch mob. "The last thing we need right now is a fucking moral, yeah? Spare us, please."

Two of the boys who'd been sorting through the bodies

stood beside him, keeping him covered. I stood up and walked towards him across the hall floor, skirting the wounded and dying.

"What does it take to kill you, eh?" I said, incredulous. "I mean, I shot you, I blew you up, you just got beaten and shot at. What does it fucking take to get rid of you?"

"Back at you, Nine Lives," he replied, with a sneer.

I reached the stage and leant on it, resting my arms on the footlights and looking up at him. I sniffed and shook my head. I didn't understand it, but I was almost glad to see him. "Shooting David wasn't the cleverest thing you've ever done, was it?"

He shrugged, then he limped over to the front of the stage and sat down, dangling his legs over the side next to me.

"Fair point." He chuckled. "Snatched defeat out of the jaws of victory there, didn't I?"

"Kind of, yeah. You do realise you're insane. Really, genuinely psychopathic."

"Probably," he replied. He paused and then said: "I blame society."

I couldn't help it; that made me laugh. After a second he joined in and before I knew it we were holding our sides, tears streaming down our faces, in the grips of the most terrible giggles. When they subsided I reached down and picked up a discarded Browning. I checked it was loaded and chambered a round.

"Still," I said. "I'm going to have to kill you now, Sean. I hope you understand that."

He looked at me and nodded.

"It's what I'd do," he said evenly.

"I just want you to know, it's completely personal. I really hate your guts and I want you to die."

"I understand," he said.

I took a step back, raised the gun and aimed at his

heart. I looked straight into his face, at his one remaining eye, as I squeezed the trigger to the biting point.

"Lee, put it down," said Matron, behind me.

I didn't move a muscle.

"Lee, please, put it down. Enough now. You don't need to kill him. I worked too bloody hard to put him back together."

Mac held my gaze. His face gave nothing away. He seemed more curious than scared, interested to see which way I'd jump. Was I finally the cold blooded killer he'd always told me I needed to be? The answer was yes, and I was going to prove it. I wanted to kill him. I was sure it was the right and necessary thing to do.

I felt Matron's hand on my arm. "Put it down, Lee. It's over."

I turned my head to look at her. Somehow I'd not noticed before now, but she'd washed her face clean of blood. I could really see her for the first time in months. Her eyes held such compassion and warmth. My stomach felt hollow and empty, but I couldn't be sure whether it was because of the drugs wearing off, the sight of her face, or the certain knowledge that I was going to pull the trigger whatever she said.

"Sorry, Jane. But I'm a killer now." I turned back to face Mac. "It's what he made me." I steadied my arm to fire. I would have done it too, but Mac wasn't looking at me any more. He was looking over my shoulder. He smiled. "Finally," he said. "Someone with balls."

The first bullet took him in the jaw, ripping away half his face. The second got him right between the eyes. The third and fourth hit him in the right shoulder. The sixth ripped open his throat. The seventh and eight took away his nose and one remaining eye. The ninth, tenth and eleventh hit his chest, exploding his heart and lungs. Then the hammer hit metal. Mac fell backwards, a dead weight.

Green, by this point standing beside me, dropped the smoking gun to the floor, wiped his eyes, and walked away without a word.

EPILOGUE

I remember the first time I met Lee. He was fourteen and it was my first day as Matron at St Mark's, my first day as Jane Crowther. I wasn't sure if it was an identity I'd be comfortable with. I'd trained to be a doctor, not nursemaid to a bunch of spoiled upper-class brats. I was nervous and uncertain.

The police had taken care of all the details, and Inspector Cooper assured me that my cover was absolutely water tight. A few years hidden away in this anonymous little school and then maybe I could resume my medical studies somewhere else. Somewhere they'd never find me.

The last words Cooper said to me were: "I promise you, Kate, it's over. You'll never have to pick up a gun again."

What a joke.

Anyway, there I was, hair freshly dyed, first day at my new school. And the first boy into the San that morning was Lee. He was awkward and gangly, with arms that seemed too long for his body, and a smattering of spots across his forehead. His hair was wild and scruffy, and his uniform was a mess. He'd hit a pothole and fallen off his bike, he said, as he showed me the nasty graze on his arm. I swabbed it clean, smeared it with germolene and slapped on a bandage. *Three years of medical training for this*, I thought, totally depressed.

But then Lee did the sweetest thing, I've never forgotten it.

"You've got a hell of a job here, you know," he said. "Your predecessor was quite something."

I remember thinking 'Predecessor'? What kind of fourteen-year-old uses a word like 'predecessor?' Certainly not the kind of kids I grew up with.

"Really? How's that, then?" I asked.

So he told me all about the Headmaster and his wife, and explained why the boys might resent me; he gave me tips on how to defuse the Head's rages, and schooled me in the tactics needed to manage the particularly difficult boys, who he named and shamed so I wouldn't get caught by surprise. He was shy but friendly, presenting himself as a willing conspirator and helpmate. By the time he left I felt much better about things.

It was such a thoughtful, welcoming thing to do. I had a soft spot for him from that moment on, I suppose.

I think back to the year after The Cull, and the broken, hard-faced wreck that he became, and I want to weep. You see, he was never cut out for leadership, not under those circumstances, anyway. He was sweet and slightly bookish, a bit of a dreamer really. Young, yes, but mature for his age and with a strong sense of right and wrong.

Even now, years later, he hasn't got over the choices he made that year. I try to tell him that he shouldn't feel bad, that what he achieved was flat out heroic. But he doesn't see it that way. He still has the nightmares. I like to think that I'm a help to him, but sometimes he suffers from deep depressions that can last up to a month, and I'm powerless then. Still, I think writing this account has been therapeutic for him.

However, he can't bring himself to write the final chapter of the St Mark's story, so he's asked me to do it for him. I'm not much of a writer, so I'll keep it brief.

We were still clearing out the main hall when we heard shouts and running feet in the corridors. Then Rowles appeared on the balcony and shouted: "Bomb!"

Everyone was very calm about it, no one panicked. I suppose after what we'd just been through this seemed kind of tame. We walked outside and made our way to the playing fields at the back. Rowles had been putting the guns back into the armoury when he'd discovered a cluster of dynamite sticks, booby trapped and wired up to a clock.

MacKillick must have left them there, as an insurance policy. If he'd survived he'd have gone down and cut whichever wire he needed to cut. But he was dead, and neither Rowles nor Lee wanted to take the gamble of choosing red, yellow or black. As we stood there debating what to do there was the biggest explosion I've ever seen. All the grenades and bullets in the armoury went up with the dynamite, practically demolishing Castle in one horrendous bang.

Sean had the last laugh in the end. If he couldn't rule St Mark's then no-one could.

The wreckage burnt long into the night, warming us as we tried to decide what to do next. Lee just sat there, silent, staring at the fire, tears streaming down his face as he watched all his dreams, everything he'd fought for, burn away to ashes.

In the morning we packed up the Blood Hunters' marquee and walked to Hildenborough, where we moved into empty houses and slept all day.

I had been thinking about what Lee had said, about me being the natural leader. Those three months at the farm with the girls had been wonderful, and yes, I had enjoyed being in charge. Lee made it very clear that he didn't want the job any more.

So I called a meeting and we put it to the vote. Should we stay and become part of the Hildenborough community, or should I take charge of the search for a new home, a new school? The vote was unanimous.

Weeks later, when we were having our final meeting to choose between two likely places, Lee took me to one side.

"I'm leaving, Jane," he said.

I told him to stop being silly. His arm and hand were healing but he still had limited movement. He needed more physiotherapy and time to recover. But he was determined.

"I have to go find my father," he explained. "I know he survived the plague, but he should have been back here by now. Something's gone wrong and he might need my help."

"But where will you look?" I asked, unable to believe this.

"Iraq," he said simply.

I begged him to reconsider, told him to wait for us to finish our meeting and then we'd discuss it. He promised he would. But when we wrapped up half an hour later, he was gone.

I only spent two years as the matron of St Mark's School for Boys. I'd gone there looking for a refuge from violence, and instead I'd found more death than I could have imagined. And more kindness, too. We took the sign from the front gate with us when we moved into Groombridge, establishing some sense of continuity. "St Mark's is dead, long live St Mark's," as Rowles put it.

I was in control and I swore this time it would work, this time everyone would be safe.

I'd make sure of it.

THE END

Scott Andrews is a critic and journalist who has contributed features and reviews to magazines like *Starburst*, *TV Zone*, *Dreamwatch* and *Film Review*, and websites like Film Focus and BBCi. He has also written comics, and two episode guides for Virgin Books. This is his first novel.

Yes, he attended boarding school as a child. This book might lead you to conclude that this left him with some issues. He also spent five years working as a teacher, some of it at boarding schools. This screwed him up even more. Despite this, none of the characters in this book are based on actual flesh and blood people, none of the events portrayed are based on real events, and St Mark's only resembles those schools he attended and taught at in as much as they share some internal geography.

He lives in London's orbit but dreams of escaping to the wilderness with his wife and daughter. He can be contacted at www.sixesandsevens.net

coming
April
2008...

Now read the first chapter from the fourth book in
the exciting *Afterblight Chronicles* series...

THE AFTERBLIGHT CHRONICLES

DAWN OVER DOOMSDAY

Jaspre Bark

COMING APRIL 2008 (UK)
JUNE 2008 (US)

ISBN 13: 978-1-905437-62-7
ISBN 10: 1-905437-62-5

£6.99 (UK)/ $7.99 (US)

CHAPTER ONE

Cortez hated the smell of whorehouses. It was so dishonest. Cheap perfume and stale sweat masking a fruitless search for satisfaction.

Cortez had always preferred torture to sex. He had little interest in the wares the girls were selling. Torture seemed far more honest to him. Just as intimate, but a hundred times more heartfelt and intense. There was so much more invested in torture.

Sex always left Cortez feeling hollow afterwards. Empty, angry and unfulfilled. Torturing someone made him feel like a god. The men and women he was paid to torture came to worship him a little more each time he touched them.

Cortez always thought it strange that in English fucking was politely called 'making love'. He had never made a woman love him by fucking her. He had made many women and men love him through torture. It wasn't long before they looked to please his every whim. To confide in him their deepest and most dirty secrets. Things they wouldn't even tell their closest friends and lovers they would whisper into his ear between the pain filled sobs of shame. The timid admissions that lovers make to each other during pillow talk are nothing like the devastating truths he had extracted from his victims.

There are no misconceptions like there are with sex. No-one is thinking about a possible future together during torture. There were no tears when Cortez ended his relationship with his victims. They didn't beg him for one last chance, or to try and work things out. They looked at him with gratitude and relief. Some of them kissed his hand as joyous tears spilled from their eyes.

When they thought about the broken and agonising state their bodies were in, Cortez's victims realised there was no greater compassion a human being could show than to end their suffering. No lover's caress brought them anywhere near the relief Cortez did when he finally ended their lives.

And yet he had always been paid for this pleasure. Which, when he thought about it, made him little better than the women who worked in this brothel. They traded in their own tawdry and limited pleasures, much as he had. Taking lovers as he had victims, indiscriminately as long as he was paid.

He didn't betray it in his face or the way he stood, but it was this that annoyed him most about Greaves taking him to the brothel. Greaves was his paymaster. He went where Greaves asked him, irrespective of what he felt.

Cortez thought it ironic that even in these times, when Allah sought to test the faithful through plague and famine, that the world's oldest profession continued to thrive.

"What's your pleasure?" said a woman's voice over the intercom at the door. Greaves bent down to speak into the metal box, leaning against the reinforced steel door. "We're here to see Mr Edwards, the owner," he said. "About a... err, monetary transaction."

"Just a minute," the voice replied. A CCTV camera, mounted above the door swivelled round to get them both in shot. Cortez was impressed by the security. It wouldn't have come cheap. Seems sex sold well even after the world had ended.

Greaves straightened up and adjusted his glasses, looking out over the ruins of the traditional stone houses and churned up lawns of what had once been an exclusive suburb of Harrisburg, Pennsylvania. "This part of town used to be real popular with the pharmaceutical execs you know," he said. "That's where all the money was out here. That and steel of course."

Cortez nodded silently. He didn't have anything of value to add. Greaves knew a lot more than he did. He was smart. Perhaps the smartest person Cortez had ever met. He was short and scrawny and he couldn't fight for shit, but the smarts Allah had granted him were as deadly as any weapon Cortez knew.

"They're taking their time aren't they?" said Greaves, taking off his glasses and rubbing his eyes. "Damn this pollen," he swore and began rummaging for his pills in the pockets of his greatcoat. He never took it off, even though it was high summer and the sweat stuck his mousey brown hair to his forehead.

"Okay, step inside," said the voice over the intercom. The door buzzed to show it was unlocked and Greaves pushed it open. Cortez followed him into a cage of reinforced steel. Four shotgun barrels were pointed directly at them. Four dangerous women, with very little clothing, had a bead on them. "Gentlemen," said a deep male voice from the shadows. "You'll be dead 'fore you even reach for your weapon. So I suggest you take out whatever you're packin', nice and slow mind, and toss it through these here bars. With the safety on of course."

Cortez didn't like the odds. He looked over at Greaves to see how they were going to play it. Greaves nodded for him to disarm. Greaves pulled out a Colt .45 from the holster under his robes and the sawn off shotgun he had strapped to his back. Greaves pulled out the snub nosed pistol Cortez had given him. He held it like it scared him.

"Is this how you put the safety on?" he asked. Showing Cortez the pistol. All four women dropped a shell into their chambers and aimed at Greaves. He went very pale. "You need to press the lever forwards," Cortez told him, remaining calm.

"It's okay, it's okay," Greaves said holding the pistol away from him. "Don't shoot I'm not gonna try anything." His hands shook as he fumbled with the safety and dropped it through the bars.

"Y'know fellas," said the man in the shadows. "There's a lot of cunts on sale in this place, but I'm not one of them. Think I don't know you're holdin' out on me? I wanna see every piece on the floor, in front of these bars." Greaves looked confused and panicked. He turned to Cortez. Cortez shrugged, bent down and took the pistol out of his ankle holster. Then he reached into his belt and removed the Bowie knife he kept there.

"That's better," said the voice. Lights came on in the reception area to reveal a hallway done out in plush velvet and gilt brocade. Edwards, the owner of the brothel, was standing at the bottom of a baronial staircase.

He was a big guy. Around six-two, six-three in height. And although he was carrying a lot of weight he looked like he could move pretty fast when he had to. He was wearing shorts, slippers and a loud Hawaiian shirt. Specs of sweat stood out on his bald pate and what little hair he had was tied in a pony tail at the back.

Edward's arms were spread in welcome and he was smiling. The type of broad smile you wear when you're just about to fuck someone good. "Welcome to the Pleasuredrome," he said. "Excuse the gals, they're not used to being up before noon and they get kinda tetchy 'till they've had their coffee."

The cage doors clicked, whirred and swung open. Greaves stepped through them and Cortez followed him. Two of the women bent down to pick up the weapons as the other two kept theirs trained on Greaves and Cortez.

"Can I you gentlemen anything to drink?" Edwards said, beckoning for them to follow him. "A little champagne perhaps, maybe somethin' harder?" The two women followed as they walked down a corridor off the main hall, shotguns still trained on them. "I'll just have a glass of water," Greaves said. Edwards chuckled. "Got ourselves a real party animal here gals." Edwards slapped him on the back. "Just bustin' your balls buddy, guess it is a little early in the day for some people, lightweights that is."

Edwards turned to Cortez, "How about you big guy, what's your poison?"

"I do not drink," Cortez said. He trusted Edwards even less for his attempts to ply them with alcohol.

"Is that a South American accent I hear?" Edwards said, probing him. "That's some beard you got there Fidel. You' ain't one of the last survivin' commies are you?"

Cortez started to lose his cool. He did not feel comfortable in this place of carnal sin and Edwards' attempt to rile him were beginning to work. "La ilaha illa Allah," he said aloud. Partly to put Edwards in his place. Partly to collect himself and ward off the stench of the wrongdoers. "Muhammadur rasoolu Allah!"

Edwards stopped at the door of his office. For a second he lost his composure, surprise burst out on his face. Then he pulled himself together and laughed as he unlocked the door. "Seems we got ourselves a Muslim girls," Edwards said and motioned for them to take a seat. "Don't have too many of those where you come from, I'll bet."

Greaves took a seat and leaned towards Edwards. Cortez remained standing. The two women kept him in their sites. "Is that entirely necessary?" said Greaves. "You have our weapons. We're simply here on business." Edwards waved a hand and the girls put their weapons at their sides. They stood at the back of the room, looking bored, irritable and tense. Not a good combination in an armed individual Cortez noted.

"Don't mind them," said Edwards. "They're only

hanging around in case you want to party when we're done. On the house of course." Edwards laughed when he saw their reactions. "What, you never had a blow job from a gall with a gun on you?" He said. "Jesus you guys like it vanilla, don'tcha."

Greaves cleared his throat. "Perhaps we should get down to business."

"Ah yes, I have some merchandise that you're interested in, I understand." Edwards leaned back in his chair and smiled his 'I'm gonna fuck you' smile again. "The big question is, how interested are you?"

"I believe I named a figure to your associate," Greaves said. "I have the money ready. Perhaps we could see her."

"Now hold on there junior," said Edwards. "You talked about money with one of my lackeys. No-one said he was authorised to agree a price. Let's just say, what you've brought today, that's a down payment."

"What!" said Greaves sitting upright, his voice carried a sudden weight of authority. "We had a deal. I've upheld my side of the bargain. I expect you to honour yours."

"Hey, hey, calm down there junior," said Edwards holding his palms out. "Now I understand how it is. You've gotten yourselves all psyched up. You probably went to sleep last night thinking about all the things you're going to do with her. And she is somethin', believe me. I don't go for injuns much myself but she is well worth a look. Whatever you've got in mind, hey that's fine with me. I'm not gonna judge you. Thing is though, you're wantin' to buy this girl outright, not rent her, and I can still earn a fuck of a lot of money out of her. She's young, she's clean and she ain't injured any. That's a big chunk out of my profits and I need reimbursin'. I got overheads you know, protection to pay. I put a lot of money into my girls."

"She's a slave," said Greaves with disdain. "You keep her chained to a wall and you feed her slops."

"Hey I'm not judging you, so don't you get all high and mighty with me you little pissant," Edwards said, his manner suddenly threatening. "We cater to a lot of exclusive tastes in this establishment. The slaves are a lucrative service. Be a lot of my customers disappointed to see her go. They might even take their business elsewhere. So you gotta make it worth my while. Hand over the scratch you brought and when you raise some more you can come back and we can talk about letting you have her."

"What if we just take our money and leave?" said Greaves.

"Now that just ain't gonna happen," said Edwards with his biggest 'fuck you' smile yet.

The two women stepped forward and levelled the barrels of their shotguns at Greaves' temple. That was their first mistake. Before they could react Cortez stepped around behind them and grabbed the barrels of both shotguns. He pulled them back and up, driving the butts into their faces.

He was right on target with the woman on his right. The butt hit the base of her nose. It exploded in a hot burst of blood and the bridge cracked, driving shards of bone into the front of her brain. She was dead before her crumpled body hit the floor.

The woman on his left caught the butt on the side of her face. There was a crack as her cheek bone broke and her right eye rolled up into its socket. She fell to the ground, dazed and twitching.

Cortez swung both shotguns round and pointed them at Edwards, just in time to see him pull an ivory handled Magnum out of his desk.

Cortez unloaded one shotgun and blew a hole in

Edwards left wrist. Edwards shrieked as his blood and cartilage sprayed the floor and he dropped the gun. He ducked behind the desk and grabbed the Magnum with his good hand, firing at Cortez's foot.

Cortez leaped back and Greaves cowered behind his chair while Edwards made a bolt for the door. He ran out into the corridor, screaming at the top of his voice. "Trixie, Fifi, Jezebel, Chelsea, get your skanky ol' asses out here! We got trouble!"

Cortez hauled up the unconscious woman. She moaned at the pain as she regained consciousness. "Where is the girl?" Cortez demanded.

The woman shook her head. "What girl? I don't know who you mean."

"She's a Native American," said Greaves getting to his feet. "She's called Anna. I know you've got her prisoner here."

"I can't think," said the woman. "I'm hurt too bad." Cortez leaned in close to her face. "Take us to the girl Anna," he said. "Or you will know what it really feels like to be hurt too bad."

"They're... they're all kept in the basement... next to... to the dungeon," she said and passed out again.

Cortez walked to the door and stuck his head slowly round. He jumped back as a stream of bullets tore up the plaster an inch from his head, colliding with Greaves.

"We can't leave," said Greaves, picking up his glasses. "They've got us pinned down. We have to make them come to us." He thought for a minute. "How many did of them you see?"

"I was too busy dodging their bullets to count."

"Edwards called out four names," said Greaves. "So there's at least that many coming for us. We're at the end of a corridor with no other exit. We're outnumbered and outgunned."

Greaves hit Cortez with his fierce blue eyes. "There's got to be a way to turn that to our advantage."

Linda could have kicked herself when she came to. If she hadn't been too trussed up to move her legs. And if her head hadn't felt like someone was doing all the kicking for her.

She was lying on her side on a cold stone floor. Her wrists and her ankles were tied behind her. She arched her back to stretch her legs and relieve the cramp in her thighs. This tightened the rope and cut off the circulation to her hands. She felt for how it was tied with her fingers. Luckily it was a bondage knot that she knew. She found the right end of the rope and pulled to release the knot. Her bonds uncoiled and she was free.

Thank God for pervy clients, she thought as she got to her feet and massaged the life back into her wrists. She was in a dark, confined space. She reached in front of her and felt what seemed like shelves and broom handles. She smelt bleach. She was in a broom closet. She'd been tied up and dumped in a broom closet.

Time to get some payback.

She fumbled her way over to the door and tried it. It wasn't locked. It opened on to a dimly lit basement. Across the way from the closet was a door marked 'DUNGEON'. She had to be in the Pleasuredrome. That's why she was tied bondage style. Sloppy of them really, her being a pro and all. They had to know she'd be able to get loose. They must have thought she'd be out for longer and were going to come back with better shackles.

She had known there was something wrong with her clients the night before. They said they were visiting traders who wanted a three-way and they had a bundle of hard cash. She should have listened to her gut though. They didn't seem that interested in her sexually and they knew their way around too well to be visitors.

They must have slipped her something after she climbed in their car. She should never have taken a drink from them. *Serves me right for being careless.*

Edwards had been after her to join his girls for a while now. Linda knew he didn't like independent competitors, but she never thought he'd resort to kidnap. She worked strictly downtown. Out of his way and away from his high end clients.

Those clients had tastes that were too special for Linda. She had no illusions about what would happen if she couldn't get out of her current situation. She knew all about the girls he kept as slaves.

She walked slowly and quietly through the basement, scanning the gloom for any means of escape. It was a huge space, and covered more ground than the building above. It had obviously been specially excavated. The only doors she could find seemed to lead either into the well equipped dungeon area or into a series of tiny cells. She didn't want to think about who was kept there. Or what the poor wretches were going through.

Over by the far wall there was something that caught her eye. She peered at it then turned away. Something drew her back however and she was glad it did. When she got closer she could see there was a hardboard panel nailed over a gap in the ceiling.

Linda fetched a wooden spanking paddle from the dungeon and pried the panel loose. About a metre above there was an outside grill. Linda pulled herself up and tried it. It was stuck fast. She tried to use the paddle to jimmy it but it broke. It would take more than one person to shift the grill.

Fuck! She was so close.

Changing tactics she hunted round and found the staircase. She made her way carefully up, testing each stair to make certain it didn't creak. The door at the top was locked, but only with a chub lock. Linda slid a thin section of the snapped paddle down between the door and the jamb, releasing the lever. Then she pulled the door open just a fraction and peeked out.

A gun went off and she jumped back, holding the door open just a fraction. This was followed by a lot of yelling. She heard footsteps in the corridor outside. She waited until they were nearly upon her, then opened the door and stuck her foot out. One of Edward's girls hit the floor face first and dropped the weapons she'd been carrying.

Linda jumped her. She knelt on the girl's spine then reached around the front of her throat with her right forearm and held the back of her neck with the left. Bending her wrist inwards she squeezed her forearms together and restricted the girl's carotid arteries. With the blood to her brain cut off, the girl kicked a couple of times then lost consciousness.

Linda got up and inspected the weapons the girl was carrying. "Come to momma," she said as she picked up a sawn off shotgun, two pistols, a Colt.45 and a bowie knife. Now she was armed as well as dangerous.

"Come on out honey," called one of the girls outside Edward's office. "I got somethin' for ya."

"I love you looong time," cried another. "Kill you quick."

Cortez was standing by the door. It was opened into the corridor to block the view of the office. Cortez said nothing. He looked over at Greaves who was going through the drawers of Edward's desk. He held up a set of throwing knives and some shackles. "Seems Edwards has some exotic tastes," Greaves said.

"I don't see how this helps us," Cortez said. Greaves smiled and handed Cortez all but one of the knives. "I need you to use these to pin our dead friend here to the door," he said and gestured to the woman on the floor. Cortez shrugged and picked up the body. Greaves applied the shackles to the unconscious woman.

Cortez propped the dead woman up against the door and held her left arm up above her. Then he took one of the knives and drove it through her wrist and into the wooden door behind. He repeated this with her other wrist and both her feet. The body hung splayed against the door, blood trickling from its post mortem wounds.

"Now give me a hand with this," said Greaves, struggling to lift the unconscious woman. Cortez picked up the woman and Greaves directed him to hang her wrist shackles from the coat hook on the door. Both women hung side by side on the back of the door. Greaves knelt down and began to remove the screws from the hinges. "Steady the door," he told Cortez.

"Now we make them come to us," said Greaves, standing next to Cortez when he had finished. "When I say go we pick up the door and walk backwards to the far wall at an angle. I'll be two steps ahead of you. Use the body as a shield." Greaves slapped the unconscious woman hard across the face. She groaned at the pain in her cheekbone and came to. "Go!' said Greaves.

Cortez lifted the door and Greaves did the same, struggling with his side. They staggered backwards with it. A hail of bullets thudded into the door. As it was at an angle most of them hit Cortez's side. The bullets tore through the thick wood of the door but the dead body stopped any that might have hit him.

As they reached the back wall of the corridor two bullets connected with the woman Greaves was using for shelter, nicking her shoulder and smashing into the back of her thigh. "Aaaaah!" she screamed. "Jesus motherfucking Christ!"

"Candy," called out one of the women who was firing. "Candy is that you honey?" Candy simply wailed in reply. "Candy we're coming darlin'," called out another woman. Cortez heard three sets of feet padding down the corridor towards them.

"Come back you dumb bitches!" Edwards shouted after them.

"Now!" said Greaves, the second the footsteps stopped. He and Cortez kicked hard and the heavy oak door, with the combined weight of the two bodies, came crashing down on the three armed women.

All three collapsed and their guns clattered out across the floor. Cortez and Greaves ran over the door. Cortez grabbed two of the semi automatic weapons and Greaves picked up the other. They ran up the corridor firing indiscriminately.

Two women standing at the top of the corridor were caught by the spray of bullets. Their bodies jerked and flew backwards as blood gushed from the holes the bullets tore in them. Cortez and Greaves reached the hallway at the top of the corridor and looked about them. There was no-one in sight.

Then Cortez heard an ominous click. He turned slowly to see Edwards with his Magnum at Greaves' temple. His wrist was wrapped with a makeshift bandage.

"Drop 'em big guy," Edwards commanded. "Or your buddy here dies." With great reluctance Cortez put down his weapons. Two of the women started climbing out from under the door, moaning and cursing at their wounds. Three more came down the staircase, all of them armed.

"You sons of bitches are in some serious shit," said Edwards.

Linda had Edwards dead in her sights. She weighed up whether to pull the trigger or not.

After tying up and gagging the girl she jumped, she'd carried on down the corridor as quietly as she could with all that weaponry stuffed in her belt.

She'd heard the catcalls and seen the gunfight in the corridor on the other side of the staircase. Edwards hid and when the two men emerged he got the drop on them. They were an odd looking couple. The little runty one looked frightened and blinked through his glasses as Edwards held him at gunpoint. The big guy with him was a bit of an enigma. He was head and shoulders above everyone, including Edwards. He looked Hispanic, but he had a huge black beard and wore robes that looked Arabic in origin. Linda had no idea what they were doing in the place. Robbing it she supposed.

Linda kept Edwards in her sight as three more armed girls came down the stairs. Then she heard Edwards say: "We're gonna do far to worse to you than was ever done to that bitch you came to buy." That decided her. She wasn't certain why, but her gut told her which side she was on.

Linda unloaded the sawn off shotgun into Edwards. Both rounds entered either side of his spine and blew his guts out the front of his body. Blood and ruptured intestines crashed into the wall opposite..

The girls on the stairs started firing on Linda who ducked back into the corridor. She heard the two guys return fire and a woman screamed, probably hit.

Linda backed down the corridor as the men charged

towards it. She was standing next to the girl she tied up when they saw her. The big guy raised his Uzi and Linda raised her hands. The runt saw the girl at her feet, put his hand on the big guy's weapon and made him lower it.

"Were you the one who helped us?" the runt said. Linda nodded. "I don't work here," she said. "I was a prisoner but I broke out."

"We need to get to the basement," runt said.

"It's this way," said Linda and showed them through the door.

She locked it behind them and used the sawn-off shotgun to wedge it shut.

"That is my weapon," said the big guy. It was the first time she heard him speak. He spoke with a South American accent that was hard to place.

"Listen," she said, "If we get out of this I've got two more you can have, free of charge. And trust me honey, I rarely give anything free of charge."

"How are we going to leave now?" said the runt. "Is there another exit?"

"There's a grill that I found, but I couldn't shift it by myself," Linda said. "It leads outside."

The runt nodded then made his way down the steps with the big guy. Linda followed.

The two of them headed for the cells. Linda watched as the runt slid open the grill on each of them and peered inside. "This is her," he said after the fourth one he came to. He reached into his greatcoat and pulled out a small device that he then inserted into the lock. He fiddled with the end of the device for a few seconds and gave it a sharp turn. The lock clicked and he pushed the door open.

Linda was surprised by the runt's reaction. He stood in the doorway with his mouth open, stunned. He looked like a groupie meeting her favourite rock star. "I can't believe I've finally found you," he said. "You've no idea how long it's taken."

Linda looked past him into the cell. The occupant wasn't anywhere near as awe inspiring as she seemed to the runt. She was a petrified Native American girl, half starved and in her late teens. She had chains on her wrists and ankles that ran through a ring in the ceiling and around a winch. Most probably to allow the client to control what position she was in.

The girl shrank from the two men the minute she saw them, curling herself into a whimpering ball in the corner. Greaves knelt down and tried to put his skeleton key in one of her ankle shackles but the girl kicked out in fear and knocked him on his back. "Shit," he said when he got up and looked at his key. "She snapped it."

"You want me to get her out of these?" the big guy said, holding up the chains. Runt nodded.

The girl tried to pull away from them and the runt tried to calm her. "Listen, Anna," he said. "It's okay. We're not here to hurt you. My name's Greaves and this is Cortez. We've come to get you out." Cortez reached out to Linda's belt. Without thinking Linda pulled the Bowie knife on him. "Getting a little fresh aren't we?" she said.

Cortez stopped but he didn't pull his hand back. "You have my gun," he said pointing at the Colt.45. "I need it to break these chains."

Linda took it from her belt and handed it to him. "You know usually men have to pay to get their pistol in my trousers," she said playfully. Cortez met her flirting with a cold stare and turned away. *Obviously plays for the other team*, Linda thought.

Cortez caught hold of Anna's wrist. She cried out but her attempts to break free had no effect. He shot each of her chains off then picked her up like a child and flung her over his shoulder. She stopped fighting, but Linda could see that Anna's eyes were full of fear and mistrust.

"Hello... hello?" said a voice from another cell. "Is .. is someone out there?" It was a woman with her face pressed against the grill. "Oh God you've got to take me with you. Please, I've got young children. There's no one to look after to them. Please get me out of here."

Linda looked to Greaves who shook his head. "We haven't got time," he said. "She'll slow us down."

"And this one won't?" said Linda.

The door to the basement began to shake as something thudded into it. "They're trying to break in," said Greaves. "Quickly, show us this grill."

"Please," the woman called out. "Please don't leave me here. You don't know what they do to me... please..."

Linda tried not to listen as she showed them the grill. She and Cortez heaved but it remained stubbornly in place. The wood of the basement door splintered and gunfire raked the floor, inches from them. Greaves joined them in their frantic efforts and the grill gave as they heard the door give way and the first set of feet start to descend.

They scrambled through the tight opening of the grill. Anna first, then Greaves then Linda. One of the women caught hold of Cortez's leg as he was leaving. He kicked her off and narrowly avoided being shot by another.

The grill came out into a parking lot in back of the brothel, surrounded by a wooded copse. Greaves and Cortez, with Anna over his shoulder, raced to their vehicle then stopped in dismay. The tires had been slashed.

"Quick, into the trees," said Linda. They followed her into the copse as the women raced around the building and into the lot. The heavily armed prostitutes attempted to give chase but they were not dressed for that terrain and the four of them soon lost their pursuers.

The copse continued in a steep slope for a while and then gave out onto one of the main highways. Greaves turned to Linda as they reached it. "We need a vehicle to get us out of the state," he said. "Can you help?"

"I may be able to," said Linda. "But why would I want to? You boys look like you get yourselves into a lot of trouble."

"Three reasons," Greaves said. "Firstly, Edwards had a lot of powerful friends who will want to get even with you for shooting him. Secondly I can pay you really well." He rooted through his greatcoat and came out with two gold Krugerrands. "This is just a down payment," he said handing them to her. "And thirdly you'll be helping to save the world."

Linda nearly laughed out loud at that last statement but she could see from Greaves' eyes that he was deadly earnest. "Follow me," she said.

Three hours and a lot of walking later they stood outside a lock up on the north bank of the Susquehanna River. Linda unlocked the door and led them inside. There, under a tarpaulin, was her baby. She tugged at the cover to reveal Bertha. A Fleetwood, 40E motor home, covered with customised bullet proof armour plating. She came complete with onboard arsenal. There wasn't another vehicle like her on the road.

"Very nice," said Greaves inspecting the custom bodywork. "Where did you get it?"

"A grateful client," said Linda. "He didn't like his next of kin so he left Bertha and her contents to me."

She opened Bertha up and Greaves and Cortez climbed in. Cortez put Anna down on a couch. She pulled her knees up under her chin and sat rocking, staring straight ahead of her.

"We've got enough gas in the tank to get us out of the state," said Linda. "Where we headed?"

"Montana," said Greaves.

"That's across the other side of the other side of the

country," said Linda. "We'll have to cross at least 7 states to get there."

"I can make it very worth your while."

"Okay it's your money." said Linda. "So Anna, is she your relative or your lover or what?"

"We've never seen her before in our lives," said Greaves.

"So why'd you go to such trouble to rescue her?" Linda wanted to know. Greaves looked over at the traumatised sex slave. She was crying and shaking and snot ran down her top lip.

"Because," he said. "She is the future saviour of mankind."

For more information on this
and other titles visit...

Abaddon
Books

THE AFTERBLIGHT CHRONICLES

The CULLED

Simon Spurrier

Price: £6.99 ★ ISBN: 1-905437-01-3

Price: $7.99 ★ ISBN 13: 978-1-905437-01-6

THE AFTERBLIGHT CHRONICLES

KILL OR CURE

Rebecca Levene

Price: £6.99 ★ ISBN: 1-905437-32-3

Price: $7.99 ★ ISBN 13: 978-1-905437-32-0

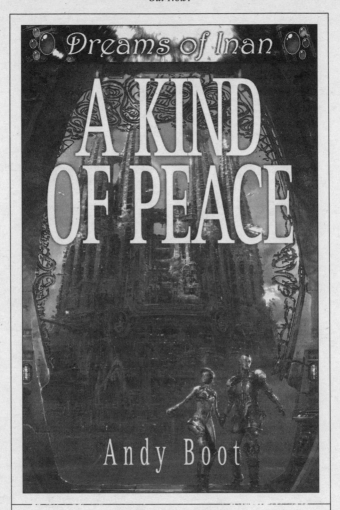

Dreams of Inan

A KIND OF PEACE

Andy Boot

Price: £6.99 ★ ISBN: 1-905437-02-1

Price: $7.99 ★ ISBN 13: 978-1-905437-02-3

Price: £6.99 ★ ISBN: 1-905437-12-9

Price: $7.99 ★ ISBN 13: 978-1-905437-12-2

Price: £6.99 ★ ISBN: 1-905437-53-6

Price: $7.99 ★ ISBN 13: 978-1-905437-53-5

TOMES *of the* DEAD

DEATH HULK

Matthew Sprange

Price: £6.99 ★ ISBN: 1-905437-03X

Price: $7.99 ★ ISBN 13: 978-1-905437-03-0

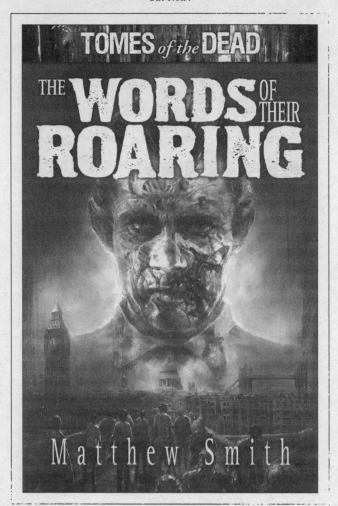

TOMES *of the* DEAD

THE WORDS OF THEIR ROARING

Matthew Smith

Price: £6.99 ★ ISBN: 1-905437-13-7

Price: $7.99 ★ ISBN 13: 978-1-905437-13-9

PAX BRITANNIA

UNNATURAL HISTORY

Jonathan Green

Price: £6.99 ★ ISBN: 1-905437-10-2

Price: $7.99 ★ ISBN 13: 978-1-905437-10-8

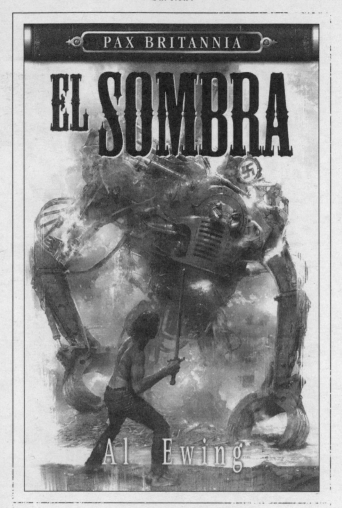

PAX BRITANNIA

EL SOMBRA

Al Ewing

Price: £6.99 ★ ISBN: 1-905437-34-X

Price: $7.99 ★ ISBN 13: 978-1-905437-34-4